# Embers in Our Past

## STEFANIE CASTRO

# Spotify

Please use the QR Code below to find the Spotify Playlist online. Listen and enjoy!

# Content Warnings

The QR code below will direct you to my website, if you'd like to check out the content warnings for Clay and Abby's story.

*Dedicated to my dreamers;*
*whatever you're holding on to, I hope you achieve it.*

*Clay*

18 MONTHS AGO

I WALK HOME, the spring air warming my skin after the coldest winter we've had in Boston in years. I make sure the coffees are positioned securely as I maneuver through the streets, bringing Abby her favorite drink, along with a chocolate croissant. She always eyes it when we go into Beans of Mass but hasn't gotten it in a few months.

We need a fresh start. I know everything the doctor said led to a slew of emotions that we are still processing, but I think having a plan is better than nothing. And having each other is what matters, no matter what. We can tackle anything —together. But that phone call the other day really set us back emotionally.

I know she has felt even more upset in the last couple of weeks. I found her sitting on the floor of our bathroom, clutching her phone, defeat written across her face. I had to pry her phone out of her hands as she shook, telling me her body failed her. The pregnancy didn't stick, confirming what the woman at the office said after we tried another round of IVF.

It doesn't matter how many times I try to erase the pain,

it's still there when I close my eyes. Each time I look at her, all I see is the pain that took over her face that afternoon.

All I want to do is fix this—fix us. But in the last few years, parts of ourselves have fallen to the side. Getting pregnant started off as a happy occasion, a fun one, if I'm being honest. In the first few months of unsuccessful attempts, we chalked up the inability to conceive as simply a timing issue. Being so young, we kept chanting the same mantra—it wasn't our time, but it will come. But as two failed tests turned into ten, it felt like I could hear her heart breaking within her chest. And her heartbreak simply led to my own.

I still remember the moment I fell in love with Abby because my heart wasn't even looking for anything beyond a mere hookup. After only a glance in her direction, all the pieces of my life that felt difficult were easier to lift. I could carry whatever problem I faced head-on because I knew she was the person I would come home to. Even when things got harder with us trying to have a baby, I knew no matter what, we would get through this together. She's my safe space, and I know I'm hers.

I reach our house and turn the key to the front door, that extra spring in my step from knowing I get the next few days off to spend with my girl. Now that the weather is improving, maybe a walk down near Gael's Stadium, our local baseball team, is in order. Even a walk along Boston Harbor might do us some good.

I think if this is leading us toward any lesson, it's about reconnecting with one another. Despite the hardships we've faced, I think moving into our future, we need to keep in mind that we are what's most important in our marriage. We can tackle this—we just need to figure out what our next step will be.

Once I walk inside, I set the bag of pastries down on the dining room table but instantly sense a shift in the air around me. Something is off. I look to my right and see a row of luggage lining our corridor.

"Abby, you home?" *Maybe she planned a weekend getaway?*

The silence that meets me causes my heart rate to skyrocket.

"Abby, baby, you here?" I swing my gaze down the hall, looking to see if I can find her. I walk further into our home only to find her sitting at the kitchen table, her face in her hands.

"Hey, we headed away for the weekend?" I move my arms around her from behind and nuzzle my face in her neck. She stiffens, and it immediately causes me to pull away to take her in.

Abby has been pushing herself away from me little by little over the last few months. I tried to ignore it, but it's in these little interactions together I realize she's become more rigid in her movements. She doesn't melt into my touch, which makes me feel completely out of place. All I've known is Abby for my entire adult life, and here I am, trying to find ways to maneuver around her like I barely recognize this version of us anymore.

"What's going on?" I feel the frog growing in my throat, and I can't help the fear it exudes in my tone.

"We need to talk, Clay." She doesn't even look at me. She speaks with her eyes cast down at the table, playing with the indents in the wood.

"Yeah? About what exactly?" I move to stand in front of her, hoping she'll look up at me. I finally give up and pull a chair out to sit next to her.

She brings those beautiful blue eyes up to mine, and I feel just a moment of hope because she connects with me.

"Clay, I don't feel like myself anymore," she says just above a whisper.

Looking at the soft-spoken version of my wife right now, it's hard to keep from comparing it with the version of her from not so long ago. Abby has always been described as jovial, always laughing, and lighthearted. She was never one to hold back her opinion, always telling me how she felt about a subject, no matter what side she stood on the topic. She was always a foul-mouthed girl who argued her opinion, and she didn't shy away from what she loved. She lived life loudly. She gave our home this light I longed for and had an infectious laugh that stayed with me after I left the house for a long shift at the station. She had this spirit that lived inside her that I loved to see grow. Her spirit was vibrant, almost strong enough that it felt infectious when she was around me.

The thing is, now that Abby and I have gone through this huge transformation in our marriage and are in a turbulent time, with so much uncertainty ahead, I've seen her really turn into a shell of herself. I can't even call her demure around me. She's just this completely different version of herself when she's with me. It's like she's indifferent, and all I can see is a dimmed version of her.

The thing about love is that I love all parts of Abby—the bright version, the reserved version, and even this hurt version. Marriage is about maneuvering through all the different avenues our paths may cross. I am one hundred percent capable of enduring this darker time if it means we are moving as one.

I grab her hand. "I know you don't, but that's why I'm here. When you aren't feeling at your best, that's where I come in. I can carry us both while you find your footing again, baby."

My unease only rises as she looks away again. It feels like a knife to the heart when she pulls her hand out of mine before she speaks again.

"I can't be here anymore," she says, her voice remaining only above a whisper.

"So, you want to go somewhere? I bet we can get a flight

booked somewhere nice. I can call my chief and get a few more days off."

"I got a flight," she says. Something about the way she's speaking to me feels like she only got herself the flight and not us.

"Where to?" Before she answers, I can already see where this conversation is going.

"I'm headed back to California." Abby is from Palos Verdes, California. She moved out to Boston when she came to college. We met at a coffee shop near campus, where I found her studying one day. From the moment I laid eyes on her, I never looked at another woman the same way. She took over my heart and has carried it with her from that day on.

"Okay. When are you planning on coming back?" I hope she gets back on a day I can pick her up from the airport.

"You're not understanding, Clay. I'm going back to California… permanently." It feels like all the air has been pulled from my lungs.

"You're leaving me?" My voice is hoarse as I speak.

"I can't keep doing this. This isn't us, Clay. We aren't these people who simply go through the motions together. We used to be full of passion and spontaneity, and now it feels so heavy. Like the weight of the world is sitting on our shoulders, and we have no clue how to get rid of it." She pulls her gaze from the window and locks it on mine. There's a finality in the way she looks at me.

"What are you talking about? We got this. I know we can weather this storm. It's one hiccup, baby. Going to California isn't going to solve this problem." I move my hand to cup her cheek.

I continue, hoping I can get through to her. "You don't even like California. You always said you feel suffocated out there." She came to Boston to escape being under her mom's control, and now she's going back? "Why would you go back there if you hated it so much? We can tackle this. *Together*."

I can hear the pleading in my voice, and as pathetic as it might seem to some, I don't even give a shit. I know deep in my heart, my wife doesn't want to leave. She wants to be here with me. I know Abby. She loves Boston. I will do whatever it takes to keep her with me.

"Clay, no. We got married young and for a huge reason: we wanted to start a family. But here we are, years later and still no family," she says, a lone tear falling down her cheek.

I bring my thumb to wipe away the tear, but she pulls away as if my touch alone is too painful. That gesture nearly guts me.

"Bullshit! This doesn't sound like you. This sounds like your mother. And we are a family, Abby. We already are one in my eyes," I tell her yet again.

I'm trying not to sound frustrated, but I am. When we sat in the doctor's office with the diagnosis of infertility, I said the exact same thing to Abby. I meant it then, and I still do. Even before starting IVF, I knew whatever the outcome, she and I were already a family in my eyes.

"Well, this isn't what I envisioned for us. This isn't my mom talking. This is *me* talking. I'm telling you this. I've already told you this. We fight so much already when that's the last thing we ever did before we started this.

"All this is happening, and we haven't even gotten anything in return. All we've gotten are injections, hormones, my crazy mood swings, medications, and disappointment. This isn't a guarantee, Clay. It's too much for me. Don't you get that? And to do all that and end up exactly where we are right now? I just can't. You deserve more, and I can't give it to you." The determination to convince herself of this nonsense is evident in her tone.

"I want you. That's all I've ever needed. Whatever else comes after having you by my side is just a bonus." I grab her hand, and she lets me touch her this time. I bring her fingers to my lips and hope that she can feel how much I love her with my touch.

For a minute I think I'm reaching her, her eyes softening as she feels my skin against her fingertips. But determination quickly takes over like a force as the walls are rebuilt behind her gaze.

"No, Clay. I can't ask that of you. And I just can't do this again and again. You say this now, but one day, it won't be enough. *I* won't be enough. I can't live a life I didn't envision for myself or for you. You're wasting your best years on someone who can't give you more. And it kills me to know I want this so much, and I can't make it happen for either of us." She pulls her hand out of my grasp and starts to walk toward the front door.

"Come on, Abby. You can't just walk away." I follow behind her. She pauses when she sees the coffee at the table but continues to the front door, opening her purse and making sure she has everything.

"I have no other options, Clay. I love you. But that's not the problem, is it? If it were an issue of love, we'd be set. We'd have enough of that to last us a lifetime. We'd have tomorrow and the next day and all the days after because our love is so strong, it would carry us through the hardest of times.

"But now I can't ignore the hole this has left in my heart. I'm not the same Abby you married. I'm damaged. I guess I've always been damaged, but I had no idea. The pain is filtering into all parts of me, Clay. I can't let you stay with me and let the resentment follow along as the dreaded enemy that's bound to get between us."

"So that's it? You're just going to speak for me and let what we've built go?" I can hear my tone get harder, and it's difficult to control.

Abby and I rarely fought before all the fertility struggles came to light, although in the last few months, I'd say we've gotten more accustomed to it. But every couple goes through highs and lows. I can't expect each day to be a walk in the park, but I honestly never thought this would be what lies ahead.

"We built our marriage on the idea that we would house a ton of kids, and now that dream is shattered," she cries out, and the anguish she holds breaks me even more.

"But, Abby, it's not completely out of the question. Dr. Levi told us she has had patients with the same diagnosis, and they came out with children of their own. We've got surrogacy and adoption as possibilities too. So, it's not like we can't ever have children." I can hear the desperation in my tone, and it's hard to let go of it.

I'm desperate to keep her home, to keep her from making a huge mistake. If she leaves, I know getting her to come back is something that will be nearly impossible.

"Clay, no!" Abby shouts. The moment she raises her voice, I'm stunned. Abby has never shouted at me. In all the years I've known her, I have never heard her speak this way. Like all the months of frustration have been bottled up, and she's hit her breaking point.

"Don't you get it? I'm done. We're done. This is over. My body—it's broken. I'm broken. I can't do this. I can't do this to you. And I can't do this to me. Not anymore. When we try each month, Clay, it guts me when we fail. Do you not get that? I feel like a failure. I feel like I'm a useless person right now. I don't know how else to say that. I feel like my body is broken. *I feel broken.*

"So yes, I'm going back to California. I'm returning to the one place I've run from because my mom said she will welcome me and care for me. I want to go back because this place I love is reminding me of pain and failure. It's reminding me of a life I can't create!" I can't tell where her tears start and where they end. She is sobbing, and my heart is completely shattered.

I move to embrace her, and she steps back.

"No, please don't. I can't. If you hold me, I'll melt right back into you, and we'll fall back into the same pattern again. I've thought about it long and hard, and I cannot keep going through the motions, especially in this house. I walk into our bathroom upstairs, and all I see is you figuring out where the next injection should go. Or in our bedroom, where what started as fun became a chore," that comparison stings to hear, "or down here, in that restroom, where we took pregnancy tests over and over again to only see one line instead of two."

I'm about to protest, but she interrupts me. "Don't, Clay. Don't say we will find a way. Each corner of this house reminds me of what we are missing. That spare bedroom is a screaming reminder. Even with the office stuff in there and no baby materials sitting on the walls, I close my eyes, and that's all I see. I have felt such sadness over everything that won't happen, and it's destroying me, Clay."

She is pleading with me to understand something I can't. I don't see each of those scenarios with the same eyes. My perspective is different; then again, I don't feel the hormones the way she does firsthand. The pain of the shots, the dream fading, or that dream dying out. I simply see a challenge I want to overcome with the woman I love.

"We've got options. I just see a future with you, baby. We can keep trying. We can take a break. Like I said, we can try surrogacy or adoption. It's worth it so long as you're with me." She's still moving while I follow behind her, begging, and then she's grabbing her bags and pulling up something on her phone.

"I get it. You see this last failed attempt as a challenge we can overcome, but you and I both know I'm saving us from having to face the uncomfortable, which was inevitably going to happen."

"But, Abby, this isn't what I want. Doesn't that matter?" I'm watching her grab her things, and I'm rooted in place.

"That's the thing, Clay. This is the hard part of it. I don't think you'd ever leave. You'd suffer for as long as is needed, and as great as that sounds, it gets old. You'd get tired of it. We can't keep fighting the inevitable. We will only drift apart anyway. So, I'm doing this for us."

She's moving her hand onto the doorknob, and I finally unglue myself from the place I'm standing. "Hold on, so you're going to California for a few weeks, then coming back? Maybe after you get away a bit, we can find a new place. Start fresh?" I know she just needs to recalibrate, and then we can figure out what we'll do next.

She shakes her head. "No, Clay. You're not understanding. I'm moving to California for good. That's what I meant by permanently. I spoke to my parents, and they said I could move back home until I can get settled over there."

"Are you serious?" I throw my hands up in the air. Her parents, especially her mom, never approved of us getting married. They were always against us dating, let alone getting married so young.

"I won't fight you on most of the things we have. I packed a few items, but you can keep the rest. We just have to figure out the house," she says, as if this is such an easy task.

"Seems you've thought of everything." I feel the bitterness lace my words.

She may have figured everything out on her end, but I don't know if I'll ever figure out how to live a life where Abby Nichols isn't by my side.

# CHAPTER 1

## *Clay*

"WHERE DO YOU WANT THIS BOX?" my brother yells as he and Ashton carry yet another load of my things into my new place.

It's been three weeks since Abby left, and the ache is no less painful. I fight the urge to respond with, "Who cares?" It's not his fault my life is in ruins. I point toward the back room and continue to look at my new space in hopes it will someday feel like home.

I couldn't take being in that house a moment longer without my wife by my side. I honestly thought she was going to spend one night back on the West Coast and then call me crying because she missed me. I didn't expect her to last one second on California soil, much less three fucking weeks. But here I am, starting my life without the partner I wanted to grow old with. This is a nightmare—living a bachelor life is the last thing I wanted for myself. Abby was it for me.

"Well, brother, I guess it's just you and me again." River brings his arm around me, pulling me into an embrace. "It's going to be okay, Clay. I promise I'll get you through it."

Right then, his puppy, Lola, comes between our legs, and

her head bumps into my calf, begging for attention. She's a ball of energy.

"She better not have an accident in here, Riv," I scold. "She already tried to pee on my mattress before I caught her."

"Oh, you haven't seen anything yet. Wait until she finds your shoes, right, princess?" He picks her up and brings her face up to his own.

She's fucking adorable, but I will not be fooled. My mother already finds her to be the most amazing gift on this planet. She's a ball of fur with the sweetest face. The moment she gets close enough to my brother, she licks his nose.

"I know you are just the cutest thing, aren't you, Lola?" he says, reserving his high-pitched voice for her. I roll my eyes.

"Don't give me that look, Clay. You know you love her too. Doesn't Uncle Clay love you, Lola? Yes, he does." He scrunches the dog's face against his and bats his eyes. It's hard to keep a straight face, and I end up laughing at his antics.

"You're ridiculous, you know that?" I shove his shoulder and walk away.

"Don't act like I don't complete you, Clay," he yells at me as he puts Lola back on the ground.

"Yes, River, you are the wind beneath my wings and all that." I make my way through my new kitchen, opening another box to grab more items to put into some cabinets.

I hear a voice at my front door, and it brings a smile to my face. Soon enough, a familiar face greets us at the entrance of my kitchen.

"Hey, Rios, thanks for joining the fun," River says as Lola gives a quick bark.

Rios bends down to pat her on the head as she licks his hand.

I make my way over and embrace my longtime friend from the firehouse. We quickly bonded over our love of running. Since I started at the station, we began a routine of meeting up in our neighborhoods to run a few miles every week. Now we run marathons and have even started clubs with other firehouses, when possible, to raise money during warmer seasons in Boston. It's been a great way to get to know other stations and connect with different houses.

"Thanks for stopping by." I thank him and get back to unpacking.

"Where do you need me?" Rios asks.

"Grab a box and have at it," I say, and Rios isn't the least bit shy and starts to lend a hand.

The two of us work quickly as Ashton and my brother continue to connect the televisions and other electronics in the house for me.

Rios and I begin discussing our route for our next run. Now that I'm living a little closer to him, we can meet up for our runs halfway, making it a little easier for the two of us in the mornings when we are off shift.

"I think that coffee shop, the one off First Street and Third, will be perfect for us to meet tomorrow. Let's say six in the morning?" Rios says as he puts a stack of plates in the cabinet next to me.

"That works. That will give me enough time to warm up." Hopefully, I can get enough sleep tonight. I have slept like shit since Abby left.

"I know things have been rocky since she left. Hopefully, as each day moves forward, you can get into a new routine in this place. This neighborhood is nice though. Nice spots with good restaurants. Walking distance to some good places too."

"Yeah, I appreciate you hanging out. And the runs are always a good way to keep my mind busy. Plus, the weather now is a good incentive to get myself out of the house. I hate when we have to meet up at the gym in the winter. Those treadmill runs are brutal." I shake my head.

"Yeah, the hibernation months are shit." He chuckles.

"How are your sisters doing? The youngest moving back

to school soon?" I ask. Rios is surrounded by sisters, and his youngest sister, Baylee, is still in college. There's a big age gap between him and the baby of the family.

"They're good… mostly. Baylee is a huge pain in my ass. Thank god she's going back to school." He rubs his hands down his face.

"Okay, the technicians have done their jobs." My brother and Ashton make their way into the kitchen. *"Die Hard* marathon is good to commence." River brings his hands together like a maniacal villain. I can't help but laugh in response.

"Really, again, with that movie?" Ashton groans.

"Why do you have to hate, Ashie?" he says, taunting him with the nickname he hates.

"You guys always watch that damn movie. Don't you get sick of it?"

My brother and I look at each other with matching looks of horror. "No!"

"Well, I'm not sticking around for this, AGAIN!" Ashton complains.

Growing up, Ashton endured many nights of Bruce Willis and our *Die Hard* marathons because we were avidly watching the movies. It was our answer to everything.

Tonight is no different. Whenever things got hard in life, we'd pop popcorn and argue if *Die Hard* is or isn't a Christmas movie, which I will go to my grave saying it is a definite fucking holiday classic. We'll likely argue a little of the same tonight, yet end up sitting back and enjoying the movie much like we always do.

The rest of the afternoon, we finish getting everything settled into my new place. I feel numb at the thought I'm back on my own. It's hard to imagine my new normal will be so lonely now, but I swallow the lump in my throat, knowing that I have to figure this out now. I look over at Rios, grateful he will meet me in the morning, and we can continue our morning runs. That distraction will continue to get me through this tough time in my life.

He has no idea how much those moments have gotten me through some of my darkest times lately. Even though we might go through our strides in silence, his presence is enough to pull me out of sadness.

Ashton and Rios head out, and I order pizza for River and me. We sit down with our food once it arrives, and before pressing play on the streaming service, River looks my way. "You know you're not alone, right?"

I swing my head side to side, feeling the loneliness of my surroundings with his words. "We live in the same building, River. I'm well aware."

"No, Clay, what I mean is, I'm not going to let you go through this alone. I love you. We're in this together, always." He clinks his beer against mine, and his words sit between us, the heaviness of his love grabbing hold of my heart.

The way my brother is my lifeline is something no one will ever comprehend. His presence doesn't take my pain away entirely, but it lessens the sting of Abby leaving just a fraction. He knows he can't cure my heartbreak but understands he's easing the pain just a little for a small portion of my day with this time together.

I will never look at life and not appreciate my brother for all he's done. He's always been my best friend through all of it. He's held me up when I've felt low. He constantly finds ways to find the lighter side of a serious moment, but he does it to minimize the weight on my shoulders. I know that's what he's doing right now.

# CHAPTER 2

*Abby*

"MOM, I promise I got everything. I need to focus on the road. I'm meeting Marissa for lunch. I'll call you tonight."

"Okay. Maybe you'll come over for dinner?"

I keep myself from sighing loudly, so my mom won't hear me over the speaker.

My mom needs to take the overbearing down a notch. I just want to stay in and read a book tonight. I'm feeling a bit suffocated. I haven't lived on the West Coast since I graduated from high school, and she hasn't given me a moment of silence since I got back.

"I think after lunch, I'm just going back to my apartment and settling in for the night. This rain is supposed to get worse later. I'll try to swing by in the next few days. Love you."

"Okay. Love you—"

I take the opportunity to hang up really quick before she tries to get me to commit to anything because that's my mother's specialty. She knows I feel guilty half the time, and she'll get me to agree to come over when I literally just said I'm not in the mood, so it's best I stop this conversation before it gets out of hand.

I'm finally having lunch with my high school best friend, Marissa, after having to reschedule too many times. She's an up-and-coming lawyer in Los Angeles, and she has been swamped with a case downtown. Luckily, she hasn't bailed on our little date yet today, so I'm hoping I don't get stood up once I get to the restaurant.

When it comes to understanding the law, I have little knowledge of Marissa's job. Even though it's the weekend, I am well aware her work follows her home. As a web developer, I helped her build the website for her law office.

I am lucky to work in that field and work primarily from home. I was fortunate to launch my own company shortly after I graduated from college and have slowly built my client list from there. The main advantage of working from home and owning my own company is the flexibility. Relocating from Boston to California did not impact my work life in any way.

I cannot say the same for my personal life. Since moving back, living near my parents, particularly my mother Collette, has resulted in a major intrusion into my personal space. If I'm not the one visiting them, my mother is at my apartment. I have so much love for my parents, but I value my alone time as well. And for the amount of time I've lived thousands of miles away from them, I've grown used to my space and surroundings undisturbed.

Whenever there is a knock on my door, I can bet money it's one of them. My brother, Frankie, used to call me complaining, stating our mother was constantly at his place. I used to laugh through the phone, telling him how lucky I was because I was thousands of miles away. Now that the tables have turned, he's returning the favor when we have our weekly calls.

Frankie and I have always had a close relationship despite being half-siblings. My mother married young when she found out she was pregnant right out of high school. My mom isn't shy about how hard it was to sustain a life with Frankie's father and how they were always struggling to make ends meet. His father left before Frankie could even form a memory of the man.

My mom met Rick, my father, when Frankie was in preschool, and they said it was love at first sight. She said my father swooped her off her feet. But my dad always tells me he had to fight for her love because my mom was scared of the same problems happening again when it came to financial stressors impacting the family.

My dad was the opposite of Frankie's though. He hit it big in the late 1980s with the start of a computer software company that took off. My dad took on the role of father for Frankie, and once I came into the picture after my parents got married, we simply became a happy, blended family. But the wounds from my mother's past still impact the way she reacts to me as I grow into an adult. It's hard for her to let go of the traumas from her past.

Frankie is now living in New York City with his wife after moving there about three years ago. I always thought he was exaggerating about the way my mother smothered him, but I called him a few months back to apologize to him, which earned me about an hour of laughter from him on the other end. I had sort of forgotten how obsessive my mother could be when living in the same city as her.

I'm surprised he didn't hang up on me when I called. For nearly six months after I left Clay, my brother was barely on speaking terms with me. I think if he had a choice, he would have chosen Clay in the divorce. I swear my brother has a bromance with my ex-husband—that's how much he loves him. I sort of get it… Clay is that amazing, and if I'm being honest with myself, I think about him constantly, even if my plan was to move thousands of miles away to start fresh.

Leaving Clay was the hardest thing I ever did. To this day, I'm still on the fence if it was the right thing to do. Each day, I wake up and wonder what I would be doing in that version of my life if I were still Abby Nichols.

I'll be the first to admit I started to lean too heavily on my mother while Clay and I were having trouble conceiving during those last couple of months. The thing people don't talk about when you're struggling to conceive is the fracture that can occur in a marriage. I know we hear about the difficulties some couples suffer through, but it's not always something people divulge.

The fertility treatments garnered so much pain that only mounted each month. At first, I thought we wouldn't suffer this divide when we chose IVF. I felt confident we could overcome anything. But then, as each test came back negative, I felt impatient. Then, as the months passed, I felt this immense sense of blame toward myself.

I would then get bitter, not sure if it was at myself or Clay. I'd look at him living so carefree and happy when all I felt was anxiety and misery. This bitterness would be laced in my movements. I was no longer the happy and lighthearted version of myself I knew people loved. Life became unfulfilling.

When we finally got a diagnosis of the fertility issues, I broke. That last epic phone call to my mother, I sobbed and broke down to the point that when I finally took a breath and she proposed I return to California, I couldn't resist the idea of being home.

Something about being in the sunshine and away from the pain I felt surrounded by appealed to me. Forgotten was the life I had when I left before college. The life where my mother was always watching what I did, and I couldn't get out of here fast enough. All I saw was a change, and I came running back. I'll admit, I wanted myself back, and I'd do anything to free the old Abby from the ashes of the sorrows I was living back in.

When I first left Boston, the newness of returning to the

West Coast felt exciting. I thought I had made the best choice. It was almost electric being here. The sun beating on me, it felt like I was shedding a new skin.

Although I loved Massachusetts with Clay, after dealing with all our fertility issues, being in that house felt like shackles were holding me down. The worst part, in some way, I felt like being around Clay was a reminder of the life I couldn't have.

However, now that time has passed and the layers of this life I've built here have dissipated, I'm now left with longing. I look for Clay around every corner. It's weird because I have never lived with him on this side of the country. But I literally reach for him in bed when I'm dreaming. I find myself wondering if he'll call when I'm working late at night. Whenever I'm left too long with my thoughts, my mind drifts to him. It's like I'm programmed, no matter where I am in this world, to be with him. That's when I realized that he is a part of me, no matter what life I build.

I made a huge decision to return to California, and I acknowledge it was a rash one at the time. I may have told Clay I had thought my decision through when I was leaving, but I know I was lying for his benefit. I wanted him to move on, but I was only wanting him to find his own happiness. Of course, I knew I was leaving my heart behind for his sake. My decision was made out of desperation to escape the memories due to failed attempts to conceive. But it was also out of desperation to escape the hole our failure was causing me inside. I let the pain lead my decision that day, and now I'm feeling a little lost, just on a different coast.

Leaving has had many good moments for me personally, though. I can't ignore the growth I've had since I left Boston. I moved out on my own after a few months of living with my parents. The independence gave me the opportunity to focus on myself and grow as an individual. In truth, it gave me the ability to return to the person I was before the struggles with fertility began. Little by little, I'm starting to get back into my love of art, although that is still few and far between.

Although my mother was eager to have me back, my father seemed indifferent. The divorce shocked him when I first mentioned it because he knew how much Clay always meant to me. And since returning, I've noticed his long glances my way whenever my mother inquires if I've started dating anyone.

I think if he were to give his opinion, he'd say he always liked Clay overall. My dad always says my happiness is his priority. No matter what, he wanted to lift the pain. Unfortunately, the pain I was feeling and still feel is simply not that easy to fix. But he's been by my side to give his big dad hugs and endless smiles when I've needed them since returning home.

I reach the restaurant in one piece, not that I doubted it. My mom acted like I was going to war with the rain forecast. She forgets I was living in Boston. The way there's a storm forecast in California, you'd think the world was coming to an end over here.

What's going to be over is my hair once I get out of the car. My long, wavy brown hair will double in size once I step foot out of my car. I can guarantee it because the waviness will only turn into a voluminous mess with the rain. I was blessed with big blue eyes, olive skin, and brown wavy hair.

If styled right, it's cute, but with humid or wet weather, it has a mind of its own, and today it seems my hair will set the rules. My hair normally cascades down my back, but on days like today, it will grow out much like the character Monica on *Friends* from the episode where she travels to Barbados and the humidity takes over.

I give my key to the valet, taking in what would be a beautiful view had the weather complied. Marissa chose a swanky new spot that is apparently one of the toughest places to get a reservation on a weekend, but dropping her name alone got us in.

Did I mention she's an influencer on top of being an attorney in Los Angeles? Yeah, apparently, being a lawyer isn't enough anymore. It all started with posts regarding local restaurant reviews as a side hustle in college, and she's "kept it up for fun," as she likes to say.

Walking into the front of the restaurant, I check my phone to find a text from Marissa telling me she's already seated in the back. I let the woman at the front know my name for the reservation, and I'm quickly escorted back. The colors remind me of everything an up-and-coming LA spot has to offer. It has trendy photo op spots, with props on the walls and wall art for influencers to take photos to upload on their socials. Throughout the restaurant, they have QR codes for people to easily find their information to upload and tag the restaurant. It's hard to contain my eye roll because everything is about social media these days.

As I follow the hostess through, I feel the buzz of the lunch crowd while taking in the decor, noting the florals on the wallpaper with the splashes of gold and black on the furniture. Even with this much life around me in Los Angeles, it's hard not to long for the special spots I found in Boston that always seemed to tell a story when you walked in, compared to ones I visit in Los Angeles.

The moment I see Marissa waving me down when she notices me walking toward her, I push it aside and give her my biggest smile. The minute I'm at arm's length, she pulls me in for the tightest hug.

"Oh, you bitch. It's been too long!" Marissa says into my ear.

"You're one to talk. It's like scheduling lunch with the Pope when it comes to seeing you!"

"Oh, stop. It's not that hard to see me." She continues to squeeze, with no hope of pulling air back into my lungs.

Finally, she lets go, and I take a much-needed breath in. I regain life back into my body, sit down in the booth, and drink a sip of water, taking in my friend from years ago.

"You look amazing, Marissa. Don't get me wrong. You always look good, but today, you look stunning. What's going on?"

"So, I, uh, I'm seeing someone." Despite the news being good, she seems hesitant to tell me.

"What? That's amazing!" I love this for her. Her last girlfriend was the absolute worst.

"Are you sure you're okay with this? I mean, I know you're going through everything with Clay and all, so I was a bit hesitant to say anything." She's still being guarded with this news, while I'm over the moon for her.

"Stop, Marissa. My sadness should not cloud your happiness. I'm beyond thrilled for you. Really." I reach my hand out and grasp hers to squeeze it. "Tell me more. When did you start dating? What's her name? When do I get to meet her?"

"Um, let's see. About a month. Her name is Josie. I hope soon." She's ticking each answer off on her fingers to keep track. I can't stop the smile on my face from spreading. "She's a wedding photographer." She smiles so big, it's pretty amazing to see. "We met at a banquet for work. She was actually filling in for a friend who couldn't be there. It was pure coincidence, and we just hit it off."

She is my closest friend, despite the years of living so far apart. We've remained close, and with all the times I've needed someone to lean on, she has never hesitated to be there for me, especially when Clay and I were going through our toughest times.

Not many know the full details of why things ended between Clay and me, except for my family and closest friends, which includes Marissa. She was always the first person I would call when Clay was working his long shifts and I was home alone crying into my pillow, wishing my news was anything but sad.

"We have to celebrate. Where is the server? I need a mimosa or something!" I try to locate someone to grab me a proper drink.

"Yes, we definitely do. Plus, I need to celebrate that trial being over too. That was the absolute worst." She rubs the space between her eyes and groans.

"Add that to the celebratory list." I clink my water glass to her martini glass.

Marissa was valedictorian of her graduating class in high school. She was two years ahead of me. We were on the swim team together, and we were fast friends when I was an incoming freshman.

She went to UCLA and continued on at Harvard Law School. She is incredibly gifted at what she does, and hearing about all her accomplishments makes me immensely proud to not only know her but to be her friend. She even finished a year ahead in undergrad.

Once I get a proper drink ordered, we move on to our meal, and the lunch continues with so much laughter that my stomach hurts.

"I forgot Carl tossed that frog down Danika's sweater during that fire drill. Then the Bunsen burner truly caught that paper on fire, and we had to evacuate!" We start laughing again, reminding me how good it feels to laugh and reminisce with Marissa.

We are the only ones left in the restaurant, and the staff are eyeing us with annoyance.

"Okay, let's be real for a second. Why are you back in California, Abby?"

I feel like reality has slapped me across the face. The entire lunch has been completely lighthearted, and much like Marissa usually does to her opposing counsel, she comes out of nowhere with her dose of life and hits you upside the head.

"What do you mean?" I feign innocence and stupidity, apparently. "You and I both know I've been back a year. Why are you asking me this now?"

"I'm not stupid. You know what I mean. I gave you the year, but we're done now. Why are you still here? I honestly thought you would have pulled your head out of your ass already." Right then, I start laughing, thinking this is some kind of joke, but when she doesn't join me, I realize she's not kidding.

"Oh, you're serious right now?" It comes out as a question, even though I know it's not.

"As a heart attack. Abby, I know what happened between you and Clay. I get it, sweetie, it sucks." She grabs my hand and squeezes. The sympathy in her eyes seizes my heart.

" I get it. You were hurting. You are still hurting. Honestly, I assumed you just needed space. I thought you'd get here and then spend a few nights in your childhood home and book the next flight back to Clay. I didn't think you'd last a week back with Collette. I mean, let's be real, that woman is a pain in my ass, and she's not even related to me." She laughs because she and my mom mix like oil and water. They have never gotten along.

Marissa continues, "But then you never left." I look over at her in shock. "No, no, no, that came out wrong. I don't mean that like I want you gone. I mean, I just thought you wouldn't want to stay here because of your overbearing mother." She pauses and considers how that sounded. "I guess nothing I'm saying sounds right, but honestly, no matter how I phrase it, your mom has a stick up her ass on the best days, Abby." She pats my hand, and I laugh.

"Please, just let me get this out. I love you, Abby. I love you like I love the law. Even so, I think you need to leave. California isn't for you." I gasp, and she rolls her eyes. "Oh, come on, don't give me that. It's no shock to you. You hate it here. Everywhere you go, you compare it to Boston. So don't give me that fake gasping charade because we both know I'm not lying. I'm stating facts here. You want to tell me you walked through this restaurant, and a part of you didn't think of Boston?"

She eyes me for a second, and I roll my eyes. As if proving her point, she sits up taller and says, "Exactly. Plus, I rehearsed this already, so I'm not wrong." I roll my eyes again because I know she probably has a typed-up sheet in her purse with actual bullet points listed.

"You gave this a shot. You put in your best effort. You made this mistake. Now it's time to go back home. Not here, but back to Boston. This didn't work out. California Abby isn't your look, sweetie. I love you, but this is a no-go for you, babe." She pats my hand.

"I really have no clue how to respond to this conversation." Seriously, is this the right way to speak to your best friend? I mean, don't long-distance besties ache for their friends to move back?

"Yes, usually they do, but I'm not longing for this version of you."

*Fuck, did I say that last part out loud?*

"In case you're wondering, yes, you did ask that last question out loud. If you were out here living life to the fullest, trying to find your zest for life again, I'd support it. Heck, even if you were just going to therapy while you try to process your grief for the life you lost, I'd be all for it. But you aren't. You're moping around, feeling sorry for yourself and trying to avoid your mom.

"But really, why did you come out here? And are you really living the dream here? Are you getting what you want out of this life? Because from what I'm seeing, you're not. You're just living in an apartment alone, with Collette invading your space half the time. Or most of the time, right?"

I look away, and she laughs. She knows my mom is over way too often.

"I'm not going to agree with you, but I won't disagree with you. And I promise to give it some thought, okay? But I can't just keep flip-flopping from state to state on a whim. I have to make this decision and stick to it. I mean, it took a lot for me to leave Boston to begin with. To return, it will have to be forever," I say.

"That leads me to my next line of questioning," she says, and I can't help the moan that escapes. "Don't whine; it's unbecoming. What about Clay?"

"What about Clay?" I ask.

"What about rekindling that old flame? Have you thought of that?" This isn't the first time Marissa has brought this up in the last year. She is obsessed with Clay. She isn't attracted to him. But, like my brother, she is not over the fact that I got a divorce.

"Marissa, I told you we are no longer together. He and I have moved on in different directions." I pull my hands apart to emphasize my point.

"Oh please, you haven't done anything. Have you even seen another dick since Clay?"

"Marissa, voice down!" I whisper-yell. Why do I choose a friend who's so crass?

"Come on. We're in LA. No one gives a shit. Penis. Dick. Vagina. Fuck. Pussy. No one cares." She sips her martini and rolls her eyes. Motherfucker.

"I honestly don't see why I have to answer this line of questioning," I tell her, looking to the side as I sip my mimosa.

"The fact you're avoiding eye contact is answer enough. Listen, I don't give a shit if you've fucked the entire western hemisphere, but you've always had a hard-on for Clay, and he's only had eyes for you. So, tell yourself whatever you'd like, but you love him. You still want him. This is still the person you're supposed to be with, Abby!" She is so goddamn stubborn.

"Marissa, can we drop it?" *Ugh! Why is she pushing this today? I mean, really.* First the move back, and now this? Why is she being such a pill?

"I wouldn't be a good friend if I didn't push you to see right from wrong. I could be a shit friend, but I don't think they make key chain hearts that say BSF: Best Shit Friend." She laughs at her own lame joke. To accentuate the point, she holds up her key chain with her half of the BFF charm she still has, the ratty BFF portion of the heart I gifted to her years ago still holding strong. I can't help the snort I return at her ridiculousness.

"You're such a smart-ass," I toss back at her.

"Oh, you love me." She continues to laugh. "Just fucking admit that was a good one. I think I'm going to make us that key chain, too, just for fun. Even though it doesn't apply because I'm fucking awesome." She moves her glass to cheers.

I cheers her because she is right about one thing, I do love her more than anything. Marissa is the one person I will always lean on, no matter what. I won't ignore what she's saying about Boston because it's been on my mind more often than not. I'll let it sit in the back of my mind for a little while. Maybe going back should be something I'll consider in the future. Being back here isn't bringing the new beginning I was hoping for.

---

The sound of the rain hitting my apartment window brings back memories of my first place with Clay in Boston. When memories like these pop into my head, it's hard for me not to think about what he's doing right now and what we would be doing if I were with him and still his wife.

I look down at my phone, and it's only then I realize the date. Oh my gosh. Our friends—Ashton and Samara—got married today. I completely let it slip my mind. Since I left Clay, I distanced myself from everyone in our friend group. I took the initiative to pull away from anyone he was friends with first. I wanted to take the awkwardness out of the equation and ensure no one felt obligated to choose between us.

I was always friends with Samara because it was easy to be close to someone as sweet as her, but it would be strange to stay friends since her husband has been friends with Clay since they were in kindergarten. I never wanted to put her in a bad spot once Clay and I were divorced. I'd seen it with other couples who had divorced, making others pick sides. I knew it would be difficult. I simply pulled myself out of the equation altogether.

Still, it's hard not to feel heaviness in my stomach when people I shared so many memories with are celebrating a huge moment, and I'm missing it. I feel like this is one of the first big parts of their lives I won't be there to witness. One of many memories that Clay will start to build without me. I feel a tear fall down my cheek.

I finish making my tea, grab my blanket off the back of the couch, and pull it over my legs. I scroll through one of the streaming services to find a sappy rom-com. Hopefully, I can lose myself in something lighthearted to keep my mind from drifting to thoughts of my life in Boston.

I finally find a movie and relax enough to pull myself into it, but soon, my thoughts drift to Marissa's conversation at lunch. It's hard not to overanalyze what she had to say, and her words sink farther into my mind.

She's not wrong that moving here may have been a huge mistake. I thought it would have been different for me emotionally. I thought I would have felt a huge shift by now, but it didn't even provide the Band-Aid for my heart that I originally thought it would. I saw my life moving forward differently once I settled, but nothing seemed to move forward the way I planned it, I guess.

I'm distracted by my mental spiral when my phone chimes, and I pick it up to see a name across my screen that I haven't seen in quite some time.

CLAY

No matter how hard I tried, every turn led to thoughts of you today 🖤

# CHAPTER 3

## Clay

I STARE at the text I just sent to Abby and wonder why I did that. I can't even blame the alcohol because I only had a few drinks hours ago. I don't see the little dots in return, but I know she's up. She was always my little night owl, working away on her computer endless hours into the night.

Abby Nichols is my kryptonite. In reality, I should get used to saying Abby Morris because that's her name again. She's back to her maiden name, and it about kills me that's our reality. She's back to her previous life, a life I never thought she'd return to. She spent our entire relationship telling me how hard she worked to start a life away from California, only to walk right back to it when things got hard between us.

It stings to feel like she threw out everything we had between us the moment things got hard. I've heard it time and time again from couples trying to conceive that relationships can crumble. I've listened to it and quickly ignored it. I never imagined we wouldn't last and believed we were invincible. I ignored so many forums that talked about the difficulties other families faced when they constantly dealt with infertility month after month.

As much as I wanted a baby, I wanted Abby more, and I'll admit that's still the case. I think what hurts is that the longer I live without her, the truth remains that Abby wanted a baby more than she wanted me. I wasn't enough for her. I was not the piece to her puzzle in the end.

She thought she knew what was best for me and made a huge decision about our marriage alone. And I'm more pissed about that the longer I'm left to simmer with that information.

How can I still love someone and nearly hate them at the same time? That's the emotional turmoil I'm faced with in this divorce. I constantly walk this line of anger and love when I think of my ex-wife. She is someone I wish I could spend forever with and forget about all in the same breath.

I'm about to click out of the text thread when I see the three dots appear:

ABBY

How was the wedding?

I feel like an absolute loser that I respond without waiting even an entire minute, betraying how desperate I am to speak to her. I also decide this is not the time to tell her about Samara and Ashton's baby news.

Perfect. The way I would expect Samara's wedding to look. Ash's smile was constant. You were missed.

ABBY

I miss everyone too. Glad it was a nice time. I bet they are both really happy. Did Kennedy trip your brother down the aisle?

No, thank goodness. I swear I thought she was going to poison his drink at one point. The way they both push each other's buttons, I'm not sure they're going to take each other out or go at it like rabbits.

ABBY

Ha! Yeah, I could see that. Well, it's raining like crazy here. It never rains in California, and the one day I make plans, it's a nightmare for my hair.

Oh yeah? Hot date?

I'm a glutton for punishment. We haven't spoken in months, and I'm torturing myself with this line of texting.

ABBY

Yeah. Hot double date with Marissa and my hair. You should have seen the looks we got. It was impressive. LOL.

How's my favorite lawyer?

ABBY

Good. She's dating someone new now. She seems happy.

That's good to hear. How about you, Abby? Did you find your happiness out there?

I'm pushing her. I know I am, but I can't help it. I need to hear her say it's better for her out there than it would be here. She left me, and deep down, I know she's better off with me. We are meant to be together, and I don't know what it's going to take for her to realize it, but I need her to open her eyes.

ABBY

I'm as happy as I'm going to be, Clay.

What does that even mean, Abby?

ABBY

It means I'm giving you a chance to find a better future. You know this. We've talked about this already.

> No. You talked, and I had no choice. There's a difference. You didn't give me a choice. I chose you. I still do.

ABBY

> Well, I choose to give you a better future, and that doesn't include me.

> That's bullshit, and you know it.

I decide calling her is a better option and ditch the texting.

"Clay, I don't want to fight." She sighs into my ear. The moment I hear her voice, even if she's exasperated by this conversation, relief washes over me.

"I'm not fighting. I'm having a conversation, Abby. That's what couples do."

"Well, we aren't a couple anymore. We haven't been for some time now. I think the divorce papers prove that."

I don't know why she has to remind me we're divorced. Maybe she does it to keep herself in check. I don't need her to bring it up because I'm well aware of our situation. The lack of the ring on my finger is a constant reminder of what I'm missing in my life. She's a daily missing piece for me.

"Yeah, I think you've done a good job solidifying that fact. Thanks, Abby." I let irritation lace my tone.

When I looked around tonight, I felt her absence in every fabric of the wedding. She should have been there. Every moment, I wanted to share a memory or a significance with her. I'm close to my brother and Ashton, but the way I felt a pull to Abby was next level.

"Clay, listen, I don't think this is healthy." Abby sounds exasperated as she talks to me.

"What?"

"Us talking to one another," she responds as if we talk on the daily.

I haven't heard her voice since she walked out on me. And

hearing it is instantly soothing my racing heart. I hate to admit it, but she feels like a comfort after a race. I still want to hold her in my arms when I feel overwhelmed by the difficulties this life has to offer.

But she left when things got hard. We never spoke again when she left our home that day, and it took everything in me not to pick up the phone so I could talk to her again. I gave her space, all communication coming in the form of texts or through our lawyers.

I thought she'd come running back. She never did. Each day turned into a week. Then a month turned into six. Now, a year later, and here we are, in a phone call, and I'm wishing I could hold her again.

Many describe marriage as signing one's life away, but getting a divorce felt more like it held that sentiment for me. I don't recognize the existence I'm living today. I'm constantly mourning the married life I lived versus embracing the divorced one I have ahead. It sounds pathetic, but the life of a bachelor is absolutely daunting to me.

"When did this happen to us? When did I become someone you couldn't stand being around, Abby? I remember when we couldn't keep our hands off one another. Now even hearing my voice is too much?" I feel a lump in my throat forming with the thought that I might be so repulsive to her that she can't handle a simple conversation with me.

"Clay, don't do this. You're putting me in an impossible position." She sighs. I can imagine her throwing her head back and rubbing the bridge of her nose like she's done a thousand times when irritated.

"I'm putting you in an impossible position? Fine, maybe this should just be it then," I throw back. "You know what? Let me leave you with this, then. You made a mistake, Abby. Maybe I should have flown out to California the moment you cooled off a bit. Maybe I should have dragged you home and told you to stop your tantrum and get your ass back where you belong. Maybe I should have just not signed the damn papers and told you no. I loved you, and I let you just leave. Shame on me. I loved you, and I still love you. I miss you. I missed you tonight. I miss you every night. So there, I said it. I am not ashamed to admit it. Maybe this was a bad idea. But I seem to be full of bad ideas. Fuck it. Have a good night. Sleep well."

I hang up. I'm breathing heavily, and I begin pacing my room. I can't believe I let her get me this upset. I have allowed all this irritation to fester for so long. I wanted to chase her when she left me and go after her. But I also know how much her mom doesn't approve of me, and I let that hinder me. I let that poison she was fed hold me back, and I stayed put. And now this is our life. This is our fate. We are apart, and we are living our lives separately. It's painful, but it's our truth.

I decide to grab my running shoes and change into my gym clothes. It's late, but maybe their gym is open twenty-four hours. I check with the front desk, and I'm in luck. I'm grabbing my things to leave the room when my phone chimes, and I look down to see Abby sent a text:

ABBY

I'm sorry.

I throw my phone to the bed and head out. I'm going to have to find a way to lock the door to the past, but she's holding the damn key.

# CHAPTER 4

*Abby*

"MOM, where are you putting this dish?" I've never seen this much food for three people before.

"Oh, you can put it anywhere on the table. Guests can grab as they go. It's not a formal thing," she says as she moves between the backyard and the kitchen, bringing things back and forth.

"What do you mean 'guests'? Who's coming? I thought it was just you, me and Daddy." This is the first I'm hearing of guests joining us. She invited me last minute to lunch over here today, and when I arrived, it looked like she was going to feed half the neighborhood.

"Don't be silly. You think the three of us are going to eat all of this? That's ridiculous, Abigail," she scoffs. "I told you; Frederick is coming over."

I drop the cup I'm holding on the ground. Luckily, it's only plastic.

"Abigail Morris, don't be clumsy!" I am fuming right now, not only because my mother remains the only person to call me by my full name but the fact that she is holding onto this damn fantasy.

"Why is Freddy coming here?" I nearly scream. I cannot

believe my mom invited my high school boyfriend over. This is so embarrassing and juvenile.

"Oh, he's a lovely boy. You know how much your father and I love him. I stopped by to see an old friend for lunch at that one place near Wilshire with that Caesar salad I love. Well, anyway, I ran into him there, and I just had to invite him over," she rambles, then looks at me with a quizzical look. "What? Was I just supposed to not invite him over? Don't be preposterous. I told you all this the other day." She absolutely did no such thing.

"No, Mom, you did not. And yes, you can just not invite him over... because we broke up! More than a decade ago!" I throw my arms in the air. "Why, Mom? Why would you invite him over?" I move my hands through my hair in an attempt to calm my nerves, but today, my hair is cooperative, with no frizz to combat like when it betrayed me during the last rainy day.

"Abigail, stop fidgeting and finish getting things set at the table. And don't be silly. Frederick is coming, and it's final. So is his sister and her fiancé."

If I thought the prospect of having Freddy over was daunting, seeing his sister Edith is going to be to be torture. She was the biggest bitch in our school, and she made my life hell. These next few hours will feel like a week. Add to the fact that Frederick is coming over, and I'm going to want to stab myself with my silverware. Fuckety fuck.

I pull out my phone and text Marissa.

My mother has gone too far. She invited "Frederick" over for lunch without telling me first.

MARISSA

Shit! And I wasn't invited? What the hell, Collette?

> That's not even the worst part...Edith is coming!

MARISSA

Oh shit! Let me tell my assistant to clear my schedule tonight. Make sure my number is under your favorites, and label me as your lawyer so they call me. Remember you get one phone call when you get arrested.

> I'm so fucking pissed at my mom. She went too far.

MARISSA

Your mom wasn't known for being subtle. Keep me posted on how it goes today. I'm around if you need me.

"Abigail, can you go inside and grab those blue napkins I left on the counter please? I think they'll be here any minute." She smiles at me, and I realize that even though my mom may have listened to all my cries over the phone when I called all those months ago, she didn't really hear me. I truly think she feels I'm cured of all the heartache now that I've settled into a new routine.

Little does she know my heart is not up for grabs. Honestly, the longer I'm here in California, the more I realize what a mistake I've made. Today is the huge nudge I needed to make me understand I can't stay here any longer.

It's been weeks since I spoke to Clay the night of Samara and Ashton's wedding. That entire text and phone conversation plays on repeat in my mind. What started as a playful conversation quickly escalated, but his words are on an endless loop in my mind.

I hear the doorbell ring, and I have to control the groan that wants to escape. I cannot believe I have to endure a lunch with my sleaze of an ex-boyfriend from high school. The cherry on top will be his witch of a sister, who I thought I'd never see again.

Maybe it won't be that bad now that we are all adults, and it will be a nice change of pace after years of hell growing up.

———

This is bad. Let me rephrase: *This is atrociously bad.*

Edith is worse than she was in high school, if that's even possible. She has not stopped talking about her upcoming nuptials and how lucky everyone is to be invited. Let me add that I am not invited, and she has not just hinted at this fact—she has told me to my face I am not getting an invitation. I can't even express the relief.

My dad has kept his mouth shut, holding back a laugh when he sees me biting my tongue to keep from screaming profanities in Edith's face. He knows how much this girl makes my skin crawl.

"So, Frederick, what are you doing for work now?" My mother has been trying to veer the conversation toward my ex-boyfriend the entire lunch, but his sister seems to love the spotlight. "Did Abigail tell you she's doing web design work?"

"No, she didn't. That's amazing. I'm working as a financial manager downtown. It's a solid gig. Maybe I could look at your portfolio. I think my company is looking into possibly doing some revamping of their site." Freddy looks over at me and smiles.

He's lost a lot of the boyish charm I was attracted to when we were teenagers, but he still has that attractive way about him as he inches closer to thirty. Unfortunately, my heart just isn't in it like it would have been. We never did the long-distance thing when we graduated because we knew it wouldn't last. He stayed back to attend college down in San Diego, and I got as far away from California as I could.

He wanted to try and work things out with the distance, but I knew it just wasn't worth it. I think I knew I wouldn't be back. Plus, it was just prolonging the inevitable breakup and heartache. Add to the fact he was always checking other girls out when we were together, I knew he'd have a wondering eye the moment I was on the other side of the country.

"Yeah, just let me know. I can definitely help out. I work remotely, so it's easy for me to hop on a video call and share my screen and present from pretty much anywhere," I explain.

"Nonsense. You can just meet up downtown and do everything in person," my mom chimes in, and it feels like she's my manager more than my mother right now.

"Actually, there's been a change of plans recently, and I'm headed back to Boston. So, I won't be as local as I have been lately," I announce. My mother gasps, while my father covers his face with his palm as if he knows this is going to cause more of a headache for him with the blowback from my mother.

This is exactly what I did when I felt suffocated by my mom the first time, and I moved to Boston. I did this same thing when I was deciding what college I wanted to attend. I was between one close to home and a university in Boston. I almost chose the one here in my home state until my mom pushed me to my limits.

It feels like I've traveled back in time. I'm eighteen and announcing I'm moving yet again, however, this time I already know it's a city I already know I love. My mother pushes too hard, and I push back. She doesn't give me space, and I make huge decisions that lead to grandiose announcements like these.

I was feeling suffocated, and regret was clawing at me, so here I am, opening my mouth and letting this enormous life choice come out of me. But frankly, I think I knew this was bound to happen after Marissa spoke to me at lunch that day.

After we talked, it slapped me in the face how miserable I was by being here in California. I really do miss the independence of Boston.

I loved that city, and I truly felt happy. The longer I'm here on the West Coast, the more the reality hits me that I want to be back in the comfort of that city and in that part of the country where I felt more at home. After this afternoon, my eyes are open, and that's where I belong.

There are moments when my mom is kind and comforting. That's how she was on the phone when I would call during my fertility struggles. She felt like a safe place. And when I first came back, that was the safe place she seemed to be. But the longer I've been here, she's become more overbearing than safe. The way my mom made it appear she would welcome me and comfort me lasted much less than I thought it would. Maybe a part of me hoped she would be less smothering and more of a friend in my time of need. Instead, she fell into old habits.

She did provide the comfort I needed to mend for a brief moment in time, but then I got my own place, and she began meddling in ways I didn't expect. It felt like high school all over again. She started to poke and prod here and there, inserting herself into my life in subtle and not-so-subtle ways. Then, the stunt she pulled today... it just went too far.

I'm aware I could pick a whole new place in the country and start anew. But that sounds exhausting. I know living in Boston was a lot when I left over a year ago, but now, I think it's time to try and go back. I've been discussing it in therapy, and even my doctor says it might be beneficial to try and see if things would improve. Running from my problems isn't a solution, and I see that clearly now. When I brought up with my therapist what Marissa had said at lunch, she asked me to dive a little deeper, and I ended up confessing how much I was missing Boston itself. That's when she helped me see moving back didn't have to set off all the bad things I was associating with the city.

I think some familiarity could be good for me. I can go back to Boston unannounced and just start fresh in a sense. I have the financial means to get by comfortably, get myself out there, and just start living my life without my mother meddling in my personal life. I can also find a new therapist with the help of my current one in order to feel supported while I adapt to my new life. Until then, I could continue with virtual therapy appointments until I find one in Boston.

The rest of the lunch continues, the tension building between my mother and me with each passing second. Luckily, Edith is too self-involved to take a hint and continues to talk about her wedding, not giving her fiancé a chance to get a word in. She carries the rest of the conversation until she, her fiancé, and her brother head out the door. By then, even my mother is ushering them out, which is a nice change for me because I have been counting the minutes until this lunch would end.

The moment the front door closes, my mom scurries back into the kitchen and begins. "What do you mean you're headed back to Boston, and why is this the first I'm hearing of this?"

I open my mouth to speak, but she continues, "And why would you let me have them come over if you were going to move back? Poor Frederick thought he had a chance with you, and you are moving back? I mean, that's heartbreaking, Abigail."

I stare at my mom for half a beat to ensure she's done asking her questions.

"Abigail, answer me!"

"Oh, I can chime in now, can I?" I can't help but feel like I'm back in tenth grade and being scolded by my mother.

"Don't start with me. What is going on?" she continues, and I hear my dad in the kitchen cleaning up behind me and decide to at least start walking further in to make myself useful if I'm going to start a yelling match with my mom.

"First, let's start with the fact that I had no idea Edith, her fiancé, and Freddy were coming today. You never told me, so I wasn't aware I had to inform you of anything." I look at my mom as I start throwing away empty plates. "Second, this is all too much, Mom. I told you when I was in Boston, I was feeling like I needed a reset. I told you everything I was going through. The news from the doctor and the infertility struggle were a lot to bear, so this is just too much, too soon. The thought of dating isn't something I have given much consideration to, especially dating on that level."

"What does that mean, *dating on that level*?" My mom just doesn't get it.

"Mom, let's say I started dating Freddy. Think about it! It's like starting at date ten, not date one. I would be jumping in from a few steps in. It's not like he doesn't know me at all. He might be thinking about kids. He might be a few steps ahead. Dating someone with this kind of baggage isn't really something he would like to sign up for. Please don't make me spell it out for you. I just don't want to deal with that. Maybe going out, going dancing, getting drinks, sure. Not something serious. You have to understand how this feels for me. Plus, have you thought about the fact that he might want kids? What about that? And how that might feel for me? I have to deal with that whole conversation then."

My mom is watching me as I'm explaining everything, and I can see the lightbulb go on as I take the time to explain.

"I've overstepped, haven't I?"

*No shit.* I don't say it, but I think it. Sometimes, it takes a moment for her to get there, but finally, she does. That's when I see the woman I came running to when I returned from Boston, crying and needing my mom to take my pain away. There's the woman who stood at the airport waiting to hug me and give me endless moments of her time so I could cry on her shoulder.

"Yes, Mom, you have. You've crossed the line from comforting to smothering. And it's just too much. I can't do this, and I think I need to go back to Boston. I think being here was good for a little while, but I now know I took on too much by running away," I confess.

"Does this mean you're going back to *him*?" my mom asks. It's obvious she was never a fan of me marrying Clay. I knew that, but since I left him, it's only become clearer. I think it's time to nip this in the bud. He was always good to me. He's always been kind and loving and never showed anything but his best to her.

"No, Mom, I think I really messed up with Clay. And I think he deserves something better than the way I treated him," I say right as both my parents pull me in for a huge embrace.

"I doubt that, ladybug," my dad says as he kisses the top of my head. My dad loves me and embraced what I had with Clay. "Clay loves you no matter what. But we stand by whatever and whomever you love. Right, Collette?"

My mom clears her throat. After a beat of hesitation, "Yes," she finally confesses.

I pull away. "I know that was hard to say out loud, Mom. I wish you would be kinder to Clay. He really is a good person, even if he isn't with me anymore. Why do you hate him?" I wipe away a lone tear that falls down my cheek.

My father clears his throat. "Collette, speak to her. Just tell her how you're feeling and explain your side of things."

I look between them, trying to understand what's going on. "Tell me what?"

My mother relents and moves some hair away from my face. "You know I was married to Frankie's father before your own father came into the picture. And you know how hard that was for me. How hard it was to get by?"

I nod.

"Well, I know I was pretty candid with how that was for us, but I didn't tell you everything. Franklin Sr. was my high school sweetheart, which I told you. I mean, I loved him so much. In my opinion, he could do no wrong. My parents begged me not to marry him, but he was the most handsome boy in school." She laughs and looks down at her hands as she twirls her wedding band around, lost in thought. "He couldn't even buy me a wedding ring, so he got me a ring pop and said that one day he'd replace it. I thought it was romantic. Can you believe how stupid I was back then?" She laughs, but it holds no humor.

"I got pregnant, and I thought it was going to be the start of forever. But Frankie came along, and it was so much harder for us than I ever imagined. Babies are so expensive. The moment he arrived, the fighting started. He had colic, and breastfeeding wasn't something he tolerated, and he needed special formula—another huge expense. This just added to the stress. Franklin, my husband, he couldn't provide for us financially. We lived paycheck to paycheck. What I didn't tell you is we sometimes had no food. We went weeks without any food." The moment she says this, I take in a breath, sadness overwhelming me, knowing my mother endured that kind of life.

"One day, when Franklin was off doing God knows what, I packed my things, ready to leave him. I had a whole plan for the next day, but he never returned. Another day passed, then another, yet he never came back. I swear he just never came home. I don't know if he just realized he wasn't fit to be a husband and father and couldn't provide for us or what. Maybe he believed he wasn't the man he wanted to be and just left. I honestly can't say. But the day he never came home was the best and worst of my life. Being a single mother was hard. But not raising Frankie in that type of environment was a blessing all the same," she says, holding back the tears I can see threaten to spill from her eyes.

"Don't get me wrong, when I look at Clay, I don't see Frankie's father. What I do see is someone who has a tough job. Clay is charismatic, a good-looking guy who captures hearts. Most of all, I see the two of you together, and it reminds me so much of my first marriage. You two are literally so much like the two of us. And when the fertility issues started and you mentioned the fighting, the parallels were there to when I had a new baby and I had issues with Frankie's dad. It's not exactly the same, but for some reason, it resonated with my past.

"I know, it's wrong to project. Your father has told me it's wrong for me to do what I've done. To compare Clay to Frankie's father because he's been nothing but amazing. He's provided and done the opposite of him in every way, but I've let my anxiety take over. I don't know why. I am so sorry. I wanted something better for you because no matter what, I don't want you to go through what I did years ago. Then, today, when I invited Freddy over, I let his ability to provide for you overpower everything. I just want you to be happy and comfortable. I think I'm trying to make you live a life without any discomfort. You are more than capable of providing for yourself, and I need to remind myself of that instead of worrying so much." She finally looks up at me and gives me a sad smile.

"Mom, Clay gave me so much. We never lived paycheck to paycheck. And I contributed too. I never said anything to make you think otherwise, did I? And the fighting wasn't ever yelling matches. It was strained because we were sad. There wasn't love lost between us because of our struggles to conceive though." I try to think back if I had insinuated something in my calls.

"I think early on, you had made a comment about him being a new firefighter and how much work he put in to not make much. You two were recently married, and my heart broke. Then, down the line, you mentioned starting a family, the fertility issues and the tension you were feeling, and it all sounded so familiar. So yes, I took it upon myself to worry. And it was my fault to make this about me. I'm sorry, Abigail."

"And I'm sorry, Mom, that you felt you needed to worry about me financially. It's completely normal for couples to have less money when they first start out. We were figuring things out in the beginning. We always knew it would be a lot of work for little return when he first started firefighting," I say.

I probably made a comment without thinking. I should have never said anything out of respect for Clay. But I was probably in shock seeing how much he earned after all the hard work he put into his training and shifts, and it took a moment to get used to it. We found our groove, and with time, he started to get raises. Had I known the extent of my mother's past, I would have understood what a trigger it would have been for her as well.

"As for our fighting, you have to understand, we were navigating something incredibly personal for us. We did the best we could. You can't judge us for something you have no personal experience in. And you can't put all of that on Clay. He was incredibly kind and was doing everything to be supportive. He wanted to do everything to ensure I was loved, when all I wanted to do was run," I explain.

My mother nods and stays silent, realizing the extent of her actions and her judgment toward my ex-husband.

"I'm going to work on improving my meddling skills though." She winks.

I laugh. "I appreciate that. Thank you."

"Do you know when you are headed back?" my dad asks now that the dust has settled a bit between his girls.

"It won't be for a little while longer. I need to get things in order and find a place back in Boston. Maybe something near the water. I always loved those apartments with a harbor view." Clay and I dreamed of starting a family and moving to a place in the city with a view of the harbor.

"Well, consider this," my dad begins. "Your mother and I are thinking of buying some property, and we could buy in Boston. You can live in the property we purchase, free of rent."

"Dad, I can't do that. Really, it's too much." I honestly thought I'd just rent something or find a roommate for a short period of time until I found the perfect place to settle.

"I think your father's right. Let us do this. I think your heart was meant for Boston. As much as I want you here, I think you are meant to be there. We were looking into doing something like this anyhow." She smiles and tucks a piece of my hair behind my ear. I wish I could bottle this feeling up when I feel her love this way. She's not always in this comforting mood.

The rest of the evening is uneventful. We come up with a plan that feels like a solid one. I text Marissa, and she seems relieved that I'm moving back. California was supposed to be permanent, but I think I always knew it wasn't where I was meant to be. Boston is where I left my heart, and I guess it's time for me to go retrieve it. Too bad the person who owns the key to my heart is one I'll never confront and ask for it back.

# CHAPTER 5

## Abby

"I THOUGHT you said you were going to help me pack?" I say as I tape up yet another box on my own.

"I said nothing of the sort," Marissa calls from the other room.

"If I recall correctly, you called and said, 'I will come over and help you pack, then we can hit up the town like two kick-ass women in LA.'" I use air quotes to emphasize my irritation.

"First off, I do not need to say kick-ass women because it's implied by my personality. Don't be ridiculous. Second, I told you I would come over and pick you up after you were done packing. If you needed me to, I could have had my assistant from the office here helping. He loves organizing things," she says as she sits on my sectional and drinks her martini.

"Where did you find a martini glass in this mess?" I look at her in shock. Did I even have a martini glass in this place?

"I didn't. I brought it with me. It's plastic." She taps on it.

"You brought a martini glass from home? You have issues," I scoff.

"Can you not be so judgmental? It's your last night in LA.

You had, like, one box to pack. Stop being so difficult." She rolls her eyes.

She's not wrong. I've been slowly packing for weeks now.

"Okay, so where are we going? You're being super secretive about it," I say.

"Not telling you. But at least I'm not driving. I didn't drive here, and you won't need to either. It's down the street from your place. I can't wait. You'll love it. So, it's perfect for us," she squeals.

Forty minutes later, I'm sitting in front of an easel with a blank canvas in shock that Marissa is about to endure a paint and wine night. She hates things like this, but she loves me enough to do it for me.

I've never done this before with friends. I've, of course, painted on canvas but I've never gotten to go out with friends to do it. Marissa is not good with a brush; I already know this will turn out absolutely horrendous for her. The memories I'll leave here with tonight will be absolutely wonderful to take with me to Boston.

It took me some time to find a place I liked in Boston, so moving wasn't as quick for me to pull the trigger. Once I found a spot I envisioned for me to move into, my parents made sure the investment property made sense for them as well.

Things moved from there, and I started the process of getting things ready in California for my move. Now that it's really happening, I've got butterflies multiplying by the second. The movers are coming early tomorrow morning. I'll be flying out on a red-eye tomorrow night and waiting for my things to arrive in Boston. I decided to stay in a hotel while my belongings are being driven across the country.

I'll be buying some new furniture for the apartment, but the majority of boxes with my clothes and dishes will be making their way over. I don't have too many large items, so there shouldn't be too many things to unpack once every-thing gets there.

Either way, knowing I'll be going back to a place that holds all my adult memories is exciting and nerve-wracking all in one. It's hard to imagine what it will be like to run into people I will know. Especially one particular person.

Clay has crossed my mind constantly as I think about Boston. I don't even know if he's seeing anyone. My brother hasn't said if he's dating, although I'm not sure he'd tell me. I asked that he not mention my return to Boston, and he hasn't fought me on this issue.

Marissa speaks to him occasionally, but she's tight-lipped about Clay's personal life. I wonder if she'd say something about Clay's dating life just to get a reaction out of me. She might tell me just to see if I'd get mad.

The moment my brush moves through the paint and I swipe it across the canvas, I feel at home. Each element of painting brings relief to my heart, and I'm swept into a new level of comfort. It doesn't matter the medium of art I practice —it relaxes my body and mind.

Marissa and I laugh too much the entire time we are sipping our wine and painting. I succeed in making my starry night painting. I wish I could say the same for Marissa. Hers looks more like a hideous, blotchy mess. It's more abstract than anything, but that's Marissa in a nutshell.

We leave the studio giggling, and my heart is full. The moment we step out into the night, the warmth of the Cali-fornia summer coating our skin, Marissa grabs my painting.

"This will look perfect in my hallway, right next to that one piece you made me when I finished law school. Remember that one, it's of Boston Harbor?" she says, and my laughter dies immediately.

"Of course I remember. But what do you mean? I painted this for me," I say, reaching for my canvas.

"No, no. This night was about painting keepsakes for each

other. You're leaving me, and I needed something to remember you by. You need something for your new apartment that reminded you of me, and this is the perfect something, obviously." She rolls her eyes.

"This is your something?" I ask.

"Yes, it's gorgeous!" she exclaims.

"Obviously," I answer, sarcasm evident.

"Hang it with pride, my friend." She pats my cheek.

It's hideous. But I know that if I don't hang it up, she'll FaceTime me and ask to see it, and if I scramble and don't show her evidence of it, she'll call me out on it. Then she'll visit, and if I don't show it to her, she'll throw a tantrum. That's just Marissa's way.

"I'll think of you each time I walk by it," I tell her.

"Obviously," she says, and she's not being sarcastic.

# CHAPTER 6

## Abby

I LOOK out at the water while drinking my coffee, and I feel at home. Although I didn't have much to unpack compared to most, it still felt like I took forever to get things out of boxes. Time has flown and I've now been here nearly six weeks. The moment I stepped foot on Boston soil, I felt like my heart was home.

As I was boarding my plane the night of my flight, I was nervous. Marissa had to talk me down off the ledge multiple times, making sure I made it on the plane when I was at the airport. I remember at one point; she even had me FaceTime to ensure I truly sat in my seat. But when I looked out my window as we made the descent into Boston, it felt like all the nerves dwindled, and my heart was beating for my beautiful city again.

My phone rings, and I smile the moment I hear the ringtone. "Hey Lover" by LL Cool J ricochets off the walls of my new apartment. Without looking down at my phone I know Marissa's voice will grace me the second I hit accept.

"How's my little Bostonian doing now that she's back in her neck of the woods?" Marissa starts without a hello.

I laugh because she always gets me to smile. "I'm well.

You know you don't have to ask me that each time you call. I've been back a while now. How are you?" I've settled in nicely now that all the boxes are finally unpacked, and I know where everything is. It took me a while to remember where I stashed all my things after throwing the final few items in any spare space I could find.

I got antsy when I kept putting off the last boxes in the corner and gave in to simply throwing items into the cabinets where I had space. I'll admit I haven't ventured out much aside from a few strolls outside and getting groceries at some nearby markets. Luckily, I haven't run into anyone I know yet, but I know it's only a matter of time. I didn't tell any of my friends out here that I moved back to the city.

I'm walking through the hallway, taking note of the ugly-ass picture Marissa painted on that last night we went out.

"This painting of yours is an eyesore, by the way. But it somehow brings the whole apartment together, I'll have you know." I chuckle into the phone.

"Oh, I bet you miss me each time you pass it." She laughs.

"You know I do. It's the best housewarming gift you could have given me." I make my way to the kitchen to retrieve my second cup of coffee for the day.

"Well, you know me, I always like to be a little different with my housewarming gifts," she says. "But that's not my housewarming gift this time around."

I think back to one of the gifts she sent us in the past. She mailed Clay and me a large pillow with a picture of herself on it for us to put in our first apartment together before we got married. It was the ugliest selfie, displaying a clay mask and alien headband. It legit made us jump anytime we moved it throughout the house. Clay got a kick moving that pillow all over the place just to see me lose it each time I'd walk into a room.

"Oh, I can't wait to see what amazing item you're adding

to my new place." Maybe it's a life-size cutout of Matt Damon or something.

"Here's the thing. It's not quite an item but an experience," she says hesitantly.

"I will not go skydiving, Marissa. Absolutely not!" She tried to get me to do it once, and I swear, as much as I love her, I refuse to do it.

"No, not that. You think I'd miss watching you jump out of a plane and not be there to witness that? Come on! No, this one you have to agree to before I tell you what it is, but remember, life is short, and we have to live life to the fullest. Also, remember how awesome your best friend is and that you moved back to your favorite city because I convinced you to."

"Oh yes, you are the best, oh wise one," I tell her, laughing between sips of coffee.

"So, you agree to my gift?" The way she sounds, I know she's up to something, but my curiosity is piqued.

"Yeah, sure, why not?" *I mean, really, how bad could it be?*

"Great! You're all settled, right?" she asks.

"Yep. Finally, no more boxes now. Free as a bird. No plans this weekend either. What's up?" Oh, I hope it's one of those ice cream deliveries or something.

"Perfect! Well, be ready at five p.m. tomorrow in your best dress. Wear makeup and heels! Because you're going on a date, my friend!"

What. The. Actual. Fuck?

"NO! Marissa. Absolutely. Not. Fuck no! I'm sick." I begin coughing to play it off.

"Nope. Too late. It's happening. I already set off the bat signal. Love you so much. I have to go. There will be consequences, and it will involve a plane and you jumping out of one if I hear you aren't ready when said date shows up at your door. So I highly recommend you do option A. Toodles."

I'm about to argue when she hangs up. Fucking ass.

First line of business: Find a new best friend. In Boston.

———

"Oh, that one is super cute. I love it!" Hilary compliments me through FaceTime. My brother's wife is one of the sweetest people I've met, and I'm currently putting her at the top of my list as a contender for the best friend position after Marissa gets fired.

"This is a horrible idea. I mean, what was Marissa thinking?" I'm going to break out in hives with how nervous I am, and my date is supposed to be here in ten minutes. Also, I have no idea who he is, what he looks like, or what his name is.

Marissa gave me explicit instructions that she would give me his name right when he's about to ring the doorbell because she's trying to keep the element of surprise. I swear she's driving me nuts.

"I think this is so romantic. What if this is the most amazing meet-cute you've ever seen? Right, honey?" She looks past me on the screen to who I assume is my brother. "I mean, this could be a rom-com, don't you think, Frank?"

I swear she has hearts in her eyes. My brother met his wife on a flight while traveling for work. Talk about a meet-cute of epic proportions. I still can't believe it. She got transferred to New York for work, and they've been there ever since.

Well, romantic or not, I'm going to get an ulcer before the night is over, and I'm going to lose my mind.

"This is awful, Hilary. What if I throw up on his shoes? What if he's the worst? What if he's boring? What if—"

"Oh my gosh, Abby, stop! There are so many what-ifs you could list, but you will never know if you don't try. Just go have fun. Either way, you get a free meal. Enjoy that aspect," my brother chimes in.

Both Hilary and I roll our eyes. Men don't get it. There's

an emotional component to all this he just doesn't under-stand, but at the same time, I know he doesn't mean anything by it, so I'm going to let it slide for now. I think he's just bitter that I'm going on a date, and it's not with Clay.

Right then, the pieces start to fall into place. Oh shit. What if this is all a ruse, and this date *is* with Clay? Fuck! What if Marissa set this up with Clay, and she's playing a trick on me? Now I'm really going to be ill.

A knock on my door sounds, and my eyes nearly bug out of my head. I whip my head toward my phone to look at Hilary, and she starts laughing. Is he early?

"It's going to be okay. You're either going to have the best time or the best story. Promise me you'll call. Either way, you look hot!" she whispers as she blows kisses to me while my brother whisper-yells in the background to be safe and she hangs up.

I smooth my hand down my dress and look back at my phone. The text from Marissa says the person I'm going on a date with is named Tucker.

The moment I read the name, I can't help but recognize it. Why does that name sound familiar? And in the same instance, a pang of disappointment hits me that the name she mentions isn't Clay.

I hear another knock on my door, so I move quickly to answer it. I swing it open and find a large, burly man with a thick red beard and forest-green eyes. Now I know why the name looks familiar because I've met him before. Shit! He's a fucking firefighter.

Damnit, Marissa! She set me up with someone from one of the firehouses in Boston. He doesn't work in Clay's firehouse, but these guys all know of one another, and there is no way Clay won't find out about this through the grapevine. This is already a disaster, and we haven't even spoken one word to each other.

"Hey. Abby, right? I'm Tucker. But everyone calls me Malloy." He smiles and extends his hand toward me.

I'm standing in my doorway, stunned in place. I can't even pretend I'm not shocked by what's transpiring right now.

"Hi. Yes, hello. So, you know who I am?" If he remembers me, he must know I was married to Clay.

"Yeah, I mean, Rios… uh, Daniel Rios reminded me when he set this up. I know your ex."

Rios set this up? How did someone in Clay's company set us up and not feel like he was betraying the brotherhood? I'm so confused. I will have words for Marissa, but I have no time for this. A text will suffice. Also, Rios's first name is Daniel? I had no idea.

"It's nice to see you again, Malloy. Am I too dressed up?" I look down at my dress and then look at his cargo shorts and T-shirt. I feel extremely overdressed.

"Absolutely not. I don't mind having a beautiful woman on my arm tonight. You might be a little cold being outside for part of tonight's dinner though." He rubs the back of his neck, seeming uncomfortable as he looks me up and down. He's still standing quite a distance away from me as if he stands too close, he'll catch cooties or something. This is off to a stellar start.

"Let me grab a sweater." I hold the door open for him as he walks in, and I run to my room to grab a cardigan. I use this time to send a text to whom I am now feeling confident is my ex-best friend:

> What in the world, Marissa!

The dots appear within seconds, but take forever to formulate a response. I take my sweet time to dig up a sweater while I wait to see what she has to say.

MARISSA

Oh my gosh! Is he hot? Have the best time.
Can't wait for details! 😊

YOU. ARE. INFURIATING.

MARISSA

Yet you still love me.

Debatable.

MARISSA

Can't wait to hear how it goes.

If I call you after this shitshow.

MARISSA

Oh you'll call. You always call, bestie.

I hate you.

MARISSA

You love me. That's what pisses you off even
more.

Damn it. She's right. Even after all this, I love her because she knows that even if this is a disaster, I need to get out—to rip off the Band-Aid and start meeting people again. I really hate that she's right.

Fine. I'll call you tomorrow.

MARISSA

Gosh. You didn't even make me sweat.
Thank goodness I became the lawyer
betyour the two of us. You're a shitty
litigator.

I'm not a litigator. I'm a web designer! I'm
going back out there and getting this disaster
over with.

MARISSA

That's the spirit!

Again, I hate you. Bye.

MARISSA

Love you too. Bye.

"Okay, I found a sweater." I hold it up like I caught a fucking trout on a fishing trip. What is wrong with me? I find Malloy looking out at the harbor.

"This view is amazing. I wouldn't leave this spot if I lived here," he says without taking his eyes off the water.

I don't remember much about Malloy, aside from what Clay mentioned in passing. Clay was never a fan. Always told me Malloy was crass and difficult. Clay complained he was rough around the edges and never fit in with his group of friends. I only vaguely remember Clay mentioning that out of all the guys, Malloy only got along with Rios because they grew up together.

Now that I remember correctly, Clay's exact words were, "condescending prick," but something about the way Malloy is looking out at the water, he's really giving off "sensitive giant" by the look of things. I know I've known him for a mere three minutes, but I've always been a good judge of character, and he's not really giving off the vibe of a person that seems rude or cocky.

"Yeah, I can't argue with that. It's nice to sit there with a good book and just get lost most of the day," I say back.

"I could see that." He smiles, completely lost in thought.

My stomach growls loudly, pulling both of us from our thoughts.

"Where should we go to eat?" I ask, both of us laughing.

"Oh, I have the perfect spot." He smiles, and it's warm and welcoming. Maybe this date won't be half bad.

———

I was wrong. This date is definitely not what I expected.

Malloy brought me to a hot dog stand. Not even a food truck, but an actual hot dog stand like one outside a baseball field. I put in the effort to be in heels, a tight dress, and full makeup as per Marissa's instructions, and I'm sitting on the curb trying not to spill condiments all over myself.

Here's the deal. I am not uptight. I'm the girl who would rather stay in, wearing my sweats, with a movie and popcorn, than wear this skintight dress. I am all about that life. I'd choose that over the skintight dress anyway. But I put in effort. I did the layers of makeup and a smokey eye. As someone who works from home and doesn't go out much, I looked up a tutorial and got the latest trend on how to curl my hair just right!

I went to the trouble to get the look down tonight, so yes, I wanted a nice night out. Ask any girl, and they will tell you that for all this work, they want effort put into their night. I didn't do all this to sit on the side of the road and eat a hot dog. I could have put tennis shoes on and some jeans with a simple tee and just grabbed a hot dog any day of the week.

It sort of feels like Malloy just thought of this random thing while he was walking over here and saw the cart and pulled me in this direction. If Marissa went out of her way to make this happen for me after such a hiatus on my end of dating, why start with this introduction into the dating world? This isn't making me feel very special.

I'm not trying to sound ungrateful, but once someone has been through divorce, they just want the effort made if they're going to start dating again. That's all. So here I am, with a significant intention to make myself look nice tonight, and this guy brought me to get a hot dog. Figures.

"How long have you been back in Boston?" Malloy asks with a mouth full of his second hot dog.

Sipping my drink, I take in the people walking by. "Almost two months. It's strange to think I've been gone because the moment I unpacked, it felt like I never left. I thought moving away would be the right move for me emotionally, but my heart just wasn't in California."

"Yeah, I could see that. I visited the West Coast once. It wasn't for me. But the weather is nice. I'll give it that much," Malloy says.

"Yeah, it does have that going for it. It's never horrible weather in California, especially in the winter when everyone is drowning in snow; they're still soaking up the sun." I smile.

That is something many people asked me about when I first moved to Boston. When we are freezing in the winter months here, they'd always be baffled that I'd choose to leave the California sun to endure the Boston cold. But once I met Clay, nothing else mattered. Now I'll see how I feel enduring all the seasons without the one person who made everything possible for me all year long.

We once again sit uncomfortably silent. I can't take it much longer, so I simply blurt it out.

"Malloy, what are we doing on this date together?"

I can't take the small talk about the weather from Boston to California. The longer we are on this date, the more it feels like he doesn't want to be here. Don't get me wrong, I don't want to be here either, but I was forced on this date. What's his excuse?

"What do you mean? We're on a date," he says like he rehearsed that excuse all day before going out tonight.

I look at him with a *come the fuck on* look on my face.

He lets out a breath. "You want the truth?"

"Always," I say before taking a bite of a potato chip.

"Please don't say that, then get all pissed when I tell you. You seem like a pretty chill chick. I mean, I get this vibe from you that we could actually be friends. I don't say that lightly because I don't have any female friends, at least none that I don't want to sleep with," he adds, and the smile that crosses his face shows off a side of him that most likely has girls falling at his feet. I'm not one of them.

"I promise I will not take offense." I cross my heart and laugh at the ridiculousness.

He blows out a breath again, nerves really taking over his behavior.

"You know Rios from Clay's station, I assume." He looks at me as I nod. "Well, he's my best friend. I've known him as long as I've understood friendship. I'd do anything for him. That being said, I wouldn't do anything to compromise that friendship. He's my ride or die."

Malloy looks away, focused on something in the distance, and nothing he's saying makes any sense. Is he saying he has something for Rios? I don't get it.

"Well, you see, Rios has four sisters, one of which is the youngest. Baylee's in her last year of college. She was always that bratty little sister, and growing up, that's always how I saw her. But something changed. When I was around her recently, I felt differently. *We* felt differently. And I think Rios noticed something."

He's fidgeting with his hands, and I can tell this conversation is only getting more uncomfortable for him. I put down my food and grab his hands. Nothing about my gesture is romantic—I'm holding onto him to show he's got someone to lean on, and he continues.

"Marissa got ahold of Rios right when he and I were in a heated discussion about his sister. I guess she's trying to play matchmaker with you and Clay. She thought she'd light a fire under your asses and called Rios to see if he could make Clay jealous. I don't know the whole story, but she called when I was over at his place.

"He put me on the spot after he hung up with Marissa. I couldn't say no because he wanted to prove a point to see if I would accept in front of his sister. The moment I told Rios I would go out with you; I saw Baylee's eyes dim. It fucking gutted me. But I also don't know life without Rios. I ended up accepting the date. Accepting the date with you was a dick move to Baylee, but the only way to prove to Rios I wasn't making a move on his sister, you know?"

He hangs his head, and I can see he's absolutely wrecked.

"You're not a dick. You care for both of them. You have a heart. There's love for them both in this situation. That's evident," I tell him. I was not expecting this crazy story though.

I start laughing. At first, it's a soft chuckle, but then it starts to become uncontrollable laughter. Malloy must think I'm crying at first, so he pats my back, but then I'm doubling over, cackling so loud, it's hard to contain myself. Tears are springing from my eyes.

"Are you laughing, Abby? What's so funny right now? I just told you I'm out on a fake date with you and that my friendship is sort of a shit show, and all this with Baylee went down, and you're laughing at me?" He seems sort of in shock, and I'm still laughing.

"Well," I'm trying to catch my breath, "yeah, sort of." I continue to laugh because this is sort of a disaster.

"I mean, I feel like I'm on an episode of *The Bachelor* mixed with that old show *Punked*. Remember that show from years ago? I mean, this is sort of ridiculous. Look at us. We are sort of disasters." I'm still laughing, wiping the tears from my eyes.

"Hey, I love *The Bachelor*. I watch it, along with *Love is Blind*, with the guys at my station. We take bets any chance we get on who's going to win."

I look up at him, and I swear he's just a big teddy bear.

"Oh my gosh, Malloy. That's it. You're never getting rid of me. We're friends for life now. I love both of those shows. I watch them religiously! Are you caught up for next week's *Bachelor*? Because I swear if he doesn't give Lexie a rose on the next episode, I might eat an entire tub of chocolate ice cream!"

"How about when he left Lexie waiting until the very last second last week?" He throws his arms in the air.

In this moment, I realize I've gained a friend in Malloy. A friend is something I can handle and something I need.

I smile up at him. "I think we just became friends, Malloy."

"Yeah, I think you're right, Abby."

"I didn't expect you to take the news of a fake date so well. But I appreciate you being so kind to me. All of this was really weird for me. Things have been a little off with Rios ever since he assumed things between his sister and me." He laughs, but it holds no humor.

"No. I need a friend. It's been strange being back, even though it feels like home in Boston more than California ever has."

This big guy looks like he could be all of five years old with the smile he gives me.

"Maybe you need to be honest with yourself though. If you really like her, you need to tell her. And then you need to tell Rios. Keeping it from him is only going to make it worse," I tell him. I don't know how to deal with something like this personally, but I can only imagine a secret like this will ruin a friendship more than help it.

"The thing is, I haven't done anything. I just have a feeling. I know she and I have this pull. I know she feels it when she's around me too. We haven't acted on it, but it's there. Obviously, it can be felt because Rios saw something between us, but I swear we didn't do anything together. I won't lie and say I didn't think about it though. I wanted to. Man, did I want to. But it's too late. She left last weekend, and we haven't spoken since. The moment this date was planned, she packed her things and left. It's probably for the best."

From how devastated he looks, I can tell that none of it

was "for the best." He seems completely wrecked from what he's telling me.

I squeeze his hand in mine. "Well, you can call me anytime. Hand me your phone." And the moment he gives me his phone, I input my number and put *Bestie* with a heart next to it.

It will be nice to have a new friend to lean on nearby. It will be a new start for me too. I needed this. It might not have been what Marissa had planned for me, but it's something my heart needed to start mending itself.

"I appreciate you listening, and I'm sorry this was the worst date ever. I just thought if I made this a shitty date, you'd think I was an ass and find me repulsive," he says, shrugging his shoulders.

"Well, I don't think I can find this repulsive," I point to his muscular frame, "but the date wasn't great." I laugh. "I hope you'll work on your dating game before taking your girl out."

"Ha, *if* I take her out, you mean."

"Oh, you'll take her out, Malloy! I'll put money on that!" I sound more like my ex-husband and his brother than I'd like.

"You're sounding like those Nichols brothers, from what Rios tells me."

"You're not wrong." I laugh to myself, feeling that familiar little ache in my chest when I think about all the little things I miss about my ex and his family.

"Listen, there's one last part of this whole date Rios had planned that you may not like though." He looks uncomfortable again.

I can't help the uptick in my heart rate. The hot dog I just ate threatens to come back up.

"Oh gosh, I'm scared to ask what you mean by that statement." I look at him cautiously.

"Rios just texted that he and some of his crew are at the bar waiting for us to show up. He had this plan that we'd stop by so that Clay would see us. I know, it's a dick move.

But it was how we'd get Clay jealous." Malloy hangs his head. "I know it's a horrible plan. I can feel it in my bones. But at the same time, I think Rios means well by wanting to see you two back together. From what he tells me, you two were really great together, if that's any consolation." He winces, and it does little to make me feel better.

"Um…" It's hard to feel relief at Rios cheering my ex and me on like that. I mean, Clay and I were the "it" couple for so long, but now we aren't, so it's not something I'm running toward anymore.

"So, you're inviting me to walk into a room full of Clay and his firefighting buddies?"

As much as that rattles my nerves, a part of me wonders if he'd still be jealous to see me with another man. I know the last time we spoke, he hung up on me. He was so angry that he might be done with me after that last call. Maybe he started dating since then. It's so hard to tell. A part of me is scared he's given up on us, which is incredibly stupid because I literally left him so he could move on. Why are emotions so confusing like this?

I must be a masochist and need to feel the pain of my own actions. Walking into that bar is selfish and incredibly wrong. Then why am I considering it? My new therapist will have something to say about it at our next session on Tuesday.

Malloy looks over at me, and I think pity is all I see reflected in his expression.

"I completely get it if you don't want to go. I can tell Rios you're not feeling good, and we can go somewhere else. He'd never know. You know what, why don't we do that, and I'll take you somewhere else. This was a bad idea. We can find another spot." He's getting up and picking up his trash. I quickly cover his hand to grab his attention.

"You know what? It's okay. We can go there. I mean, I'm bound to run into Clay sooner or later, right? I mean, we're friends, right?"

I see Malloy's shoulders relax. "We don't have to do this. Rios is a shit for coming up with it, and I'm a dick for even bringing it up to you. The more we're getting to know each other, I'm feeling oddly protective over you already, Abs." He throws his arm around me, more like a big brother being protective than in a romantic gesture.

I shake my head. "No, really, it's fine. We can go."

"Are you sure? I mean, this could go horribly wrong. The more I think about it, this is probably a clusterfuck of a situation. But if you do want to go, I'll protect you against all the firefighters." He throws another smile that I bet melts all the hearts in Boston.

I can't help but love the feeling of Tucker Malloy protecting me with his arm around me, and in no way do I feel the flutters of my heart like I do when I think of Clay's arm around me.

"I haven't seen my ex-husband since I was last in Boston, so I really have no clue how things will go. I will apologize in advance for whatever is said," I say, grimacing at the thought.

"Ha, that's fine. What's the point of having all these muscles if I can't keep my date out of trouble anyway." He winks my way. "Plus, it gives me an excuse to let out some aggression. Hell, I'm frustrated anyway over Baylee, so I wouldn't mind focusing on something else for a little while." We begin walking toward his parked truck.

"Please don't hit Clay." My eyes bug out of my head for fear a fight will break out the minute these two are in the same room. I can already feel my heart rate doubling.

"I get that Clay may have a bad impression of me, and maybe I haven't been on my best behavior around him and his friends, but I'm really not that guy. I swear. I'm a big teddy bear, I promise. I love hard, including my friends, Abby." He pulls me close, and he's right—he does feel like a teddy bear.

It's a short drive to *Jenson's*—a local spot owned by

Tommy, a retired firefighter from Clay's station. I used to come down here back when we were married.

The moment I walk into the place, I feel Clay before I see him. Making my way inside, I can see he's with River and a few of their fellow brothers at a table on the other side of the bar.

I see eyes on me, and my stomach drops when I am recognized. I walk a few steps in and take a look around. I scan the place, and that's when Clay's eyes lock with mine.

He was mid-sentence with his twin, River, when he stopped talking and now sits there like a statue staring at me. His face turns to stone as he takes me in. I assume, at first, he thinks he's imagining me, like I'm a figment of his imagination. Malloy bends down and whispers something in my ear. Honestly, I have no clue what he says because I am solely focused on the man I once called my husband.

All I see is Clay, much like when we were together. I can see the second he registers the proximity between me and Malloy, presuming that we are "together" as his body hardens.

Rios says something to the table, and Clay stands. River has to hold his brother back. I realize what a huge mistake this was, and I wish I had thought this through because from the anger I see in my ex-husband's expression, nothing good is going to come from this encounter.

I should have known this would implode if he was here, but I guess I was naive to think we could be civil in a public setting. I don't know why I assumed such a thing because I was an idiot not to even warn him I returned to Boston in the first place. I've been an idiot about a lot of things lately.

I see something move through River's expression, and I feel the guilt even more. I always loved the dynamic between the brothers. They loved me so much. Even though they are identical, I fell in love with Clay, whereas with River it felt like I gained a brother of my own. He was truly a protector, and he was someone I leaned on in so many ways.

I know Clay confided in him after we divorced and told him how we struggled to conceive, and I know he was heartbroken to hear how things crumbled between us. But seeing the devastation on his face now, what I'm doing here with another man, a firefighter nonetheless, is breaking his heart just as it is his twin. I wish they understood this is not at all as it seems.

As I'm moving through the bar on autopilot with Malloy ahead of me, I'm pulled out of my thoughts when I hear Clay's voice. "What are you doing here with my wife, Malloy?"

*My wife.* The knife feels like it's being pushed further into my chest. I'm hurting him even more, and it's the last thing I wanted to do tonight. Rios knows this isn't what it looks like, but he's doing nothing to explain it. Why did he set this up? And why isn't he intervening? My gaze shifts over to Rios, but he doesn't make eye contact. This is getting worse by the second.

I should have texted Clay that I was headed to this bar or that I was hanging out with Malloy as a friend, but this thing with Malloy and Rios's sister isn't my story to tell. So I'll honor Malloy's secret and simply allow this to be a friendly interaction because, to me, it's nothing more. Too bad both men don't let me chime in, and it begins to escalate before my eyes.

"Last I checked, she no longer wears your ring on her finger." *Wow,* Malloy is really asking for trouble. It's taking everything in me not to rub the spot between my eyes to calm the throbbing that's starting to erupt there. The headache I'm going to get from this is going to explode and never die down. I just want to leave this bar and go home. I honestly want to erase this date from ever happening.

I remember Tommy from when I'd come to this bar with Clay, and he's always welcomed me with the warmest hug and the sweetest smile. But today, he's got a serious expression and hasn't once glanced my way. His eyes are glued to Malloy, and I know he's focused on avoiding a fight in his bar.

Without looking at me, Tommy says, "Hey, Abby, why don't you and your date head somewhere else. Let's not cause any trouble right now, yeah?"

I couldn't agree more, so I rub Malloy's forearm in hopes of getting his attention. It's not the first time I've touched him in an affectionate way, signifying a friendly connection, but that's not how onlookers perceive it. Unfortunately, it gets Clay's attention, too, and I see his gaze directed to where my hand connects with Malloy, and I swear I think Clay is going to blow.

I whisper to Malloy, "Maybe we should head out. This was a bad idea. Let's grab some ice cream at that place we just passed."

Hopefully, Malloy isn't set on standing his ground and staying. When we were having dinner earlier, he didn't come off as someone who would push too far out of stubbornness just to prove a point.

River decides to speak up and adds, "That's a great idea. Why don't you listen to her." It's not hard to miss the disappointment in his tone. It's directed at me, and I deserve it. I don't know if I'll come back from this one in the Nichols' eyes.

I broke this line of trust, not only with Clay but with River too. I love them both in such different ways, and I wish things could have been different. But no matter what I hoped this relationship could have been between us, I caused this rift. Tonight, I have gotten confirmation that he hasn't moved on. A part of me, the part that has saved that piece of my heart for him, is relieved. That selfish piece of me wants to scream that I want him back. And yet the other part now feels relieved that he can now move on. He deserves more than me. No matter what, though, I need to apologize once things settle down later tonight.

Finally, Malloy grabs my hand and begins to walk toward the exit. Before I break my gaze away, I mouth an apology to River. I really am sorry. No matter what future any of us hold, I love Clay. I will always love him. What we shared is sacred to me. It might be hard for people to understand the choices I made, but I made them out of love. Maybe some think I made them out of selfishness. Some even believe I was being stupid. Without the full story or without walking in my shoes, they can believe what they'd like, but I did what I feel is best for Clay's future. I am truly thinking of him.

The moment we get outside, I finally take a full breath of air. It felt like I was suffocating in there being surrounded by Clay and all his friends. It took everything in me not to grab Rios by the ear and have a word with him because he acted like he wasn't a part of this little charade with Malloy. Granted, he had no idea Malloy let me in on the little secret that was concocted, but still, he looked completely innocent in there. If Clay ever finds out why I was with Malloy tonight, I don't think Rios would be so calm.

"I hate to do this, but I think I'm going to ask you to drop me off. I don't think I'll be great company. Plus, I think I should clear the air with Clay before this gets worse."

"Yeah, I get it. I'm sorry. I hope this doesn't complicate things more." He seems completely gutted at my pain, and we look like old friends versus two people who just started this friendship a few hours ago.

"I really appreciate you sticking up for me back there. I know those guys give you a hard time. Rios would be lucky to have you date his sister." I walk over and give him a hug, even though I'm half his size, and he swallows me up in an embrace.

We pull apart and make our way over to his truck.

"I'll drive you home." He opens the passenger door for me, and I struggle to get my short legs up into the raised cab.

"Actually, do you mind dropping me off somewhere instead? I think I should clear the air first." I decide it's best I get this over with now, or I'll never get a good night's sleep.

"Yeah, no problem." Malloy closes the door and makes his way to the driver's side.

The drive is quick, and the conversation is easy. I don't have many outside of the friends I share with Clay. We'd been together so long that we've shared most of our acquaintances since we were in college. When I moved back to California, I kept to myself, assuming most of the people I left in Boston were going to choose Clay over me.

"I really appreciate you hanging out with me tonight. And you're pretty cool about me being into another chick while I was supposed to be on a date with you," Malloy says, a playful smile gracing his features.

"Honestly, I was really nervous about tonight. I didn't even want to go. I would have backed out, but when Marissa puts her mind to something, it's sort of hard to say no. Hearing you didn't really want to be on the date was a huge relief. And I got a friend out of it. Now I don't feel so lonely in this big city," I say, meaning every word of it.

We reach my destination, and he parks his truck and cuts the engine. The moment he turns toward me, I can tell something heavy is about to come out of his mouth.

"I hope you don't mind me asking, but why exactly did you and Clay get divorced?" he asks, and I can tell he's uncomfortable. I really don't want to end our night on this note, but I also know he was vulnerable with me, and I should have the courtesy to give him a morsel of my truth as well.

"I won't go through every ounce of my painful past right now, but the plain and simple of it all is, I can't have kids. Clay and I got married young—like right out of college young. I knew he was it for me. And we wanted to have kids. It was our biggest dream, and the moment we put those rings on our fingers and claimed forever together, we started trying. He lost his father young, and I think he craved as much time being a father as he could. I always dreamed of holding my son or daughter in my arms and wanted to start that chapter in my life as soon as I could.

"At first, of course, it was fun and exciting. But with each failed test, the excitement dwindled, and it became a defeat and heartbreak. At first, we didn't think much of it. We were trying to just have fun with the process. It was hard, though, not to feel broken each month of failure. Finally, we went to see the doctor. We got answers, and it turns out I have a condition that makes my chances of getting pregnant non-existent." I practically whisper that last part.

It's still painful to say out loud. I look out the window, not sure if I feel shame or anger or maybe a little bit of both. It's hard to process my feelings, even after all this time. I'm a healthy person, and I've always taken care of my body. In high school, I was a star athlete on the swim team. I continued to value what I put into my body as I got older and always ate balanced meals. So, it was a shock hearing that my body betrayed me in such a way.

"I'm so sorry, Abs. Did Clay react poorly when he heard? Is that why you broke up?" I see Malloy's jaw tick, and it's hard not to laugh at his protectiveness coming out. My new friend is already such a ferocious bear when it comes to me, and I love it.

"Oh gosh, no. The opposite, actually. He treated me like I was so fragile and wanted to make sure I was okay. He was ready to tackle this and try anything to ensure we could add to our family. He was willing to do fertility treatments, adoption, surrogacy. I couldn't do it anymore. I was the one who left him," I admit.

"I don't understand," Malloy says.

"Yeah, that's how Marissa reacted," I say, laughing to myself, "and in some ways, I am trying to figure out my reaction as well. I guess I really do see myself as broken. It might be silly, but I really don't want Clay to feel stuck with me. I wanted him to get a chance to have a baby with someone. With me, he would most likely never get that. IVF is a long shot, really. And then there's surrogacy, sure, but even that is not definite. Then there's adoption. Those are all great options, but I just got spooked when I saw some online forums, and most were more like horror stories of how things could go wrong, and I just couldn't handle it.

"Then the fights we were having from not being able to conceive naturally were weighing on me. Add in the fights we started having from all the hormone injections and failed attempts. I can't imagine what might be in store for us if we had an adoption go wrong. Or a failed surrogacy." I start to fiddle with my fingers in my lap, my gaze down as I recall my fears from that time.

"Maybe it was me not being able to handle it. I don't know. I just couldn't take it, and I ran. I did the worst thing to him and left." I sigh and shake my head. "Maybe it makes me a horrible person, but I also didn't see another way. I wanted him to find his happily ever after. And I just didn't think that would be with me, so I forced him to let me go."

Malloy grabs my hand and squeezes. I appreciate he doesn't try to say anything. He just sits with me, and the silence in his truck soothes me.

Finally, I take a deep breath and look over at Malloy. "I think I should head over and wait for him."

"There is no way I'll let you wait in there alone," he replies, and I look up and roll my eyes as a response.

"Don't roll your eyes at me, Abby." He sighs. "Listen, you can go sit on the steps," I'm about to chime in, and he holds his hands up so he can finish his thought, "and I'll sit in my truck and wait until he gets here, okay? I'll stay in the background just to make sure you're safe until he gets home. I just want to make sure you're unharmed while you wait. I can't, in good conscience, leave you here alone."

I stare at him, trying to look annoyed, but in reality, I find his behavior sort of adorable. I finally relent and nod, then lean in to kiss his cheek and hug him.

"Thank you for being the best guy friend ever. You truly are a prince charming, just not mine to keep." I pull away and open my door. Before closing it, I look over to Malloy and tell him, "Thank you so much for getting me out of the house. Next time it's sweats and a movie night in, alright?"

"It's a date." He winks back.

We exchange phone numbers before I walk toward the steps and take a seat under the stars. The air is cool, so I pull my sweater over me and rub my legs while I sit on the steps to wait.

I'm not there long, looking down and taking in the cracks in the asphalt in front of me, when I hear rustling by my side as someone walks toward the building.

I look up to see the only hazel eyes to ever capture my soul staring back at me.

# CHAPTER 7

## Clay

"WHAT ARE YOU DOING HERE, ABBY?" How can my heart long for the same person who it also breaks for?

I'm still fuming after seeing her hand rubbing Malloy's arm, trying to calm him down. It's my arm she should be touching. It's my nerves she should be calming. And when I look down at her hand, I should still see the ring I put on her finger.

She's mine, and she's out there trying to be claimed by someone else. I'm fucking furious, and she's sitting here acting like it's another ordinary night. After everything she put me through, she didn't even have the courtesy to tell me she came back to Boston.

When she said this city reminded her too much of the pain, the reality is that I remind her too much of the pain. She kept saying she was helping me by leaving. No. She left me because I was the problem.

"Clay, I wanted to explain—"

"I think your actions explained enough tonight. You can go." I'm being cold, which is the exact opposite of my norm with her, but I have no clue how else to respond. But what does she expect from me? This stings. I'm not too sure what hurt more: her deserting our marriage or seeing her with Malloy—a fucking firefighter. Who does that to someone they claim to have loved?

I walk past her into my building and up the stairs. I can hear her steps following me as I make my way up to my floor. I unlock my door, hoping she won't follow me in, but I can feel her warmth behind me.

Her presence feels like an electric current passing along my spine, and it's hard not to react to her. If this were our past, I would pin her against the wall and run my nose along her jaw, watching her skin react to my touch. I'd hold her down with my palm and feel her pulse quicken as I pumped into her. All those little movements would excite me, and now they only anger me, making me wonder if another man now has that power with her while I hold memories of us together instead.

"I'm sorry for showing up there. Malloy and I are just friends. I had no say regarding the date. I had no idea it was him before he got to my place. I swear it isn't anything more than that with Malloy—"

"What do you mean? Did he force the date on you?" I turn abruptly before making it further into my apartment. She stops, nearly colliding with my chest. Thank goodness she stops herself before she makes contact with me because if her skin touches mine, I don't know if I can keep from touching her back.

"No, of course not. I mean, I was set up on a blind date," she explains, staring at me, her eyes going wider. She pleads with me with that gaze of hers, and I try to decipher if she's being honest. She's always been my weakness. It's taking everything in me not to step closer and devour her the way I'm tempted to do when she's this close to me.

She's so close, I can smell that sweet vanilla scent I've longed for all these months she's been away. Now that I have this one part of her in my proximity, I'm starting to wonder if other parts of her remain the same. Does she still taste like cinnamon because she loves chewing that flavored gum? Does she still wear matching panty and bra sets because it bothers her to see them mismatched? Did she wear them for *him*?

Fuck, now I'm pissed again.

"Damn it, Abby, why did you have to go out with someone I know? Do you have any idea how this feels? Put yourself in my shoes." I throw my keys onto my table and storm into the kitchen.

I open my fridge and realize I forgot to stock up before my last shift, so I have nothing stronger than water. I slam the door and rest my hands against the cool stainless steel. Soon, I feel her hands against my shoulders, trying to soothe me.

"Don't. Don't touch me." Too bad Abby has terrible listening skills because she continues to move her hands along my shoulders and down my biceps.

"Clay, please look at me," she pleads, just above a whisper.

"I can't. I'm fucking furious right now. You broke my heart when you left, and tonight, you fucking shattered it." I'm about to move away when I feel her kiss between my shoulder blades above the fabric of my shirt.

As much as this pisses me off, my dick doesn't seem to care that we are supposed to be on the same page. I feel my cock stiffen behind my zipper.

"What are you doing, Abby?" I ask with thickness in my throat. I keep my back to her, afraid of how I'll react if I turn around.

"I told you, Clay. I was set up on a blind date. I didn't know Malloy was my date until I opened the door," she says, still planting kisses along my upper back.

"Then why did you go on the date after you found out it was a fellow firefighter?" I ask, still needing clarification, although my mind is starting to wonder if an answer really matters at this point because all I want to do is turn around and devour her.

"Because Marissa wanted me to go out and distract myself a little. She didn't know who the date was with either. She just reached out to someone to set me up with a person in Boston, and Malloy happened to be that person."

That's a small world.

Abby's hands start to move down my sides to the hem of my shirt and begin to drift under my shirt. I don't know if we are riled up because we are emotional after tonight or we just missed seeing one another, but the tension between us is intense. I can't resist the temptation anymore.

I finally turn around and meet her gaze. I see fire in her eyes, and there's no innocence looking back at me. She wants this just as much as I do.

"What do you want, Abby?" I ask as I move my hand through her hair, pulling her head back and drawing a moan out of her.

"I want to remember what it's like to be touched by you," she says.

I move my lips close to the shell of her ear. "Oh yeah? You know what I think?"

I hear her breath hitch.

I continue, "I think you want me to remind you why I'm the only man at that bar you should be with."

She whimpers in response, and I smile. I nibble her earlobe and see the goosebumps break out. It's such a turn-on that she's so reactive to my touch, even after all this time apart.

I glide my tongue along her jaw until our mouths connect. The moment our lips come together, it feels like coming home, and electricity ignites. I have missed her and this feeling of love with the person I know is my forever.

I push that feeling aside, knowing this isn't what we have anymore, and let the intensity of our kiss ignite the flame that exists between us. Her moan is swallowed by my own. She rolls her hips into me, and my length hardens even more for her.

I turn her around and pin her to the fridge. I bring my hands to hers and intertwine our fingers together, moving our hands above our heads and pin them there.

I roll my hips into her, then pull my lips away enough to look her in the eyes. "I think a little reminder of who this pussy belongs to would be a good place to start tonight."

I'm feeling greedy and angry. I think she's going to comply with my demand with a simple nod until she answers, "Then maybe you should feast on me for a while to show me what's yours."

The smirk she throws at me only confirms the confidence she's returned to Boston with, and it's hard not to find it incredibly attractive. I guess she gained something in her time away. That timid version of Abby that left all those months ago has faded, and I see that beauty I have always loved rising back to the surface. Deep down, I knew she was going to return.

Without giving her an answer, I bring her dress up above her ass, pick her up to sit on my counter, and rip her panties. They are black lace, and the fury that engulfs me at the thought another man may have seen these tonight takes over.

"This is my pussy, Abby," I say as I throw the panties over my shoulder and get on my knees.

I spread her knees wide and bring my lips to her core. I give her no warning and move my tongue to her center. She screams from the contact, her feet coming to my shoulders for support, opening herself even wider. Her hands find my hair, and within seconds, she's moaning, screaming my name, telling me not to stop and that she's coming.

Like hell, I'm going to stop. I continue until she's riding my face so hard and fast that I nearly come myself from the mere satisfaction of hearing her pleasure.

I kiss the inner portions of her thigh while she's coming off her orgasm. When I look up, I take in all that has happened while I was lost in Abby's pussy.

Her hair looks like she's been well fucked from however many times she's run her hands through it, and she must have pulled her tits out of the top of her dress. She sees me staring and begins to put herself together.

"Absolutely not. We aren't done here." I pull the strap back down and bring my lips down onto her taut nipple. I use my free hand to grab onto the other breast, kneading and squeezing it. Fuck I've missed her breasts. They're the perfect size for me.

I lick and nibble to the point she's writhing beneath me, and I swear I might combust. I move on to the other one, giving both equal attention.

I let go, and she protests, so I explain, "We need a bed for what I have planned." I grab her ass, and she wraps her legs around me.

We waste no time, and she kisses me. The intensity of each connection is electric, and there's nothing light about the way we are kissing.

The moment we get to my room, I throw her onto my bed, and it's abundantly clear I am way overdressed right now. I begin toeing off my shoes and socks while Abby removes her dress.

The moment we are fully naked, it's like we are animals and pounce on one another. Abby decides to take over, pushing me to lie on the bottom. The moment she gets me in position, she grabs my cock and lines me up. She sits on my dick achingly slowly, and the moment she's fully seated, we both moan.

I grab her tits and pinch her nipples, and she begins riding me. I'm so fucking deep; I know I'm hitting right in that spot that gets her to climax the fastest. Her hands are on my chest as she starts to set the pace. I hold onto her hips, matching her speed, and it feels absolutely incredible.

"Fuck, Clay, right there. You feel so good. Harder, yes, you're so deep," she says, and it's fucking unbelievable.

I can feel her squeezing my cock when she starts to come, and I can't hold out any longer and fall off that cliff right along with her. I pump into her so hard my vision goes dark.

Abby rolls off me, and we both lie there, looking up at the ceiling. A minute ago, the sounds of our skin slapping and our moans filled this room, but now all I can hear are our breaths catching up to us.

"That was… that, um, wow," she says, laying her arm over her eyes.

"Yeah, that definitely was something," I say.

Abby and I have always had good chemistry—there's no denying that. But this time was different. Maybe we both had pent-up frustration or had a lot of time apart and missed this connection with someone familiar. Or perhaps we simply are good together. Whatever it is, it works. I miss it. I miss us.

But no matter what it is, it's over. I'm well aware of that.

For the rest of the night, we explored each other's bodies as if we had the rest of our lives to do this. We didn't talk about the date she was on, and I accepted her word that it was a blind date she truly knew nothing about. Honestly, we're divorced. It doesn't matter past her explanation.

The next morning, I wake up to find Abby gone. Her side of the bed is cold, and so is my heart.

# CHAPTER 8

_Abby_

"EXPLAIN RIGHT NOW, or I'm hanging up." I'm giving her five more seconds, or I'm literally putting a post up on social media stating I'm looking for a new best friend. Marissa's little stunt went too far.

"What's the big deal? So you went out and got a free meal out of it. Who cares?" How can she be so nonchalant about it? It's a shame she and my brother haven't spent more time together.

"Who cares? Marissa, I care! Do you even know me?" I yell into the phone, exasperated that I have to explain myself to the one other person who knows me better aside from Clay.

"Listen, you had to get out there, Abby. You were stuck in a rut. Come on. You were mopey! I had to do something, or you were going to be the crazy cat lady!" Marissa whines into my ear.

"No, I was not. Plus, I'm allergic to cats!" I throw back.

"Fine, but you were going to get a goldfish or something and start talking to it and then never leave the apartment. Come on, tell me how it was, but let me switch to FaceTime—"

Before I can interject, it's already ringing, and I accept. I'm confused by the image in front of me until I realize she's sitting at her desk at work with a bowl of popcorn.

"Are you eating popcorn right now? What am I? Your entertainment?" My mouth is hanging open.

She doesn't even look guilty, and I swear I'm going to change my number after this and never contact her again.

"What the fuck did you do, Marissa? I'm returning to how I started this call with—explain yourself!"

"Fine—calm your tits! Geez, someone needs her kitty tickled." She has the audacity to roll her eyes and pops another popcorn into her mouth.

"Don't get mad." She looks over at me and corrects herself. "I should say, don't get angrier, but I may have called in reinforcements and reached out to Rios on this one."

I grind my molars. I already know this. She better get to the part of why. She's not even from Boston, so why is she interjecting herself into Clay's circle of friends?

As if reading my mind, she says, "I met Rios at your house one of the times I came into town. He was at a barbecue you had a while back. River was there, and a few of the guys were hanging out. I thought it would be good to have his contact if anything ever happened in case of an emergency and I couldn't get a hold of you."

I try to think back, but we've had a few gatherings in the past, and I was on my journey with IVF. I was dealing with so many things with Clay and trying to have a baby I wouldn't even think twice about mixing all my friends together in a social setting and forgetting about it until now.

She continues. "I reached out to him and sort of asked about punching the best-friend card to see if he was interested in trying to get you and Clay back together again." I'm about to protest when she adds, "I know, I know, I overstepped. But you have to understand, it was hard to see you miserable. Hearing you heartbroken on the phone is one thing when you were in Boston, unable to fulfill your dream to become a mother. But seeing you here in Cali without Clay? You have no idea how hard it was for me to see you like that."

I see it then. My best friend has tears in her eyes. There's no joking in her expression staring back at me. The humor is gone, and the act I was putting on when I was living on the West Coast was a failure, and she saw through my facade. She saw my pain. *Shit.* I bow my head.

"I'm sorry, Abby. I know I did something unforgivable last night, sending you on a date with another man. But I honestly did it to push you back into the arms of the man I really think you deserve to be with."

"But why did you have Rios set me up with a firefighter of all people?"

"Hold on, what?" She worries her brows, mid-chew.

"Yeah, the guy you had Rios set me up with was Tucker Malloy, another firefighter. He doesn't work in Clay's house, but he's only about twenty miles out of town. They know one another. He's Rios's best friend," I explain.

I think the screen is frozen because Marissa is staring back at me silently.

"Marissa, you still with me? Did I lose you?" I start to touch my screen to see if I lost signal.

"I'm sorry, I think I heard you wrong. Did you say Rios set you up with another firefighter?" She laughs, but it sounds sort of maniacal like she's losing her mind.

"Yeah, that's exactly what I said," I respond, putting my phone back against the wall.

"That motherfucker." She grabs her laptop and begins to log on.

"Um, Marissa, what are you doing?" I ask, panic lacing my tone.

"What do you think I'm doing? I'm texting Rios."

"Why?"

"To give him a mouthful," she says. "Please tell me you

did not run into Clay. Oh, no. Please tell me the night ended early. No, no, no. Shit." She looks over at me. "Fuck, Abby, what happened?"

Her eyes are wide, panic taking over.

"Put the laptop aside and let me finish. There's still a lot more to say," I explain to her.

She puts her computer aside, but I can tell she is itching to give Rios a piece of her mind.

"Malloy took me on a terrible date to a hot dog stand. It turns out it was on purpose. Rios was sort of a prick who purposely chose Malloy to take me out. He cornered Malloy to take me out to prove a point. I guess Malloy has a thing for Rios's sister, and when you called asking to reconnect Clay and me, Malloy was with him, so he thought up this plan. Malloy went along with it because he didn't want to disappoint his best friend. In doing so, he hurt Rios's sister. It's a whole thing for them, and unfortunately, Clay and I got caught up in it.

"Malloy felt bad and confessed the whole thing to me when we were out. But then we still had the rest of the date to fulfill, which meant going to the bar Clay was. By then, I knew what was going on. I mean, I didn't want to hurt Clay, but I also can't lie and say I wasn't a little interested in seeing him," I admit and look up to see Marissa's reaction.

"Oh my gosh, Abby, you didn't!" She throws popcorn at the screen.

"What do you mean? That was what you wanted!" I yell back.

"Yeah, but you went in knowing exactly what I was doing, you dirty girl!" she says, a smirk playing on her features.

"Well, what do you want me to say? I mean, I was curious, and I sort of wanted to make him jealous. I know, I'm a horrible person." I bury my face in my hands.

"No, you're human, Abby. I get it!" she admits, but it doesn't make me feel any better saying it out loud.

"Well, the moment we walked into the bar, my stomach plummeted. I swear, the look on Clay's face said it all. I swear, I broke his heart. I saw the way he looked at Malloy and me, and all I saw was his heart shattered across the floor. I made a huge mistake walking in there with another man. I felt awful. And I was thinking if he saw me with another man, he would finally be able to let me go and move on. But it still didn't make me feel any better." I throw my head back and groan. "Why am I such a ball of conflicted emotion!"

"I think you're fucking psychotic, really," Marissa chimes in, and I swing my gaze at her and give her the bird. She laughs and winks at me.

"Well, at least now you know you broke his heart, and that's that," she says, and I look away, trying to hide the way my cheeks flame.

"Um, what's that?" she says at the camera, and I keep looking out the window, hoping she lets it go.

"What? The reflection of the sun on the water? It's beautiful, no?" I say, hoping the view does it.

"Absolutely not. I live in California. I see enough fucking views. Don't bullshit me, Abby. Look at me." I move my face toward her but keep my eyes up at my ceiling.

"Motherfucker! There's more!" she shouts.

"No!" I respond.

"Bullshit! Tell me!" she demands.

"Ugh! Fine!" I say. "There's more!"

I scratch the back of my head and take a long drink of my water. I feel incredibly parched all of a sudden. Finally, Marissa complains, "What the hell? Are you getting ready for a marathon?"

"Okay! Goodness!" I put my cup down and smooth my hands on my thighs, calming my nerves.

"Well, I felt awful about the whole bar fiasco. Plus, I couldn't, in good conscience, let Clay think Malloy was really my date, and I wanted to clear the air. So I waited for Clay to return to his apartment," I say, although the last part was very much whispered.

"I'm sorry. Did you say you waited for Clay to get to his apartment?"

"Yes." I stand straighter, chin tall.

"You dirty bitch. You fucked him, didn't you?" She is so vulgar.

"Maybe." I look down at my nails, not making eye contact.

"Maybe? You don't remember?" she asks.

"I don't kiss and tell."

"You don't fuck and tell, apparently."

"Listen, that wasn't why I went over there. I wanted to explain myself. He deserved to know I wasn't on that date to hurt him. I just said it was a blind date. That's what he needed to know. I didn't tell him about Rios or about Malloy and Rios's sister. That's not my story to tell. I don't want to get involved in their station's drama. I just wanted him to know I was not there to hurt him."

"Did you tell him you were there to make him jealous?" Marissa points out.

"Well, no. We started off talking, then things shifted, and the moment I touched him, I guess we just forgot about words. I mean, Marissa, the minute I felt his skin beneath my hand, all bets were off. I swear it felt like an electrical current moving along my palm. I forgot how electric we were together," I explain, and I can still feel that tingle at the memory of him.

It had always been like that with Clay. Unfortunately, I forgot how special it could be as the moments together felt more rehearsed the more we kept trying for a baby those last few months together. It's sad to admit that now. I never thought we would get to a point where our lovemaking would be anything other than breathtaking. We were always this force together. Until one day, it just felt like the weight of the world sat between us. At least, that's how it felt for me.

My therapist in California said that's common to feel. The battle we start to have within our mind with the blame falling on ourselves becomes increasingly burdensome. I felt like I was the reminder we were struggling. I couldn't run from myself, so I ultimately felt like a huge problem in the relationship.

"Hey, Abby, where did you go?" Marissa pulls me from my thoughts.

"Oh, just thinking of things in my past." I give her a small smile.

"Did Clay say something before you left?"

"No, I left before he woke up. I didn't want things to get too awkward. I knew it was a one-time thing between us. I thought it was best I leave," I say, shrugging my shoulders.

She gives me a sad smile in return.

"I know I overstepped a bit here." I give her a *you think* look, and she amends her statement.

"Okay, okay, I overstepped by a lot. But I still stand by my statement that you two really are an amazing team. I know you went through something tremendously hard together, but I think there are options you could face together to make the family you want," she reminds me yet again.

"I know, Marissa. It's not that I'm not open to adoption or surrogacy. It's just that the fighting with Clay was far from who we were already, and we had just scratched the tip of the iceberg with IVF. Imagine if we had continued. I just couldn't do it anymore with him. It was too much. We were great until we weren't anymore.

"And I just had to let him go. We loved hard. But it just wasn't working out anymore, and I had to walk away. I love him. I really do. But I love us enough to say he deserves better than what we were doing to each other." I think it's fair to say I love myself enough to know I wasn't myself anymore either.

"For what it's worth, I'm sorry I put you through last night. I honestly had no idea Rios would pull that stunt. It came from a place of love from me. I hope you know that," she says.

"I know, Marissa. I get that it came from a good place. And a part of me thinks Clay and I needed last night too. We needed to say goodbye. We needed one last time together. But it doesn't mean it didn't hurt to say goodbye. Because it's still a part of my life I'll always mourn," I admit. It hurts to know I'll wish things could have turned out differently. Someone will live a life with Clay that I wish I could have fulfilled for him.

Marissa and I say our goodbyes. Many might expect me to be upset at her for interjecting herself into my personal life like she did. But I don't see her actions as malicious. I see her as someone who simply wanted to see me happy. She saw me sad and wanted to help fix my pain. I think I would have done the same if I were in her shoes.

I walk into my kitchen to refill my glass of water, feeling a little lighter, even though I should feel absolutely wrecked after what has transpired the last twenty-four hours. As I'm pouring more water, my phone chimes, and I expect to have some long text from Marissa. I'm surprised to see a text from Samara:

**SAM**

I just heard you're back in Boston, and I had to hear it from River. WTH Abby. You could have reached out.

I wasn't kidding when I said I cut contact with everyone when I left. I shared all my friends with Clay. We pretty much grew into adults together, and our friends were all connected. The only people I kept were Marissa and my brother, although I know Frankie speaks to Clay on a weekly basis. I miss Sam the most of all my girlfriends in the city.

> Hey Sam. Yeah, I got back a little while ago. If it's any consolation, I hadn't told anyone. How are you?

SAM

> You know these guys gossip worse than us. Plus, River may have lost fifty bucks to Ash. You know they had a bet going. Ash is over here gloating. 😒 Why didn't you text me? I would love to see you, but now I'm on bed rest. Which means you have to take pity on me and come visit me.

That's right. I saw her announcement on social media not long ago that she was expecting not just one baby but two. A boy and a girl. I acknowledged the announcement with a like and a comment but left it at that. I keep my time on social media minimal and don't post content of my own anymore.

It's always hard to see those sweet baby announcements. I used to long to be one of those people who got to make a post with an ultrasound photo saying Clay and I would be parents. I imagined what ours would look like. The sting those photos bring now is a hard pill to swallow.

It doesn't mean I'm not happy for Sam and Ashton because I know what amazing parents they'll be. It just takes time for me to get used to it. Now that I'm back in Boston and she has reached out, I can't ignore her. And of course I'll go see her. But hopefully, she'll give me time. If she's on bed rest, she'll need to do just that—she can't be bombarded by visitors while she should be caring for herself and growing those precious babies.

> I was still getting situated. And I'm sorry you're on bed rest. Congratulations again. Yes, once you're settled and ready for visitors we can set something up. Rest up and I'll see you at some point in the future.

SAM

Nonsense. You'll be hearing from me because I'm already bored on bed rest. I'll see you soon. Love ya and glad you came to your senses and came back to Boston. You've been missed, not just by Clay.

Thanks for reaching out. Rest up. I hope Ash is taking good care of you. Love ya lots and sorry for not reaching out when I got back.

SAM

You don't have to apologize. I get it. But you're my friend too, and I've missed you. You're stuck with me, Abby. Don't let what the boys have intimidate you into thinking we can't still hang out.

Hearing Samara say that makes me tear up. I kept telling myself I didn't need to keep the friends we shared, but knowing she wants me around makes me feel something I didn't realize I longed for. I guess deep down, I need Samara and this friendship more than I actually acknowledged.

Thanks Sam. I appreciate you saying that. I missed you too. Rest up. We'll catch up soon. Hugs to you and Ash (and those babies).

I put my phone down and feel a tug at my heart. Maybe all my worries were for nothing. Being back around Clay's social circle could be better than I initially thought. Last night was probably just a little hiccup, and it will be smooth sailing from here.

# CHAPTER 9

## *Clay*

THE POUNDING on the door wakes me from a deep sleep. I swear it feels like my eyes are lined with sandpaper when I blink them open. Why is someone waking me at this hour?

I turn to look at the clock and realize it's nearly twelve o'clock. Fuck. I was supposed to be ready to eat lunch at my mom's house.

The pounding begins again, this time accompanied by my brother's voice on the other side of the door. We might share genetics, but he's grating on my nerves today. I toss the sheets off me, not even bothering to throw a shirt on.

It's been a few weeks since my night with Abby, and I still feel her presence in my apartment. I can't shake the feeling of her all around me. My foul mood is an indication that I miss her even more now that I know she's back in town.

My sleep has been shit, hence the pumice stone that lines my eyes each morning, along with the endless coffee I have to drink to keep them open. On shift, I feel like I'm either focused on the job or my mind wanders to her. I can't seem to do anything but think about what she's doing. Knowing she's here, in my city, is wrecking me.

I swing the door open to find my brother's smug face,

knowing full well he's probably well fucked by his girlfriend. They go at it whenever he's around her, and I swear I've never seen him happier. I couldn't be more thrilled he's found his forever in Kennedy, but how in the fucking hell has the universe done this one-eighty on us?

River used to fuck anything with a pulse, while I was the settled one, and now he's two steps away from putting a ring on it, and I'm over here thinking about possibly entering the dating scene again. I can't even deal with this shitty reality called my life.

"Fuck, Clay, you're chipper this morning," my brother starts, and I answer by trying to shut the door on him. I haven't even said anything, and he's already judging me.

He laughs and stops the door from closing. I don't even bother waiting around and start walking toward the kitchen, needing caffeine before getting myself ready.

"Can you text Ma and let her know we'll be late? I need to grab a quick shower." I get a mug from the cabinet. "Want a cup?"

He shakes his head. "Seriously, what crawled up your ass?"

I scratch the stubble that's grown on my chin as I watch the coffee brew in my machine. "Abby," is the only response I give him.

"Oh, ass play? I bet Kennedy would be all for that. She's all about being dominant in the boardroom, but she likes her man being the dominant one in the bedroom when I do this thing—"

I cover my ears and start singing loudly.

I glare at my brother and see him throw his head back and laugh.

"Fucking filter, River. Goddamn it. No one, especially me, wants to hear about your bedroom kinks with Kennedy." I throw a packet of sweetener at him.

"You're such a baby when you aren't getting any, Clay. Goddamn." He throws the packet back.

I'm being a complete asshole right now. He's right; I'm whiny and quite irritated and just can't seem to figure my shit out. I've been in a piss poor mood since Abby left my apartment that morning after we had sex.

I don't know if I'm mad we went at it like fucking hormonal teens who couldn't keep it in our pants, or if I'm angry I'll never get to have her to myself again. Maybe it's both. I'm utterly confused with my emotions.

I put my hands on my kitchen counter and hang my head. "You're right, and I'm sorry."

My brother comes over to comfort me, rubbing my shoulders. He's got this sensitive side that many don't get to see, or at least I think he does until he whispers, "Could you say that a little louder so that the recorder on my phone could catch that to prove that I'm right?"

I smack him on the shoulder, and he laughs. I can't help but laugh with him. If he's good for one thing, it's to get me to loosen up a bit. My brother is the one person who can always lighten my mood.

"Seriously though, you haven't heard from her?" he asks, knowing damn well if I had, I would have told him first.

"No. I think, even without words, we know last time was it. It's not healthy. As much as I didn't want the divorce—actually, I still don't—if her departure the next morning from my apartment is any indication, she doesn't want to explore anything further with me. I can't expect she wants to reconnect, and I'm not going to assume, much like she keeps making assumptions about my feelings. I can't be friends with her. I just can't bear it, so we have to cut things off. She needs to build her own life back in Boston. We can't do this whole hanging out together thing," I say, grabbing my cup of coffee.

"I get that. I still think it sucks what she did, going out with Malloy," River says.

"Yeah, from what she said, it was merely a blind date. But I don't understand why she would continue the date with him once she saw who it was. She had to know how much that would hurt me. And then for them to come to *Jenson's*? That was way too far." I try to shrug it off, still feeling my muscles tense at the thought of them standing together at that bar.

"Either way, I think a warning would have been nice," River says.

If my brother is one thing, it's protective of the people he loves. He loved Abby like a sister. The minute she left, he was incredibly hurt, but his priority was to make sure I was cared for. He never once talked poorly of her. But after seeing her with Malloy, all bets were off. He knows all the shit Abby and I went through, but even that didn't give Abby the excuse to pull the stunt she did.

I was hurt to see her out with Malloy. Although the explanation was short, once she explained what happened, I believed her. Knowing Marissa, I'd buy that she would set her up on a blind date. But the more I think about it, the more I know that if the tables were reversed, I wouldn't have gone on a date with someone who would affect her the way Malloy affects me. Seeing her on a date really opened my eyes to the fact that this is inevitable. I realize now that I have to pull my head out of my ass and get myself out there. I have to start dating.

Even though I know I need to start dating, I don't want to. It's exhausting, and I just don't feel like doing it again. I hate going on dates and possibly enduring weird silences. Dating Abby feels like ages ago, and we simply clicked. What if I never find that with someone again? The idea alone is daunting, which leads me to my current mood.

"Yeah, I won't argue with you there. A warning would

have been fucking awesome. A simple 'I'm back' would have also been nice," I say in return.

We sit in silence until our mother texts us a GiF of Anger from *Inside Out*, and I book it to my room to get ready. No matter how old we get, I will never not be scared to be reprimanded by my mom.

―――――

"No, Ma, I don't think Cindy from down the street is a good match for me anymore. We shared a cookie in third grade. I think we might have grown apart since that groundbreaking moment of love." I give my brother a pleading look but he's eating his corn like he's never had the vegetable in his life. The smirk on the fucker's face tells me he is enjoying this conversation too much.

"Kennedy, sweetie, you don't have any friends you can set my Clay up with?" My mother continues her harassment.

I look at Kennedy, my glare murderous. We have always had an unspoken bond, and I swear if she does me dirty, I will never forgive her. Luckily, she seems to read between the lines on this one.

"Honestly, I don't. I'm the boss, so I have no friends at work, and anyone outside of work is married or dating someone. I'm sorry, Mrs. Nichols." She cowers a bit when my mom gives her that look only moms have perfected.

"Sweetie, you call me Mom because my River will be marrying you. He's not dumb enough not to." She smacks my brother upside the head, which earns her a loud, "Ma, why?" but our mom ignores him. "Or you can call me Mary."

Kennedy was late to join us for lunch because of her meeting. I thought the minute Kennedy arrived, it would steer my mom's focus away from me and my dating life, but Mom has been adamant I should be the center of attention today. She has gone through a list of my elementary school love interests, if you can even call them that... I was in grade school, and we still have middle and high school to go through, apparently. I should have had more coffee to prepare for this.

"Ma, why are we doing this?" I ask. Did I say something in my sleep last time I dozed off on her couch or something?

"My sweet, Clay, you are so sad. I can see it in your eyes. Even Lola has noticed, haven't you, sweet girl?" My mom looks up to speak to Lola.

I look to my right, and my brother's golden retriever, Lola, rests her head on my arm. That's right, Lola is my brother's dog. The fucking dog is mopey around me. I guess I've caused my brother's dog to become depressed.

"Every single time Lola comes back from your place, she's all sad," River says with a mouth full of food.

"River, stop being gross," Kennedy says, pointing to her mouth.

"What is it, Skip? You want a kiss?" he says as he makes a kissy face at her.

She rolls her eyes and moves her face farther from him.

Mom snaps her fingers to grab my attention like I'm some sort of preschooler. "Clay, listen to me. I'm your mother, and I know what's best for you. I love Abby. She is precious, and I miss her too. But I think it's best to start moving forward, not back. Maybe one day, things will circle back to her, but now, it's time to move on and start dating again," my mother says, bringing her hand to her chin and looking at me with so much hope.

"So, you think diving back into the dating pool with someone from third grade is my best option?" I ask, trying to hold back a laugh. Too bad my brother has no self-control.

Soon enough we are all laughing, including my mother, at one point wiping tears.

"Okay, you're right. Maybe she's not the right choice. But will you at least try? I mean, it could be a good idea?"

"Listen, Ma, I get it, and I appreciate the concern. I do. It's just not the right time for me. I'm not quite ready. Okay?"

She reaches out to grab my hand, and I grab hers.

"Okay, son. I get it. I love you."

"I love you too. And I know you only do this because I'm your favorite," I tell her.

"You are," she says, knowing it will get a rise out of River.

"I'm right here!" he yells in return.

# CHAPTER 10

*Abby*

"BIANCA? Really? She's a two-faced piece of work!" Malloy yells at the television, pointing his spoon as if the contestants of *The Bachelor* can hear anything he's saying.

I'm laughing as I devour my own pint of rocky road ice cream and cuddle into the couch a little more. Today is the first snowfall in Boston, and I turn my head and take in the white flakes as they fall outside my window. I've loved this time of year since I moved out here for college years ago. Some things don't change.

"You're really passionate about his choice," I tell Malloy.

"Oh, come on, she was the wrong choice. You and I both know that Cora was the right choice for him. She looked at him like he hung the moon. I'm so fucking pissed right now." He throws his spoon in his tub of ice cream and smacks his hand down his face. He's really maddened over this. I rub his back to console him but still can't help the laugh that escapes.

I never thought I'd be spending my evening watching *The Bachelor* with Tucker Malloy. I look over as he yells at the screen as if the season finale of the show is a World Series game. It's comical, but the moment I laugh, he glances at me and glares. All it does is make me laugh harder, and he throws a pillow at me.

"This isn't funny, Abby. He's making a huge mistake," he says right when his phone chimes. He looks down and grunts.

"Is it her?" I already know it's Baylee.

"Yes. She is just asking how I am." But then he throws his phone down.

"You can't just ignore her. It probably makes her confused and hurts her feelings, Malloy."

"I know, but I'm in an impossible position. I might be pissed at Rios, but it doesn't mean I want to complicate things further. I need to figure things out with him first," he tells me as he removes his ball cap and runs his fingers through his hair, a telltale sign he's irritated.

I move to put my ice cream on my coffee table and stand up. My muscles ache from sitting for too long. I stretch and start to clean up our mess. There's pizza and snacks thrown about everywhere.

"Listen, ignoring her is only making her question everything more. Give her some sort of answer so she doesn't wonder what she did wrong. She's young and figuring things out too, so remember that," I say as I move through to the kitchen and throw things away.

"I'm going to run to the restroom," I tell him as he's grabbing the trash bags from the kitchen trash bins.

"Let me take these out for you," he says, not giving me room to protest.

I make my way through my apartment and into my master bath. The moment I get into the restroom, I realize why I was feeling like absolute crap earlier today. Since I learned about my fertility struggles, I have had random periods, with my cycles never matching up. My ovulation is incredibly sporadic at best, so I have no clue when I'll get a period. I've tried to track it, but I'm not really regular anymore.

The discomfort I was feeling earlier today felt like period pain, but it also felt a little different, so I ignored it. I guess it was exactly that. This must be a lighter cycle, so I grab what I need and take a few pain relievers in hopes my cramps won't keep me up throughout the night.

Hopefully, once Malloy heads out, I can still get some work done. I have a few projects to finish up, and I always do my best work at night, so I will likely be up a few more hours to get some extra projects lined up.

When I get back out to the living room, Malloy has the couch back to normal, all the pillows and blankets folded, and the ice cream cleaned up. He's honestly been a breath of fresh air since we've sparked this friendship.

"You doing okay?" he asks.

"Oh yeah, just going to get some work done." I doubt our friendship has hit that point of telling him about my cycles.

"Do you ever sleep?" He chuckles.

"I'm a night owl. The ability to make my own schedule has its perks. I don't have to get up early, so I just sleep in if I work too late. Plus, now that it's snowing, I might just stare out and watch the snowfall." I look back out to see some of the snowflakes, even though the darkness keeps me from seeing them as easily.

"You really love the snow, don't you?" he says, looking out to the same view as me.

"Yeah, that California sun just doesn't scratch the itch quite like a New England snowfall, you know?" I think I was honestly born on the wrong coast.

"Well, enjoy the view. I think it's going to last a few days from what they said. You have enough groceries?"

Malloy is constantly asking me if I need anything when he's headed into the area. It's been nice having him as a friend.

"I'm good. All stocked up. Thanks though," I tell him.

It's weird having this close of a relationship with someone and having zero feelings for them romantically. We've made comments about it—how much easier it would be if we cared for each other in that way, but that there's just no spark.

"Well, I'm crashing at Rios's house." That comment causes my eyebrows to rise.

"What? When did things improve there? I thought you were giving him the cold shoulder?" I ask.

"I technically am, but I needed a place to stay with the snow and all. I told him he owes me, even though he doesn't quite see it that way. We've spoken a few times about his poor attitude, but I think it will just take time for him to see that there's nothing going on with his sister and me. I think he's under the impression something did happen, and I'm lying to him."

"But what if something does happen? What then?" I ask because that could really blow up in Malloy's face.

"Honestly, I just can't see this ending well if I went there. Right now, I'm just trying to fix things. That's my focus. I'm not responding to her so that I can get things back to how they were. I just need my best friend back. It's what I've always known, Abby." The way he looks at me breaks my heart. I can see the agony in his gaze.

I nod my head, knowing he's truly conflicted. I'm here to support him, not judge him. If he needs my support, that's what I'll do for him.

"I get it. I'm here for you, no matter what." I bring my arms out, and he crouches down to pull me into a hug. I feel like I'm being suffocated as he squeezes me.

We walk toward the front door, and he asks, "So what should we watch next? I don't know what I'll do if we don't have this disaster every week to complain about. Plus, now I'm out fifty bucks. I had all my money on Cora," he whines.

"Are you a Nichols now?" I laugh, even though a part of me is gutted comparing him to my ex-husband.

"Well, I won't pretend that his little habit hasn't rubbed off on me, even though I barely know him. But I can't help it, and I couldn't resist doing the same thing with my guys at the firehouse. Plus, I thought I would win this one," he says as he walks out of my place.

"Yeah, I get how you get hooked on it."

"There has to be another show we can pick up next week." He waves as he presses the button to the elevator.

"You mentioned watching *Love is Blind*. Is there something similar to that? I mean, there has to be something else," I say.

"We'll think of something. I'll ask the guys at the station."

"Have a good shift tomorrow night. I'll try to think of another show in the meantime as well. Also, consider what I said about Baylee. Don't leave her hanging."

With that, I shut the door, walk toward my computer, and hunker down next to the window to soak in the snowfall.

———

"Yes, Mom, I think a flight to New York for Christmas is best, instead of meeting in California. Plus, it feels like Christmas on the East Coast. It's eighty degrees on Christmas sometimes in Palos Verdes," I tell my mother while I'm on a call with her figuring out our plans for the holidays.

We've been making plans extremely last minute this time because my sister-in-law was waiting to hear back on possible work commitments that have now become a reality. She cannot leave the city, and we are all coming to her. At first, my parents were hoping I would still fly out to them in California and then see my brother afterward, but I think I have convinced her to head to them so we can meet in one spot.

"Listen, I've gotta run. I'm headed into the market to grab some things for dinner. Love you, and please book your tickets because it's not that far from now. I already got my flight booked earlier." I hang up quickly as I move through all the people walking down the aisles. It's a zoo today, probably because I waited way too long to get out of the house, and now it's rush hour, and people are all out of work and doing exactly what I had intended—prepping their meals for the evening.

The moment I turn down toward the butcher, I see someone who causes me to freeze. I swear all the air is sucked out of me. Damn it. I was not prepared to see Clay right now. I bring my hand to my chest and try to calm myself. I can feel my heart beating erratically.

He turns his head in my direction, and then I realize my panic is for nothing because it's not Clay, it's River. Our eyes lock, and what used to be that playful side of my brother-in-law is non-existent when he realizes I'm standing in front of him. I see his jaw tick, much like his brother's did that day at the bar when I stood next to Malloy.

I decide to be the bigger person and take the few steps to eat the distance between us.

"Hey, River, how are you?" I tuck my hair behind my ears, holding the basket that I have yet to fill with food with the opposite hand.

I can tell River would rather ignore me, but it's not in his nature. He takes a breath and then decides not to be rude.

"Abby," he says curtly, and I think he's going to turn and walk away. I realize I'm nervous because what used to be an easy relationship with someone I considered a brother is now a strained one. I don't know why I expected us to remain the same because I caused this, but I guess I hoped for better.

"I'm sorry, River," I decide to say. It might get me nowhere, but it can't hurt.

River closes his eyes, and I see his shoulders sag a bit.

"Why are you sorry, Abby?" he asks.

"I'm sorry I hurt you. I'm sorry I hurt Clay. I know it's

hard to believe, but I did what I thought was best for him. I know it's difficult to understand, but I honestly thought it was the best thing for everyone involved," I bite my lower lip, "and I'm starting to learn now that maybe I wasn't being fair to anyone."

He stares at me for a few beats. River is identical to his brother. He's got his brother's dark-brown hair and hazel eyes, which today are leaning more toward green than brown. They've got those broad shoulders and muscles from carrying all that equipment from their jobs. Their smiles show off their dimples and their perfectly white teeth.

They're both more fit for models and turn more heads than I would like to admit, but I've always been more attracted to Clay than River. It's weird that two people can look like clones of one another, yet I could only be drawn to one of them. My friends thought my attraction could be interchangeable, but that idea always felt weird to me.

My relationship with River always felt more like a brother, and I wish it could have stayed that way. Of course, I understand his anger and resentment at how I acted. I left his best friend. He should be upset. If he weren't, I think that would be more concerning. But right now, it still stings.

"I appreciate you saying those things. Just out of curiosity, have you said them to Clay? Because as great as it is to know you feel this way, I think it would be better he heard it from you, than to hear it from me," he says. I know they share everything, and I know he could go straight to him and repeat what I just said. I don't expect him to. I didn't say those things so that he would be my messenger. That was just for him.

"I didn't tell you that so you could give him the message. I wanted to apologize to you. I don't expect us to go back to the way things were. But I wanted you to know I am sorry. And I do miss you as my brother."

"I miss you too," he tells me. "And for what it's worth, I

know he misses you still. It's not too late. But what you did with Malloy was low."

"I swear it wasn't a real date. It was—" He stops me.

"Yeah, I heard. I still had to say it. It was fucked up on multiple levels. But showing up was still something you chose to do, and I think you should know I was not okay with it. Things could have gotten out of hand. Clay was really pissed. And I know how that night ended." He gives me a Cheshire cat look, and my cheeks flush.

"Yeah, well, we're not talking about that." I look away.

"Listen, I'm glad you're okay after everything you two went through. You have to understand my loyalty is always with my brother, Abby. If you need anything, I'm here. You know that, right?"

I clear my throat, hoping to clear the frog that's trying to creep up.

"I appreciate you saying that. Thank you. I've, um, been thinking about your mom. How is she?" I ask.

"Oh, now that I'm dating Kennedy, she won't stop bugging me to propose to her. She's been loving having her around. Though I think her favorite family member is still Lola." He rolls his eyes.

Lola was still more puppy than adult when I saw her last. She was stealing River's shoes and chewing anything she could.

"I bet Lola is much bigger now. Please give your mom my love," I tell him. Mary was always so kind and loving when I was part of the family.

"I definitely will." I notice how he doesn't tell me to come by and see her. A part of me hurts knowing I won't get to see her, but that's the pain of divorce.

"Listen, I should go. Kennedy cooks like she's feeding fish in the ocean. The girl doesn't understand the concept of measuring salt. So, I need to get home and make dinner. It was good seeing you, and I appreciate you talking to me. I hope with time things will settle down some. Take care."

I nod but don't say much else. He's grabs the wrapped-up meat the butcher put on the counter a while ago. River nods and walks past me. I stand there a while, processing every-thing that transpired. It's hard to navigate divorce, even though I'm the one that asked for it. It continues to have highs and lows even after time passes.

In our case, I didn't leave because I lost my love for the person I married. I simply feared he'd lose his love for me. But I ran away. It's something I'm working on in therapy. I can't really turn back the hands of time, so I'll keep doing the work and hopefully not make the same mistake twice if I ever get the chance at love again.

# CHAPTER 11

*Abby*

IT DOESN'T MATTER how many times I redesign this site, the company isn't happy. I may need to step away and come back to it because I'm starting to get frustrated. Luckily, I've got some time, and I'm only working because I have nothing else to do. I've been feeling under the weather lately—this Boston cold already something I am ill-adjusted to—so I'm in my sweats and eating some soup, hoping to feel better before the week ahead.

I'm about to turn on some mindless television when I get a call from reception.

"Hello, Ms. Morris?"

"Yes, this is she."

"You have a guest down here by the name of Kennedy Sparen asking to see you."

I wasn't expecting to see Kennedy. I've always known her because of Sam. They are the closest of friends. Because of Clay's relationship with Ash, I tagged along, and, in that time, I befriended Kennedy through Sam. I loved spending time with her, and we always had a great laugh. They always welcomed me in their friendship, never making me feel like an outcast, and the two of them always included me in their little jokes. But I never hung out with Kennedy alone. I can't even think of a time we were ever in the same room together without our other friends.

Although Sam reached out when she found out I was back in Boston, I haven't seen her yet. She has asked if I'll come visit, but I finally came clean regarding how difficult it would be due to some of my struggles to become pregnant. I know she's in the stage of becoming a new mother, and I don't want to taint this beautiful time for her. I have to be honest with my own feelings that self-care is important. I was straightforward with her, and the truth didn't hurt as much as I thought it would. Giving her the cold shoulder would be harder, and she was more receptive than I thought.

She was understanding and kind to my situation. Even though Sam and Ash were aware of our fertility struggles prior to the divorce, I never went into much detail. I felt it was such a private matter, and, in some ways, I was a little embarrassed. I decided to shed that layer of skin and let that vulnerability shine through as I spoke to my old friend.

This is a "me" problem, and I've stayed consistent with my therapy sessions here in Boston. I should have seen someone the minute I started my IVF journey because it would have saved Clay and me a lot of headaches in our marriage. I know I can't undo the damage I've caused in the past, but what I do from this point forward is what's important. I'm aware of that now. The way I view my fertility journey from this moment on can be more positive, including my journey through welcoming my friends in on how my fertility struggles have impacted me. Including Sam in on this was a huge step in the right direction.

I hear Leonard's throat clear on the line, pulling me from my thoughts.

"Oh, yeah, you can let her up," I tell him, then hang up the phone.

The moment I disconnect, I look around, processing the

mess of my apartment. I have junk everywhere, my apartment looking more like a junkyard than living quarters. I quickly start running around, picking up the take-out ramen I have thrown about, along with the random books and magazines I've let pile around. I haven't even taken a look in the mirror and just hope for the best when there's a knock at the door.

I look down to find a stain on my shirt and roll my eyes at myself. I should have spent the time changing my clothes instead of cleaning the apartment, but she'll just have to deal with the mess that I am. She caught me off guard.

I open the door to the woman who looks like a cover model. Kennedy Sparen is the woman I want to be when I grow up. Too bad we are the same age.

The minute she takes me in, she winces. "Sam didn't tell you I was coming, did she?" she says in lieu of a greeting.

"Um, no?" I respond, more as a question than a statement.

"Damn her and that new-mom brain," she huffs out.

"She had the babies?" I ask in complete shock. I had no idea, but I also haven't checked in for a bit.

"Oh my gosh, yes! It's been a crazy few weeks. The day she had the babies, River got injured, and it's been a bit chaotic. Everyone is fine though. Sam is great, exhausted, of course, and the babies are wonderful. Doing well and discharged from the NICU. I have pictures if you want to see. I have many because Ash thinks every angle of a photo makes a difference." She laughs.

I open my door wider and motion for her to come in. I hold onto the door because I feel a little lightheaded. Kennedy notices me closing my eyes and calls my attention.

"Abby, you feeling okay? You look a little pale." She grabs onto my arm, and I just nod.

"Oh yeah. I think I've just been working too many hours on this project. This site I've been working on is driving me crazy. Long hours and all. It's sort of kicking my ass." The CEO is an absolute dick.

"Can I get you some water or something?" I ask, trying to be a good hostess, even though I have no clue why she's here.

"Oh no. I'm imposing. I just wanted to swing by and see how you're doing. I know we aren't really close, but Sam is sort of busy with the babies now, and I thought we really don't know one another," she says, and I have no idea where this is coming from.

"That's nice of you," I reply a bit hesitantly.

"Ugh, River says I'm a shit liar. I can't really pull it off, can I? I have a shit poker face, I think." I just stand in place as she word vomits in front of me. "Here's the deal: Sam asked me to come by and check on you. She was on bed rest for the longest time. She wanted to see you but couldn't just get in the car and stop by. Then she went into labor, and now she is sort of lactating everywhere." She makes a face, which makes me want to snort with laughter because Kennedy is quite funny.

"So here I am. She's enlisted me. I know you might not want the person dating your ex-husband's twin brother, but I promise I won't choose sides. River's a bit pissed. I hope you don't mind me admitting that to you. But River can fuck off— my words to him, I swear—I love him, but he's a bit angry right now about Malloy and this whole date/non-date thing you went on. I told him he's being a baby about it and to let it go."

"Let me get this straight—you want to be my friend?" I ask.

"Yeah, I do." She smiles at me. "Is that weird for you? To be friends with me without Samara around? Because she thinks you need a friend, but she also thinks she can't give too much attention right now. So I told her I'd love to come hang out with you if you'll accept me as a consolation friend!"

I continue to just stand there in silence for a bit too long.

"It's weird. I get it. It's the ex-husband's twin brother thing, isn't it?" she asks, and I start laughing.

"No, it's not that. I just wasn't expecting this at all today. That's all. I'm sorry, I'm a mess, I feel like a slug, and this is unexpected. I had no idea Sam had the babies; I feel like a shit friend, and I just feel like the opposite of the person I am supposed to be right now. That's all. I have no idea when I became this person." I start laughing, and then it morphs into crying. What the fuck is wrong with me?

"Oh my gosh. No, don't cry. Shit, where are your tissues? Fuck." She starts rubbing my back, and I'm still doing this weird laughing and crying thing like a lunatic in front of this new friend of mine who barely knows me aside from the random times we've hung out.

I start waving my hand while walking to my couch and sit, then I bury my face in the pillow from my couch. "Mh emoshunns ahr ehvrwherr," I mumble.

"I have no idea what that was you just said," she says softly, trying not to be rude.

I lift my head. "My emotions are everywhere. Don't mind me. I'm a mess," I say while I try to calm myself down.

She moves my hair away from my face as I wipe the tears from my cheeks.

"It's okay. It's probably been a long day. Can I make you some coffee or tea? Or do you feel like getting out a bit?" Something about the idea of going out on a walk sounds like the best idea, even though it's probably cold enough to freeze the tears I just shed to my face.

"Actually, a walk around the water sounds like a nice idea. You don't mind?" I ask.

"Not one bit. Why don't you grab warmer clothes. It's pretty cold out today." I hop up and run to my room, thinking fresh air will do me some good. Without even realizing it, I'm slowly getting my friend circle comprised in Boston again after I felt completely alone. I thought I could come back here and blend in without anyone to support me. How wrong I was because I'm incredibly grateful I have people to lean on.

———

The walk around the water is just what I needed. Apparently, River got injured on the job and had to take some time off to rest and recover. Luckily, it wasn't anything serious, and he is back at work. It seems her relationship with River is the real thing, and they're fully committed to one another. They seem happy together, which is surprising because all I remember of their interactions was the two of them fighting to the point that I thought the cops would be called.

As we approach my building again, I see a figure from afar that looks familiar. The closer we get, I see it's Rios.

"Hey, Rios, what are you doing here?" Kennedy asks, just as confused by his presence as I am.

"I was just walking by and saw you two, so I thought I'd be courteous and wait to say hello." He smiles, but I know he's full of shit.

"Listen, I need to get back to that project before it gets too late. I appreciate you stopping by. Thanks for giving me your number, and let's grab lunch soon," I tell Kennedy.

"It was really nice. I don't live too far from here, so we can meet halfway or something." She pulls me into a hug.

She nods at Rios, and the Uber she ordered while we were on our walk pulls up. She hops in and waves as the car drives away. I wait until it turns down the street, then bring my attention back to Rios.

"What do you want?" I ask, no kindness in my tone. I can't help the irritation that laces my words.

"You have every right to be pissed," he says as he follows me inside my building. I walk ahead of him into my lobby.

"I know I do, hence why I'm walking away from you." I'm proud of myself. Prior to this last time I left my mother in

California, I had lost a lot of the person I felt I was. I was turning into a person who would have let people like Rios walk all over me, probably allowing him to trample over how I was really feeling. I just felt numb.

But that Abby will no longer resurface. I was raised to stand up for myself, and Rios needs to know what he did was not okay. I'm livid with him. What he did with Clay and with Malloy, who is now my friend, was wrong.

"I'm going up the elevator, Rios, so I'm going to ask again —what do you want?" I cross my arms and wait as the elevator descends.

"I was hoping you'd give me a moment to explain myself," he says, and I look at him, literally hoping he will do just that. What does he think I'm doing, standing here waiting for him to write me a letter explaining his actions?

"Okay, then use your words, Daniel." I use his first name, throwing him off. Most of the guys rarely use their first names in acknowledgments at the station, so when I do it now, he straightens his spine as if I'm scolding him the way his mother would.

"Listen, you have to understand, Malloy was messing around with my sister," he starts.

"Bullshit. That's you assuming, and you know it," I say in return.

"Fine. I think there's something going on with Malloy and my sister. When Marissa called, I used the opportunity to test out my theory. The minute he accepted the date, my sister stormed out of the room, and an hour later, she left and returned to school. If that's not proof enough, then I don't know what is."

"Wow. Too bad you're not a fucking detective, Rios. You could really do well at the precinct down the street," I spit out.

"Were you always this assertive with your opinion when you were with Clay?" he throws back, and I swear I see red.

"Are you fucking serious right now?" I whisper-yell. The elevator dings and opens, but I ignore it and continue to stand in the lobby, my focus solely on Rios. I will not go up to my apartment with this guy and infest my building with his poor attitude.

I point my finger into his chest. "Here's the thing. You need to get your facts straight. For your information, Malloy is my friend, and like it or not, I care about his feelings, so I will not sit here and give you all the facts. You're going to have to figure shit out for yourself. If you can't open your eyes and see he cares for you and respects your friendship, that's on you. But wise up, Rios.

"What you did was not just disrespectful to Clay, but a million times fucked up to Malloy too. Both of them deserve an apology for what you've done. Malloy fessed up to your stupid charade from the get-go when he went out with me. But don't come here acting like the protective brother when we both know you are in the wrong. You were just being an ass and trying to puff out your chest and show your best friend who was in charge in a situation you had no say in. And when it comes to Clay and me, please don't interfere. We're good without you getting in the middle. I don't need you meddling. Now, please, go home. I have work to do."

"I assume you gave Marissa a hard time too?" He has the nerve to act like he has some footing to bring up my best friend.

"You've got to be kidding me? I'll have you know; Marissa did not consciously choose to make Clay feel like shit with another firefighter on my arm. You get that, right? She asked for your help, and she trusted you." I point at him. "Yes, she went too far, and she realizes that. But she really does want us back together. I don't know if that's actually what you wanted here. I think you had one motive and one motive only. You wanted to see if your sister was messing around with your best friend. You saw an opportunity, and you took it. Marissa saw two friends who were hurting, and she wanted to push them back together. That was it. What was your intention here? Really?"

Rios needed to be put in his place. Hopefully, he takes my advice and figures his shit out. He has no right to interject himself in my life with Clay, nor in whatever is going on with Malloy and Baylee. Although, Malloy better fess up if something does arise with Rios's sister at some point in the future because a secret could cause a big rift between the best friends.

Before I turn to leave, this rush of nausea comes over me, and I have no time to react. And, like the exorcist, I vomit all over Rios as my grand finale.

*Well, that's one way to make him pay for being a dick.*

# CHAPTER 12

*Abby*

"OH MY GOD! I'm so sorry!" Mortified. That's the only word to describe how I'm feeling right now.

Tears are clouding my vision, but I can see Rios standing before me, my lunch visibly soaking his shirt, stunned in place. The smell alone is threatening to spill more of my contents out of me. Luckily, one of the employees from reception comes running over.

"Ms. Morris, here, let me help you." She's got a basin in her hands and a few tissues.

The moment the trash bin is in front of me, I start throwing up some more. What am I, a never-ending pit? This is so embarrassing.

Once I get back to my apartment, I'll most likely never leave the confines of my home ever again. Maybe I can move out of here and never return. This is the worst day ever.

Rios is going to have a hell of a time telling this story. Then again, he's going to have to explain why he was here, and I doubt he wants to do that, so maybe he'll keep his trap closed about my exorcist debut.

Once my lunch and possibly all the meals I've consumed

in the last month have stopped making a reappearance, I finally bring myself back to standing. My gaze meets Rios, and he's still standing there, unmoved because he really has nowhere to go. I mean, he's covered in vomit. I sort of feel bad for him, but karma's a bitch, right?

"Listen, I don't have any change of clothes, but maybe I can help you clean that up. I can at least wash it for you or something?"

Rios takes the opportunity to slowly move the sweater over his head. Luckily, it didn't soak through to the undershirt, but it's too cold outside, so I'll do what I can to help him get cleaned up in my apartment.

"Here's a bag for clothes." I look down at her badge and see her name.

"Thanks, Serena," I tell her. She nods and walks back to the front of the lobby.

The elevator dings, and we walk in. He hasn't said anything, just silently stands on the opposite side of the metal box as we ascend to my apartment.

We get to my floor and walk out to the hallway. The moment I get my door open, I walk straight to my washer to hopefully get this mess fixed up. After I get his sweater into the machine, I walk to my restroom and get myself cleaned up. I must be coming down with something. Hopefully, I didn't pass it on to Kennedy too.

I walk back out and find Rios sitting on a stool in my kitchen.

"Can I get you some water?" I ask, opening my fridge in hopes of finding a ginger ale.

"How far along are you?" Rios asks.

I quickly straighten and close the fridge.

"Excuse me?" I ask. We barely know each other for him to be that forward with his question.

"I have four sisters. Three of which I've watched go

through this. You're knocked up. How far along are you?" he asks again.

"I'm not pregnant." I laugh. "If we hadn't started off on the wrong foot, Rios, we'd be friends because you're funny. That's a good one. I can't get pregnant."

"I'm not trying to be funny, Abby. I'm serious. I think you're pregnant." He's not letting this go.

"Well, you're not letting this sink in. I. Can't. Get. Pregnant," I repeat.

"Like ever?" Is this guy dense?

"Rios, are you trying to piss me off even more or something? Do you need me to call my doctor to prove it to you?" My laughter dies off because now this guy is pissing me off.

"Abby, I know you think I'm an asshole, and I guess I am, but I'm really asking you. Are you one hundred percent unable to have children or something? I'm asking because you already didn't look great when I saw you with Kennedy. Then you threw up on me. I have this gift of knowing when people are pregnant. I knew when all my sisters were pregnant before they even knew. So yeah, I think you're pregnant." He says this like he's some sort of pregnancy whisperer.

"I don't think I'm a *pregnancy whisperer*, but I think I've got some sort of sixth sense about it," he says, and I realize I must have said that last part under my breath.

"There's like a five to ten percent chance I can conceive naturally without the use of fertility drugs or hormones." I roll my eyes.

"That's not zero, Abby," he says like I don't understand math.

"Someone paid attention in math class." Apparently, I took my asshole pills today.

"Don't be a smart-ass. It's unbecoming. Plus, you know what I'm saying. You should call Malloy and tell him. He'll be thrilled."

"What are you talking about?" I look at him like he grew a second head.

"Well, haven't you been spending a ton of time together?"

"Yes. Can I get pregnant from osmosis now?" What the hell is he referring to?

"What do you mean?" he asks me.

"What the hell do *you* mean?" I throw back.

"You're telling me you two really are *just* friends? All this time, he's been telling the truth?" Rios looks at me like I'm lying to him.

"Yes, Rios, Malloy is being honest with you. Why would he lie? He's an honest person. We are just friends. Malloy is a good person. Pull your head out of your ass and realize you have a good friend by your side. We are friends, that's it!" I smack my hand on the counter.

"I'm so tired of you making Malloy out to be some lying friend who betrayed you. Stop making him feel guilty over nothing. He's a good person. Believe him when he tells you that he is who he says he is."

Right then, I see the realization hit him.

"Fuck. You're right. I've been a dick," he says.

Right then I say, "I know you have!"

We stand there in silence, my arms crossed as I give him my meanest glare.

"Well, what are you going to do, Abby?"

"About what?" I say back.

"The pregnancy!" he says in frustration.

"What, are you an OBGYN on your days off? There is no pregnancy!" I yell.

"Oh my gosh! I will buy you a pregnancy test myself." He gets up and stalks to my front door.

"*Oh my gosh*, please don't. I do not need any of those ever again. I'm done looking at those stupid pink single lines." I follow him as he makes his way to the door.

"Fine, you can sit here and stay pregnant and sick while I

know you're carrying someone's baby. By the way, I'm really good at predicting gender as well. So I'll guess that when you're ready too." He opens the door, and I stare at him and roll my eyes.

"You're very wrong about this, Rios. Don't worry about me, I promise."

He stares at me for an extra beat.

"Why are you staring at me? It's creepy."

"I'm thinking," he says.

"Well, don't. You might pop a blood vessel." I'm on an "absolute jerk" roll this afternoon. Maybe it's being around Rios.

"Girl. Definitely a girl. You're giving off girl vibes."

"Wow, you really don't get how this works, do you? I tell you I'm unable to conceive, and you just dig the knife deeper, don't you?" I tell him, my mouth hanging open.

He walks over to the elevator, about to press the button, but then turns around and comes back to my front door.

"Abby, I know you have this horrible impression of me, and rightfully so. I get it. I showed my worst side to you. Honestly, I'm disappointed in myself. Hopefully, I can find a way to prove to you I'm a pretty good guy. I mean, well, most days. But I'm serious. If there is any chance you could be pregnant, find out. It's important. You need support. You're alone here, right? Your family is on the West Coast, no?"

"Yes, but I am not pregnant, Rios. I swear. I got my period a while ago."

"Are you sure that wasn't implantation bleeding?" he counters.

"How in the world do you know about implantation bleeding?" Is this guy for real?

"Four sisters, remember?" He smirks.

He stalks over to the elevator and, this time, presses the button. He salutes me on the way in once the doors open and finally goes inside.

I close the door and go about my day. I'm finally feeling better once the ginger ale hits my system. I get my house in order a bit and put my computer at the kitchen table in hopes of getting some work done before I decide to call it a night.

An hour passes before there's a knock on the door. I check the peephole and see Rios standing on the other end. It's only then I realize he probably wants his sweater back, and I never even put it in the dryer.

I swing the door open and am immediately greeted with a plastic bag.

"What's this?" I ask.

"It's the damn test," he says, sounding annoyed either with himself or with me.

"I told you—"

"Yeah, yeah, do what you want with it. But at least I know I did all I could. Also, I had a sweater in my car, so you can just give it to Malloy, and he can give it back to me." He turns back and is already leaving my floor.

"Rios—"

"I know. You're welcome." He waves without looking at me.

I smile, knowing he might actually have a heart deep down. He's just been a bit prickly lately.

———

It's been hours. Four hours if I'm being honest, and I just stare at the damn box. I can't even open it.

The last time I had one of these in my possession, all it did was bring heartache. I hate these damn boxes. I hate the significance of the fucking contraptions they house. I hate the line. I don't even say lines plural because, for me, it's never been two lines. One fucking line is all I've ever seen staring back at me. I don't even know the feeling of two lines.

And I know what my future holds. One fucking line. But

now what Rios has said—that damn pregnancy whisperer—is on repeat in my mind, and I need to know. He brought me the test, so I need to take it. It's like an addict who needs another hit. I remember having these tests in my house, and I would take all the tests like I needed to see if each one had the same result—as if one would differ from the other.

Things got so bad for me once that I pulled apart one of the digital ones that said "Not Pregnant" because I didn't believe the inside lines would actually match what the digital reader said.

I had read on one of the online blogs that an expectant couple had tried, and their digital test said they were not pregnant, but then they pulled the test apart, and it was, in fact, false. The digital reader had been faulty, and the inside had two lines, but the digital portion had read it as "Not Pregnant." They were indeed pregnant, and they were now happy parents to a nine-pound baby.

I had become so obsessed that I was pulling apart digital pregnancy tests. That's probably when I hit my rock bottom of the fertility treatment world. I was miserable and aching in a way no one could comprehend. So yes, this moment in time, this paper box, signifies a lot of different emotions for me. It really hurts to look at a test and feel such animosity toward an object. Especially when, just a few hours ago, I was blissfully unaware of so many things.

Before Rios said anything, I never imagined anything would bring me to this bathroom looking at this pink and white box again. I only believed I caught a little bug. But now my mind has taken off, and it's dangerous where it is going now. Because in this little box in front of me, my dreams will soon implode into a million little nightmares that will crash once again. So I'll simply stare at this box for a little longer and let the dreams float above me. I'll let myself live blissfully content in this world where possibilities run endless—where my heart is still sort of whole.

I'm so entranced by this carton in front of me that my phone startles me when it rings. "Hey Lover" vibrates off my bathroom walls, and I feel just a little relief that my best friend might be able to calm my nerves.

"What is so urgent it warranted all caps, Abby? You trying to give me a heart attack over here?" she says into my ear.

"I'm staring at a box of pregnancy tests and trying to talk myself into taking one." I decide not to waste any time and cut straight to the point.

"Okay, let's back up a bit and start from the beginning," Marissa says, and so I do. I tell her everything from how I've been feeling sick all the way to my vomiting on Rios this afternoon.

For someone who is usually full of comebacks and arguments, silence is all I'm met with on the other end.

"Marissa, say something," I demand.

"Let me understand this: you were married for years and fucked like all the time, and it resulted in no baby. But you got together once on a random night without measuring temperatures or doing any treatments, and you're saying you might be pregnant?" This is typical Marissa. She has to lay out all the facts. Like her brain has to process everything out in the simplest terms.

"Yes, it would seem so if this turns out to be true, which I think is unlikely," I respond.

"Way to stay positive," she retorts.

"Marissa, what do you want me to say? I'm kinda freaking out here. I mean, what the hell? This is really a lot to process if this turns out to be positive. But it won't be positive, so why am I freaking out? I'm probably stressed. This project is a mess, and I'm sleeping like crap. It's just a lot going on!" I start to pace my bathroom.

"Okay, then just take the test," she says matter-of-factly.

"Okay, I will," I respond.

"Okay, then do it, and I'll wait."

"Like while you're on the phone?"

"Well, isn't that why you wanted me to call? To do the test with you? I mean, why this whole show of things?" I hate that she knows me so well.

"Fine, wait here," I say, putting the phone on the counter on speaker.

"Like I have any control over where you put me." She laughs into the phone.

"Smart ass!" I yell.

I grab the box, my hands shaking as I walk into the en-suite toilet. I just stare at it a little longer, the packaging still unopened, until I hear Marissa yell out, "Just fucking open the box, Abby. I know you're scared, but you're not alone. I'm here. I'll be here with you. You're not going to go through it alone."

Her words help me muster the courage to finally pull the tab open, and I grab the test out and rip the foil packet. When I'm finally done peeing on it, I cap it off, put it down on the counter, farther away from me, and come back to the phone.

"Did you do it?" Marissa asks.

"Yeah," I respond.

"How do you feel?"

"All the emotions."

"Tell me what's your biggest fear."

"That I'll crumble," I admit.

"Then I'll pick you up." And that right there is the sole reason she's my best friend.

"Distract me, please," I tell her because my heart is racing, and I fear it might leap out of my chest.

"I think Josie might be the one, and I might puke just putting that out in the universe," she says.

"That's amazing, Marissa. That's a huge step."

"It is. It's also making me feel like an adult of all things." And that makes me laugh.

"You're an attorney. You've been an adult for a while."

"Yeah, well, I think being an attorney always felt like the one thing I'd succeed in, but a relationship never felt manageable for me. Apparently, this is my uphill battle. And it's working, and I feel like a real adult," she says, and my heart soars for her.

"I'm happy for you. I really am."

"Thanks. I'm happy for me too. I'm also quite scared." She chuckles, and I can sense her nerves. It's weird to hear her nervous in any way because Marissa exudes confidence in every aspect of her life. I guess this is the one thing she needs to put a little more effort into.

"Is the time up yet?" she asks, and I look at my watch.

"No, but with these, sometimes it will show a faint line. I can just look. Let me grab it," I say and move to the right to grab the test.

I had put it face down when I brought it to the counter. I am still not ready to shatter the little bit of a dream I am holding onto, so I drag the test down the counter without flipping it over. It's ridiculous to think I am back here, hoping I'm pregnant with such slim chances yet again, but here we are.

I close my eyes and throw my head back. I keep telling myself I've made peace with it. It's a lie. I know that single line will simply shatter my soul, but like Marissa said, she'll pick me up. I've seen that single line so many times and survived that outcome each time before. Today is no different. I'm ready.

I put my head back down and flip the test over, and I stare at it. I bring the test closer and blink a few more times. I drop the test and go searching for the box. This must be an ovulation test. I think Rios bought the wrong one. Fucking men.

I find the container and check it. Nope. It says pregnancy on it. Maybe it's expired.

I flip it around, and it isn't expired either. What the actual fuck is happening?

"What the hell, Abby? Can you talk to me? Did I lose you? Are you still with me? The suspense! Girl!" she yells.

I can't find my voice. I'm speechless. This isn't happening. All those years. All those failed attempts. And now I'm staring at a test, and it's not one line. It's two lines.

Two. Dark. Fucking. Lines.

# CHAPTER 13

## *Clay*

I'M SHAKING my head at the thought of the date I just went through and the way my mind wanders to the one question that keeps coming back to me: is this how it's going to be now?

How did I go from being married roughly a year ago to going on dates with a dog food tester? I mean, where the fuck do I make a U-turn and go back to what my life was?

The thing is, now that I've had some perspective, I realize what Abby and I had wasn't at all in a good place at the end of our marriage. We had become shells of ourselves because life has an ugly way of showing how difficult it can get. And it was hard for us those last few years.

It's been a few months since I saw her come into the bar with Malloy, and the thought of that still gets my blood boiling.

Even though I'm well aware it was a blind date, it's still hard for me to get the image of her with another man out of my head. And the fact it's someone I know is hard for me to shake.

I feel my hands ball into fists by my side, remembering her walking out with him latched onto her arm. I remember my gaze staying on them for the entirety of their exit until they were out of my line of sight.

The aftermath of that night is cemented in my mind, and it's something I'm constantly pulling myself out of each time I find myself hovering over her number on my phone.

I've reached a stage of pathetic if I'm being completely transparent. I love her. My love for Abby has not diminished, nor has my anger—at that night or even the year prior, with her blindsiding me with a divorce—deterred me from giving her my heart. I never got it back, actually. She left me behind, and she never sent back the most valuable pieces of my heart and soul.

I've been in love with Abby Morris since the moment our eyes locked years ago. That cold Boston day when a twenty-year-old version of myself was still in college and needed the caffeine to get through my midterms.

I walked into Amazonia's Bean Co. naïve and looking for the strongest shot of coffee, only to come out knowing I was going to marry that girl. She sat in a corner with her beanie pulled over her ears, yet her eyes locked with mine the minute I walked in, and I haven't looked at another girl the same ever since.

We instantly connected, and from there, my heart started to beat outside my chest. She became my everything, and I became hers, until one day, all that shifted, and I was no longer what she needed. Or, from what she told me that morning when I got home, was that looking at me only reminded her of the pain and the loss of the life we should have been leading.

I think that right there gutted me more than anything else she did or said regarding the divorce. Knowing that when I looked at her, I saw beauty and love, but when she looked at me, all she saw was sadness and an emptiness I couldn't fill— it felt like the ultimate slap in the face.

She left me, walking away from all we made together,

because life decided to deal us a shit hand. I thought we would get through everything together, no matter the heartache, yet I was on that island alone. While I was finding ways to connect to her, she was finding ways to separate herself from me. The distance just kept growing until she chose to leave.

She walked away from not only me but our future. She told me she didn't feel like herself anymore; therefore, she couldn't be with someone who was in love with a different version of her. Little did she know I loved all the various parts of her, even if she didn't understand them.

Hell, I would have walked the surface of the sun if it meant she was waiting for me on the other side. For so long, I looked at all my buddies and felt lucky to have so much stability with the woman I chose to call my wife. We did everything together until the day came when she felt like she would rather walk alone instead of by my side.

That's the thing though; she left me behind, and I'm here like a love-sick fool, and I don't know how to pull myself out of it. I've looked into the future, and all I see is Abby by my side. I've tried to look at someone new, hoping I would find something, anything, to pull me into a new love. But I'm starting to think my heart is permanently broken. It feels like it beats differently now that I lack her presence daily.

River is now in a place where he's happy and looking at his girlfriend like she is everything to him, and I'm now living a life I don't recognize. I have no jealousy toward my brother and Kennedy. In all honesty, it's been fun to see him fall head over heels for the one girl who drove him mad for so long.

I walk up the steps to my apartment, and the loneliness feels like it engulfs me even more when I make my way up the elevator. My brother used to live in the building, but now he's all cozy with Kennedy at her place.

Each time I step foot in this building, I'm reminded I live

here, in my sad little apartment, because my life went to shit. I'm completely stuck in the past, even as I go on dates trying to forget about the woman who stole a part of me, only to never give it back. Recently, I've been going out in hopes of finding something new to latch onto, but I always feel disappointed when they don't live up to my expectations.

I feel no rush to get home, so I nearly miss the elevator doors opening on my floor. The moment I walk into the hallway, I feel her before I see her. I squint my eyes, rubbing them to ensure I'm not hallucinating.

But there she is, as clear as the day I met her. Abby's sitting in front of my door. I keep forgetting she's back in Boston, instead of across the country in California.

I straighten my spine and try to stay strong, hoping my heart can handle this close proximity. But nothing prepares me for the words she's about to utter. She opens her mouth, and I feel the pull this woman has on me when she simply looks up at me with tears pooled in those big blue eyes and says,

*"I'm pregnant."*

# CHAPTER 14

## Clay

I FEEL stunned in place as I try and process her words.

Pregnant. What is she talking about? I'm just processing that she's sitting outside my door, and she's telling me she's pregnant?

There's no rulebook on this. What do you say to your ex-wife, who you've loved most of your adult life, and she just tells you that she's pregnant?

I finally snap out of it and do the only thing I can do: I extend my hand to help her off the floor of the hallway and open the door to my apartment and allow her in.

I still haven't said a word. I watch her walk into the apartment and my heartbeat is thrumming through my ears.

Once inside, I walk straight into my kitchen, trying to ignore the fact that the last time I saw Abby, we were in a very similar situation in this very same space.

I go to my fridge, but this time, I'm well stocked with something stronger than water. I grab a beer, twist the top off, and throw back the bottle, hoping the cool liquid will tame the heat that's taking over my skin right now.

Unfortunately, I feel like I'm on fire from the inside out. My heart is racing, and I fear it might pump out of my chest wall. I lose all sense of time, but I know I'm silent for far too long, my back to Abby as I process what's going on with the bombshell she just dropped in my lap.

"Clay, say something," I hear from behind me.

I turn around and find Abby standing near my sink, her hands folded in front of her, a tentative look on her face.

I finally find my voice and speak up.

"I don't know what to say without sounding like a dick," I finally confess.

That's my truth at the moment. I swear, many questions are going through my mind, and many of them sound horrible. The first one is, "Is it mine?" I know it's awful to question that, but it's a valid one to bring up. But even thinking it makes me feel like an asshole, so speaking it out loud would only make me feel worse.

"Let me guess, you want to know if it's yours? You think I'd come to you with another man's baby?" She looks disgusted I'd think that low of her.

"Abby, can you at least put yourself in my shoes? Just for a minute, try to make sense of this entire fucked-up situation if you were me," I tell her because this is a lot to process.

"Try to process this as me right now, Clay!" she yells, tears falling down her cheeks. "Do you know how hard it was for me to take the fucking test? It nearly gutted me to even open the box. I thought I was just sick with a bug of some sort. I never imagined I was pregnant. And by my calculations, I've been pregnant for weeks too," she says, now pacing my kitchen.

Then she stops and looks me dead in the eyes. "And yes, it's yours. I haven't slept with anyone, not even before that night, alright. I have only been with you since we started dating. So, it is one thousand percent yours. I have no doubt in my mind." She inhales a shaky breath, bringing her hands through her hair, clearly, the agony of the entire situation taking its toll on her.

I place my beer on the counter and put my hands in my pockets, trying to calm my nerves. "So now what?"

"I don't know, alright! I'm fucking confused, Clay. If this were two years ago, I'd be ecstatic. Hell, I'd be completely ready and over the moon. Now, I'm losing my mind. Life is a mess right now, yet it's still everything I've ever wanted. But I can't ignore the fact we are no longer a *we*. This baby is coming into a completely different situation, and I'm utterly lost on what to do." Desperation laces her tone. "So I'm confused, yet completely excited."

"Abby, you're not alone in this. It's not like I'd desert you. It's my baby too. We'll make this work. We'll move back in together, and we can finally be the family we wanted to be. We belong together. This is what we wanted," I start to say, but right then, she stops and looks at me.

"Clay, no. No, that's not, no." She's pacing the kitchen. "We are not just jumping right back into things. No." She starts shaking her head.

"What do you mean, no? Abby, I love you. I've never stopped loving you, and I know you love me," I tell her, confused by this stubbornness she hasn't let go of.

"Clay, this baby doesn't change the fact that we are still divorced. I've been working on myself. I am trying to work on growing as a person, to stand up for myself and not ignore the work I need to do to better the person I need to be. Not only for myself now but for our child. I need to think of this baby," she says, placing her hand on her belly.

"Wait, so you think being with me hinders your ability to be a better person? I keep you from being a better person? Since when?" It feels like she's slapped me across the face with that comment.

"No, Clay, it's not that. Listen, I get that the divorce threw you for a loop. And I'll admit that, looking back, it was irrational at the time. I see that now. I've been working with a therapist since I left you, and I understand I should have handled that differently. But it's done, and I've realized that since leaving, I've needed to focus on myself more. I need to put in the work to improve myself. So I can't just jump back in. I'll set myself back. I was a shell of myself in the end when we were married. I want to continue my self-growth while I'm on this journey. This pregnancy doesn't change that," she counters, and it doesn't change the sting her words have left behind.

"But you're going to need help, and being together while you're preparing for the baby is probably best," I tell her.

"And you can, but I don't think living together is the best option, Clay. You can help, and I'll tell you when I need you. But you can stay in your corner, and I'll stay in mine."

I pull my fingers through my hair. This woman is infuriating at times, and it's taking everything in me to stay calm and not say more. But I am really trying to keep my words to myself because I don't want to say something I can't take back.

"This discussion isn't over," I tell her.

"It is, Clay. I didn't come here to discuss living arrangements. I came here because you're the father, and I didn't think it was fair for you to hear it from Rios or something," she says, then covers her mouth.

"Why the fuck would Rios tell me you're pregnant?"

"Shit! Damn, pregnancy brain is a real thing! Fucker!" she yells. "Ugh! So Rios ran into me, and I accidentally threw up on him, which is a whole other story I don't want to get into." She waves her hands in the air. "That being said, he got all pregnancy whisperer about it, saying that I was pregnant and I didn't know it and talked about how he knows when someone is pregnant and all that. I laughed in his face. He doesn't really take no for an answer, by the way—he's annoying like that—"

"No shit," I say in response because Rios is definitely pushy like that.

"So after I told him I was likely just sick with a stomach bug or something, he went to the store, on his own accord, mind you, and brought back a pregnancy test. I swear I stared at that thing for the longest time. Marissa yelled at me to take it—"

"Marissa was there?"

"No, she was on the phone. I finally took the test, and I really thought it was going to be negative. I mean, do you know what a mindfuck it is to see those damn tests always show one line for years? I mean, obviously, you do, but for me, Clay, dreaming of being a mom and then never getting to be one and then finally getting to see two lines and not having you there with me? It was like the biggest dream in the most devastating of circumstances. It's like my heart was soaring and breaking all in the same instance." She starts to cry, and that's when I can't stand it anymore, and I move to her and pull her into an embrace.

She always fit perfectly into my arms. I kiss the top of her head, and her arms tighten around my middle. I let the vanilla scent of her hair waft up, and it just takes me back to all the times I came home from work and held her close after long shifts at the station. She was always my purpose, and now, I don't really know what we are to each other. But now we have a new purpose that goes beyond my love for Abby.

I pull myself away from her a bit so we lock eyes.

"You know that if Rios knows, we need to get ahead of this, right? He's got a big mouth, and he'll tell people. I really want River to hear this from me before he hears it from anyone from the station."

Abby nods and fully pulls away, leaning up against the counter again. The proximity feels like tiny impulses setting me off, and if she feels even a fraction of the same thing, I think she's trying to stand farther away to keep anything from happening between us.

"I, uh, got an appointment with my obstetrician for tomorrow late morning. Are you able to make it?"

"Yeah, I don't work until the day after next. Is it at that fertility doctor's office or Dr. Amri's office?" I got so used to her fertility doctor's office that I can't even remember the last time we saw her regular OB-GYN.

"It's Dr. Amri. She will technically do the delivery if things are okay. Once we confirm the pregnancy looks good, then we can tell your brother. Also, Rios only bought me the test. He doesn't know it was positive, so we have a little time. But I agree, if he sees you and you even look slightly gleeful, he'll suspect something. Hopefully, he doesn't say anything to Malloy."

"And why the fuck would Malloy have something to say?" Now I see red and feel my molars grind.

"Calm down, Clay. I told you we are nothing more than friends. Actually, we're like best friends."

"You're best friends with Malloy? You want me to believe you braid each other's hair and shit?" I cross my arms and still can't dispel this tension in my shoulders. Malloy just gives off the asshole vibes.

She rolls her eyes. "You can drop the alpha vibes, Clay. It's unflattering. Malloy is really great. He's been a wonderful friend, and we hang out all the time."

She walks past me toward the door. I don't know why, but that makes my blood boil. Before she reaches the front door, I grab her hand and pull her to me. Her intake of breath shows me she's not as immune to me as she likes to pretend to be.

I pull her close, and we are mere inches from one another. I continue to walk her backward toward the front door, her back hitting the door. I bring my nose to her hair and inhale.

"You know, Abby, I think you know how much you drive me crazy talking about another man. And you like seeing me get all alpha male over you. That's alright. Because no matter how much you fight it, I'll know you're carrying my child inside you." I get really close to that sensitive area right below her earlobe, where I know all her senses take off. "Just remember one thing…"

She waits and then finally relents and answers with a simple, "Mmhm?"

"It's a shame we won't be living together because I hear those pregnancy hormones leave a woman quite thirsty." I don't touch her at all, but I breathe slightly on her neck, just enough to set her off and leave her wanting more. The moan I get in response has me smiling back when I pull away.

Her eyes are hooded when I stand up and move back a bit. When she finally realizes what just happened, she glares at me.

"Good night, Clay." But there's no kindness to her voice. I know I riled her up enough to leave her pissed off and wanting more.

I guess I'm going to have to pull a few tricks out of the River handbook now because Abby is fighting this attraction between us. I'm on a mission, and if there's one thing I know for sure, I will have my family back before this baby arrives.

# CHAPTER 15

## *Clay*

I **LOST** my father when I was five years old. I don't focus on that too often because he was taken from me in such a tragic way. I was robbed of his laughter and his love, but I don't view my time on this earth as time where I've been unloved.

My mother and my brother have shown me the best kind of love. And for the short years I had my father, he showed me the truest form of what a father's love should be. He loved my mother with all his heart. And he gave my brother and me the best parts of him.

He died in the North Tower on 9/11, and our lives forever changed that day. But he lives on within myself and my brother. I will carry on his legacy in my child. When I saw that little flutter on the ultrasound this morning, it felt like I saw a piece of my dad on that screen. It was as though all the steps I've taken in this life led to that moment.

Without hesitation, I grabbed Abby's hand and squeezed. We both let the tears fall, knowing no matter what we did from that moment on, we would do it with that little baby in mind. That's led me to this moment here.

I told Abby I needed to see my mother before telling River. At first, we had decided to have my brother and Kennedy stop by to let them know. But it only feels right that I see my mother first. I want to sit her down and let her know she will be a grandmother. Plus, I need to explain what's going on with this complicated situation with Abby and me. I need have a conversation between my mother and me—alone.

Luckily, Abby didn't protest. She felt a bit tired, so I dropped her off at her place, and she said she'd come to my apartment later to meet River and Kennedy. It felt strange after such a huge appointment to leave her behind at her apartment. I remember dreaming up a huge celebratory lunch or dinner after a possible positive pregnancy ultrasound. But today, we simply celebrated in the office, and then we went our separate ways. Everything is sort of going differently than expected. But I guess we are just doing everything the way we feel we have to this time around.

In reality, we are letting things be as natural as possible.

I pull up to my mom's place and cut the engine. It's cold, and my mom is nowhere to be found outside. I didn't let her know I was coming, so I hope she's even home.

I hop out of my truck, run to the front door, and ring the bell. I hear her movements inside and breathe a sigh of relief.

The moment she opens the door, I see the concern take over her features.

"Clay, everything okay? Is River alright?" I know my brother's recent accident has left everyone on edge.

"He's fine, Ma. I promise. Can I come inside? It's cold out here," I say, tucking my beanie over my ears for added effect.

"Yeah, hun, come on in." She opens the door farther, ushering me in.

I move inside my childhood home and take off a layer of my clothing.

"What's going on?" she asks as I follow her inside to the kitchen, where she pours me a cup of coffee.

I take a seat at the table and accept the cup of the steaming hot liquid.

"Can't a son come hang out with his favorite mom?" I say, giving her my best smile.

"You're full of shit, much like your brother." She laughs and pulls out her chair.

"You and I both know River is way worse than me." I give her a look, and she throws her head back and laughs again.

"Kennedy is a godsend for dealing with him." She chuckles. "But seriously, what's up?"

The way my mom looks over at me, I feel like it blankets me in so much love, all my worries feel protected with her.

"Abby's pregnant," I blurt out.

My mom was bringing her cup of coffee up to meet her lips but stops. She looks over at me and then brings her mug back down, staring at me until I finish.

"It's mine, by the way. You're going to be a grandma. Congratulations."

I don't know if that was the best way to go about it, but now that I told her, I feel a lot better. She looks to be in shock, so I start to wave a hand in front of her face.

"Ma, you okay?" Her stunned expression is worrying me.

She sits there, still quietly staring at me, then finally snaps out of it.

"I'm sorry, I think I'm having a stroke. Did you say you got your ex-wife pregnant?" She looks at me, and I'm not sure if she's mad, sad, or excited.

"Yes." There's no point in beating around the bush.

"I'm going to be a grandmother?"

I smile. "Yes."

She smiles. "Are you sure?"

"Yes, Ma, I'm sure. We went to the doctor this morning."

Tears well up in her eyes, and she pulls me into a hug. She whispers into my ear, "Your father is looking down on you and shining all his love onto that baby. I just know it, Clay. Just be ready for River to spoil that little one, though, and to force them to call him Dada."

That brings a laugh out of me. I know my brother will definitely push hard for that.

"So, you're not mad?" I ask her.

"Why in the world would I be mad?" She pulls back.

"Because it's Abby. I know how upset you were when she left."

"I wasn't upset at Abby though, son," she says.

"What do you mean? You seemed pretty upset when she left Boston." I remember quite vividly when I called my mom, letting her know Abby had packed up and left me. My mom was pretty torn up about it.

"Clay, you're my son. Seeing you upset left me quite angry in general. You are always going to be my priority. Abby was like a daughter to me, so of course I was upset. But once you explained everything that had happened, I grew a soft spot for what she had experienced.

"It doesn't mean I didn't feel bad for the heartbreak you had also felt. You had suffered with her as well. Infertility is something you both experienced. Then the divorce was hard on both of you. But that kind of heartbreak, not being able to get pregnant, is really hard for a woman." My mom bows her head.

"Do you know firsthand how it felt for her?" I ask my mom.

"No, not firsthand. Not in that way. I once had a friend—someone I was really close to, who stopped talking to me when I was pregnant with you and your brother—who suffered the way Abby suffered. Unfortunately, she didn't have the same outcome Abby is now having. She never got a baby of her own. Plus, surrogacy wasn't what it is today." She sips her coffee, her gaze drifting off, deep in thought.

"I remember meeting her for lunch, my excitement palpable, to tell her the news I was pregnant." Her smile grows. "I brought the ultrasound with the written-out A and B from the tech on it." My mom's smile drops. "I still remember pulling it out of my purse, and the moment I opened it up on the table, my friend, Jasmine was her name, stood up and stormed out of the restaurant. I was so confused. I had no idea she was struggling. She later called me and told me why she got so angry.

"Then she told me that she couldn't be my friend anymore. Of course, I was so upset. Here I was, excited about my babies, and I wanted to share the news with everyone. It's hard to relate to someone's pain when we are here, happy to have babies to give to the world. In time, I started to understand how it could be perceived. I grew more sensitive the more people I met who struggled.

"Then, when I lost your father, although the situation was completely different, I think I started to understand the grief a bit more because I saw couples getting to do things. I was grieving your father, and when I saw people loving on their spouses, I had feelings of 'Oh, they're so lucky.' I started to realize that it's all in how we see our situations."

I look down at my mug and reflect on how hard life has looked for Abby for so long. I realize how difficult it's all been for her. And how all this might still be. It's all an adjustment for her. Even with it being exciting, it might be tough to get used to.

"So, as much as you're my son, she's still my daughter in a way, Clay. I just see things a little differently for her. I feel for her in many ways. I'm sensitive to her pain. But I'm really excited for you both, sweetie. This is great and beautiful news." She grabs my cheeks and kisses my forehead, much like she did when I was a little boy.

"Have you told your brother yet?" she asks.

"No, we're telling him this afternoon. I just wanted to come by and tell you myself."

"Well, aren't you a sweetheart."

"I had to win some points," I tell her with a wink.

"You're my favorite today." She chuckles.

"Only today?" I feign shock.

"Lola is the winner on all the days, Clay. You know that," she says as if that's not already known.

I can't help the chuckle that escapes.

I finish my coffee and head out, needing to get home before Abby makes her way over to welcome Kennedy and River.

# CHAPTER 16

*Abby*

I CAN'T STOP STARING at the image of the tiny human I'm carrying. I mean, most of the fruit in my kitchen is bigger than this baby, and yet, this little human already holds my entire heart in their hands. How is that possible?

"We made that," Clay says, standing behind me at his kitchen table. He's just as taken by the little being as I am. I think it felt even more real when we saw the flutter of the heartbeat. Once we heard that swoosh overtake the room, our hearts melted, and we knew we would never be the same.

After the ultrasound, we were ushered over to see my obstetrician in her office, where I had more than a "few" questions. I swear, the moment I thought I was done with my questions, several more popped up. At one point, Clay said she was better off giving me her email address so I could compose a detailed document with bullet points because we would take up her entire day.

She was quite shocked to see us. I think she was as excited and surprised we conceived naturally as we were. She explained that although rare, it can happen for people with my diagnosis. In our case, luck was on our side that night, and we should consider ourselves fortunate it happened naturally. She also said we should get a lottery ticket on our way home. She was the only one laughing at her joke because it's still hard to wrap our minds around the fact that a baby is coming, and yet we are no longer together.

Lost in thought, a knock sounds on Clay's front door, and we quickly fold up the ultrasound photos and tuck them into my purse for the time being. We invited River and Kennedy over prior to the appointment in the hope of letting them know about the pregnancy.

Clay was right about Rios. If he indeed let this slip, River would be none too pleased to find out he was going to be an uncle from someone at the firehouse instead of from his own brother.

Clay hurries to answer the door while I stay seated at the kitchen table. I hear River greet his brother, followed by the sound of paws moving across the wooden floor, quickly finding me at the table.

Lola brings all sixty-plus pounds of her loving self to me and gives my arm a big lick. I can't help the laugh that escapes, and I scratch the back of her ear.

"Well, hello, sweet girl. It's been so long since I've seen you. You're such a pretty princess." I greet her, and she leans into my touch.

"Hey, Abby, I didn't expect to see you here." Kennedy comes in, bending down to hug me tight. She pulls away and gives me a sly smile.

"Yeah, good to see you, Kennedy," I say, trying to keep my reason for being here a secret. I really want Clay to do most of the talking.

I hear the guys laughing and straggling behind, so it takes a minute for them to catch up, but when they do, River halts when he sees me, looking over to his brother and then back at me.

"What's going on?" he says, appearing concerned when he sees me sitting at the table. Lola remains seated next to me as if sitting guard to protect me, sensing I need a shield right now.

"Sit down, you two. Do you want something to drink?" Clay asks, motioning to his fridge.

"I'll take some water," Kennedy says, while River yells, "Same."

"You look better," Kennedy says when she swings her attention back at me.

"Were you sick, Abby?" River asks, concern taking over his features.

"Yeah, feeling much better." I direct my gaze at River. "I was a bit under the weather, but better today." I smile.

Clay comes back with two bottled waters and sits down next to me. Kennedy and River sit side by side and give each other a pointed look.

"So, what's going on?" River asks, hesitant with his questioning.

"Well, we asked you here because we have some news to tell you," Clay begins.

"I fucking knew it!" River declares while Kennedy breaks into a huge grin.

What's happening right now?

River picks up his phone and seems to type something out.

"Goddamn it, Skipper. I fucking hate losing!" He throws his phone down and sulks.

Kennedy looks all too satisfied when she gazes at him, then puts her hand on his bicep and says, "Don't worry, baby, I'll do that thing you love later, you know, with my tongue, where I—"

"Okay, no thanks!" Clay shouts, throwing his arms up to shut this conversation down. "You know I hate having a mental picture of both of you doing anything sexual in my head. Damn it. It's there. Thanks, Kennedy! Also, you bet on us? What the fuck, River!"

"Kennedy started it!" He points at Kennedy, and my eyes double in size.

"You said we were friends!" I shout.

"It was before I went over the other day, I swear. I just had a feeling when I saw Clay all sad and stuff a few months ago. I just had a feeling I'd see you guys get back together, so I made a friendly wager. I hate seeing River win, so I bet him, and here we are!" She smiles, all too proud of herself.

"Well, send the money back!" I tell her.

"What, why?" she says, disappointment lacing her tone.

"Because we aren't back together. Bet not won!" I tell her, sticking my nose up, much too happy these two aren't making money off us today.

"Then why are we here?" River says, now seeming annoyed even though he didn't lose money.

"Because we're having a baby!" we shout at them.

That stuns them both into silence.

River rubs the back of his neck, mimicking his brother's mannerisms. His eyes bounce from me to Clay. I don't know what kind of reaction to expect from him, and the longer the silence stretches, the more nervous I become.

Finally, Kennedy stands from her chair and makes her way over to me.

"Congratulations to you both!" She reaches me first and pulls me into a hug. "You're going to be the best mama," she whispers into my ear, and I feel the lump in my throat form right then and there.

She pulls away and walks over to Clay, giving him a hug and whispering something to him as well that I can't hear. I see Clay embrace her tighter and say thank you.

Once they pull apart, Kennedy turns to River. "Say something to your brother!"

River snaps out of it and stands, quickly moving toward Clay and pulling him into a tight hug. The two hold each other for a long moment. It's during this stretch of time I let my mind wander to the fact that they must be thinking of their father. They have little memories to share of the man who molded a small portion of their lives, but so much of who they are today comes from the legacy he left behind. It's hard to have these big moments without thinking of their father and the milestones he would have loved to be a part of.

When the brothers pull apart, I hear them clear their throats, and it's hard to hold back the tears that break free from my own eyes. They both shake it off as if they weren't emotional.

"I'm going to love the hell out of that little one. They will think I'm the best, and you know it might even call me 'Dada' before you," River says.

"The fuck they will." Clay socks River in the shoulder, making him laugh.

There's a lightness in the room until River looks at me, and the moment settles a bit.

"Congratulations, Abby. I know this must bring a mix of emotions for you," River says. I see a bit of confusion cross Kennedy's face. I don't know how much of my relationship with Clay he has shared with his girlfriend, but he must have kept a lot of it close to the chest because she doesn't seem too privy to it at the moment. I decide to fill her in because there's no sense keeping her in the dark.

"It's no secret to anyone in this room that it's been difficult for me to get pregnant. It's sort of a miracle I was able to conceive, so this is sort of a shock right now," I say, and Kennedy simply gives me a small nod. I appreciate her letting that settle things and not asking for me to elaborate further.

River cuts in, "So who's going to tell Collette, and can I be there when you do?" The smile that stretches across his face is one of pure giddiness.

I see Clay throw his head back and close his eyes, and my shoulders slump. In the chaos of finding out about my pregnancy and telling Clay, I sort of let the rest of the announcements slip away. I haven't even let my mind go to the thought of having to inform my parents.

"Damnit. How long can we go without telling your parents, Abby?" Clay asks.

I glare at him, knowing full well my mom will sniff this out of me within one video call. I'm a terrible liar.

"What's wrong with your parents?" Kennedy asks, not quite understanding the issue.

"Oh, I think they're great. Her dad loves all of us, but Collette, you see, doesn't quite love Clay here. She does love her some River, though, doesn't she, Clay?" River pats Clay on the shoulder and smiles. "She absolutely wishes Abby picked me in the brother pool. She's always doting on me and asking if I've gotten enough to eat and everything." He sits down and leans back in his seat, crossing his arms behind his head, letting that big head of his rest in his hands.

"I'm amazed your chair doesn't fall back, seeing that your head is as heavy as a bowling ball with that ego of yours weighing so much," Kennedy says, rolling her eyes as she sits down next to him.

I can't help but chuckle, but the nerves have settled back in, thinking about how we will tell my parents about the baby.

"What if you just ask them to come visit? That way, it gives you more time to figure out how to break the news. I bet they'll be thrilled and supportive," Clay says, grabbing my hand. "Plus, the whole grandbaby thing will cloud any other emotion anyway."

"Hold on, are you two back together?" Kennedy asks, while River swings his chair upright and points his finger to where Clay's grasping my hand.

"No," I say, confusion lacing my features. "Why?"

"Well, you can't get all handsy like that and expect it not to raise questions," River says.

Clay keeps looking at River with a confused expression,

then realization seems to dawn on him when he looks at Kennedy. "You dicks. No, don't come at us asking about our relationship status so you can go and get your payout. Stop with your stupid bet!"

"You're no fun, Clay!" Kennedy pipes in.

"You're becoming as bad as him," Clay says.

"Well, I hate when he wins, so you could help a girl out!" she yells back.

I watch them volley back and forth, my eyes pinging from left to right across the table as they continue to throw jabs at one another.

"Enough, you two! Can we please focus on the matter at hand? I need to figure out how to tell my parents because I do not want to be stressed right now. It's not good for the baby or for me." I look at Clay, and he rubs my back.

Right then, River points at us because of the signs of affection, and Clay gives him the bird. I hold back a laugh because the two of them might be nearing thirty, but their maturity is closer to sixteen.

"Okay, what if you invite them for a visit and you simply do a little lunch—which I can go grab for you—and just tell them? Nothing fancy or crazy extravagant, and that's it. Done. Then it's out in the open, and you can feel supported, and I'm here for you to have reinforcements. Your mom can yell at me if she wants. I can handle it. No problem. Then River can swing by so your mom can dote on him for a bit. It's perfect." Clay smiles, and River smirks because he's all about being doted on.

As he finishes, Kennedy gets a call—"I'm so sorry, I have to answer this for work,"—and picks up her phone and walks into the kitchen.

"I think it's a great idea. May as well do it in person. If you go out there, your mom will try to make you move back to California, and Collette is sort of all about getting her way.

That way, you're where you're most comfortable and can say what needs to be said," River explains.

"You don't mind doing that? Like being available to grab the food and even be tormented by her if she gets a bit difficult?" I ask Clay.

"For you? No," he says, brushing my hair away from my eyes and tucking it behind my ears.

"Perfect, so it's settled. Mother dearest is coming to Boston then?" River asks.

"River, I told you not to call her that, remember?" I whisper-yell.

He holds his hands up in surrender. "Sorry, sorry, you're right. She's a saint. I'm sorry." Although he's not the least bit sorry. He's smiling and knows exactly what he's doing.

I turn my attention to Clay. "And just so you know, before I left California, my mom did say she would work on being kinder, so I do hope she fulfills that promise when she comes out here."

"I don't expect anything from her," Clay says. My mom was never blatantly rude to him, but she wasn't overly nice to him either. She was always just indifferent, even when he put an effort to make her feel welcome. I hope she'll attempt to make him feel appreciated because even if we are divorced, we are now going to co-parent together.

"What about telling our mother, Clay?" River asks.

"Oh, I went over there after the appointment." Clay smiles.

"Without me?"

"Yes, River. I didn't know I had to include you in my pregnancy announcement with Mom." He rolls his eyes, and River looks offended.

"We're twins, Clay. We do everything together," River explains. "I'm truly hurt, man." He puts his hand to his heart. "I would have waited for you."

"Really? So when Kennedy announces she's pregnant,

you're going to call me, ask me to head to Mom's house, then have me be a part of your pregnancy announcement like I'm a part of this whole thing with you and Kennedy?" Clay asks.

"Of course!" River says, with no hesitation whatsoever.

"River, I love you, but you're full of absolute shit. There is no way Kennedy would do that. Plus, that's not a twin thing to do. It's a 'you and Kennedy' moment, not a 'me and you' moment. I just wanted to sit with Mom to explain to her what was going on, that's all."

"I'm completely fucking with you." River laughs. "I never expected you to have me there. I just wanted to see you talk your way out of that one. I loved every second of that."

He throws his head back and laughs as I roll my eyes. It's hard to understand how Kennedy handles this Nichols brother half the time. He's too much.

"Hey, I'm going to grab some water for Lola. The bowl still under the sink in the kitchen?" he asks.

"Yep. The cabinet to the left, last I saw," Clay answers.

"Perfect, thanks." River gets up and heads over to the kitchen.

I turn to Clay. "You're sure you're okay with all this? I mean, it's a lot to take in."

"It's happening, no matter how fast or slow it's going, Abby," he says as if this isn't a huge adjustment.

"Well, we still have a lot to talk about."

"Yeah, like the living arrangements and the fact you're being stubborn about it."

I huff and roll my eyes. "Not this again." I sit back in my chair and rub my temples.

"Oh, we haven't even scratched the surface, baby. You can't resist my charms," he says, and I'm not sure if he's still talking about just moving in or about something else entirely.

I'm about to press him on the subject when I hear a commotion in the kitchen.

"River, what are you doing on the—get up from the floor.

What are you—No, not another fake proposal. Goddamn it! You're such an asshole!" Kennedy yells.

I look over at Clay, and he can't contain his laughter. Those two are either going to kill one another, or they're perfect for each other. Either way, they're entertaining to watch along the way.

# CHAPTER 17

*Abby*

"I GOT EVERYTHING ORDERED, and I'm going to go grab the food after I go change at home. I'll be back in about two hours. That should give you some time with them. You good here until I get back?" Clay asks as he's about to leave.

"Yeah, don't worry about me," I yell back as I get a water from the fridge. "Their flight is about to land, so the timing should be perfect."

I round the corner as I untwist the lid of the water bottle. "I'll tell them the news, and hopefully, they'll be too happy to focus on anything but the good news. You'll arrive right after I tell them they'll be grandparents. It should be fine. I'm nervous, but I think I would be no matter what."

Luckily, I just look like I've eaten a massive burrito for lunch and not that I'm pregnant, so I'm still good with some oversized clothes to mask the pregnancy from them on this visit.

"Well, call or text me if anything changes." He gives me a hug and then a quick kiss on the lips. We both freeze and stare at one another.

"What was that?" I ask him, frozen in place.

"I think it's just a habit. I'm sorry," he says, although he's still standing mere inches away from me.

His eyes look down at my lips, and I swear he's about to kiss me again, and I won't deny I want him to. I'm horny as hell with these damn hormones running amuck through my body. I'm leaning closer to him, giving him permission to take another taste of me, when his phone pings and breaks the spell.

He curses a small "Fuck" under his breath and pulls away. The moment is lost.

"I should go," he whispers and is out the door before I can say a word in protest.

I stand staring at the door Clay just walked through, wondering what to do with my feelings a little longer, then snap myself out of it.

Clay was kind enough to come over early this morning to help get the place ready for my parents to visit. I had offered for my mom and dad to stay here for their visit, but they insisted on staying at a hotel nearby.

I still wanted to make sure everything looked nice for them, so he helped me get some flowers and get the area tidied up before they came for lunch. They offered to go to lunch, but I thought something at the apartment would be nice and make it easier to relax and talk to them in private.

While I'm going through the apartment to ensure everything is set, I decide to call Marissa real quick.

"Hey. Did Mommy Collette arrive safely?" she starts off the greeting.

"She isn't here yet."

"Oh, I can't wait to hear how it goes. You have got to give me the play-by-play. Make sure to protect Clay for me. His face is too pretty to let her vicious claws get to him." She chuckles into my ear.

"Play nice, Marissa," I say, rolling my eyes.

"Your mom has got it out for him, although I have no idea why. He's always been so nice to her."

"I know. She's always played favorites, with River being the contender between the two."

"I know. I could tell." Marissa laughs. Each time Marissa was around, she would sit back and watch it all play out, entertained by the way my mother doted on River and ignored my ex-husband. It was quite fascinating, although infuriating.

I'm walking through when there's a knock on the door.

"Marissa, hold on, I think Clay may have forgotten something," I tell her.

"Oh, I bet he forgot something, alright." She laughs in my ear.

"You're ridiculously dirty, you know—" I swing the door open and hear, "Surprise!"

"Marissa, let me call you back," I say and immediately hang up without letting her respond.

And a surprise it is. My parents greet me from the other side of the threshold, arms out wide, ready for a hug. My mom is the first one to pull me in. She squeezes me tight, and I swear all the air in my lungs is pushed out of me.

My dad follows with another hug, this time not as strong as my mother's. I'm still shocked to see them standing there, especially since they aren't supposed to be here for at least another hour or so.

"What are you doing here? Your flight just landed? Or am I following the wrong flight information?" I scroll through my phone to open the app and see their flight landed two minutes ago.

"We caught an earlier flight so here we are!" my mom says and does jazz hands as if she's popping out of a box or something.

"Wow, what a nice surprise," I respond. My nerves are multiplied because I had everything timed out as I was going to tell them I was pregnant, then Clay would show up shortly after. I sort of needed a little safety net per se. Now I have a lot of time from now until he gets here. *Shit.*

I'm not great at fibbing. They'll sniff out there's something more to my reason for asking them out here. I remember in high school, I attempted to lie when I'd go out with friends when I told them I was studying, and it was always a disaster. I once concocted such an elaborate lie that started with studying at my friend's house and ended with us at the circus. I was grounded for three weeks for that whopper.

"Are you going to let us in? We want to see this place," my mother says.

"Of course. Sorry, where are my manners?" I say, my nerves getting the better of me already.

I motion them inside, and they walk through the foyer and into the apartment.

I notice they don't have their bags. "Where is your luggage?"

"Oh, we already checked into the hotel and got our stuff in our room. We arrived hours ago and already showered. I had to freshen up," my mother says as she takes the place in.

"Wow. Did you take a red-eye or something?" Because that's quite an early flight in.

"Yes. We thought it would be easier for us to settle with the jet lag and all," my mom replies as she takes in the surroundings, stopping at the window to take in the view.

"This view is incredible. The pictures don't do it justice." I can't argue with her there.

"I know. I could stand here for hours," I tell her as I walk up to the window right by her side.

I can tell she's looking at me, not at the view.

"Sweetheart, what's going on? We know something is bothering you. I told your father we had to get over here quickly because our girl needed us. We are here for you. Do you need to come home? We can help you get home, sweetie," she says, rubbing my back. "If you're second-guessing your decision, there is no shame in that. We can pack things up, no questions asked."

"Collette, don't smother the girl. She is doing fine. I told you she's fine. Look at her. She's glowing. She seems to be managing well on her own," my dad says while standing on my mother's other side.

Yes, Dad, I'm glowing because I'm growing a human. Obviously, I don't say that out loud, but I sure think it.

"Well, yes, Daddy's right. I am doing well, but there is something I wanted to talk to you about," I tell them.

"Is it the business, Abby?" She swings her gaze toward my father. "Rick, I told you I thought something was going on with her company." My mom's concern is etched all over her face. I hold back the urge to roll my eyes because my mom can be quite dramatic.

"No, it has nothing to do with the company," I say.

"What is it, honey? Don't worry, we're here to help, whatever it is." My mother grabs my hands, and I can feel her slight tremble. She's so nervous, and I feel bad she's so concerned. I decide to rip the Band-Aid off.

"I'm, um, pregnant." I give them a tentative smile like I'm a teenager and sort of feel like one at the moment.

They both look at me with bewildered expressions, and silence stretches for minutes that feel like hours.

Eventually, they speak at the exact same time.

"I'm sorry, what?" That comes from my mother, while my father asks, "Who's the father?"

"Clay's the father, and I'm pregnant." I shrug my shoulders.

Again, they both stare at me. Because nothing is quite going the way I planned, another knock sounds at my door. Who the hell is it now?

I leave my two shell-shocked parents standing near the window and walk to the front door.

I look through the peephole and find two of the last people I expect to see waiting on the other side. I swing the door open, somewhat relieved to see their smiling faces.

"Hey, so sorry to bother you while you're probably running around preparing for your parents to arrive, but he forgot his house keys somewhere, so I thought I'd grab them. He got all the way home and noticed they weren't in his pocket. I was nearby, so I told him I'd grab them." He swings his gaze up and sees my parents standing behind me.

"Oh, hey, Mr. and Mrs. Morris." River waves while Kennedy smiles by his side.

"You son-of-a-bitch!" my father declares and starts storming over to the door.

River's confused expression takes over his features as he watches my father coming toward him. "I'm sorry, what?"

"You have some nerve coming over here after you knocked up my daughter, especially with your new girlfriend in hand." My father starts yelling, face red, finger pointing in River's direction.

"Daddy, no, no! This is River, not Clay! Stop!" I hold my arm out to keep him from doing anything stupid.

My father has a heart of gold, but he has a shit time telling twins apart. Even after all these years, he still can't tell River and Clay apart. I get that they are quite similar, but most people can see their minor differences once you spend enough time with them. My father is not one of those people.

For years, he would speak to Clay and call him River and vice versa. There were multiple times when one would sit for entire conversations and pretend to be the other to simply keep from offending him. I would blame old age, but my mother said my father had neighbors growing up, and he never could tell them apart, and they lived next door for twelve years. It was a story my grammy told many times, crying with laughter because it never got old. He's a lost cause.

"Mom, Dad, this is Kennedy, *River's* girlfriend." I give my dad a stern glare.

I turn to Kennedy, sympathy lacing my features. "Kennedy, I'd like you to meet my parents, Collette and Rick Morris." I then mouth *I'm sorry* to River, and he gives me his big eyes, showing off the gold flecks in his hazel irises. He and I know my dad was pretty close to punching him for hurting his little girl.

Poor River was almost on the receiving end of Clay's assault. My dad would never have heard the end of that. Clay might love that story later, though, because he's always the one being scrutinized by my mother, and River's always being doted on.

My mother shakes Kennedy's hand and proceeds to give River a big hug because I swear she thinks River is the best thing in Boston. I roll my eyes at the gesture. My dad walks over and introduces himself to Kennedy properly and apologizes to River, his tail between his legs while doing so. My arms are across my chest, embarrassed by my father's behavior.

"Yeah, so we just swung by because my *brother* called." It's hard to hide my snort at the emphasis on the brother part. "He forgot his keys here. Sorry to interrupt." River tucks his hands in his pockets, hoping I'll grab what he needs so he can leave.

"Oh, let me grab them," I say and hurry to find them. Luckily, they're easily visible on the kitchen counter, and I snatch them up and run back to hand them off to River. "I'm surprised you don't have a copy of them," I say as I'm walking back to the front door.

"Yeah, I don't know what happened to my set. I guess we need to fix that little issue. Thanks so much. We're going to get going." He grabs Kennedy's hand, and they book it out of here. I swear I see a puff of smoke following them.

I turn to my dad. "Was that really necessary?"

"Seriously, Rick, that boy is so sweet," she says, and I look at her like she's high on glue.

"Okay, you're one to talk, Mom!" I say as I shut the door.

"What do you mean?" she counters, and I walk off.

"You both need to sit down, and we are going to talk this out before Clay gets here with the food." I point to the couch, and for the first time, my parents look like the children, and I'm the parent scolding them for being out past curfew.

They both take a seat, and I sit opposite them on the loveseat.

"Listen, I know a lot has happened with me lately. I went from being married to Clay to now being divorced with his child. I was living in California, and now I'm back in Boston. I know I struggled with my fertility stuff for so long, all of us thinking I couldn't have kids to me now saying I'm pregnant. Believe me, I'm as surprised by this life I'm living as I'm sure you are. But I'm living it," I say because there is nothing about this that happened the way I had planned.

"I need you to understand that I'm doing this. Clay and I will co-parent this baby together. We haven't figured every-thing out yet." My mother tries to interject, but I hold my hand up.

"I'm talking now. I know you probably want to step in and take hold of certain parts of my life. I get it; to you, I am your child, but Mom, Dad, I'm going to be a parent now. I have to figure this out. You have to trust me to be one in my own way. I came running home, and I allowed you to coddle me. I was wrong in doing that, and I realize that now. I need to do this on my own, sort of. I'm doing okay here. Don't you see that?"

My parents look at each other, and then they swing their gazes at me. My father is the one to speak. "Yes, sweetie, we see that. It's hard, though, being so far away. When you were going through all those struggles and hearing your mother cry after she'd hung up the phone with you, it was hard. I kept my mouth shut because you know your mom. She's outspoken enough for the both of us.

"But it hurt me too, seeing you in pain. We wanted to fix all your cracks, so just realize how hard this is for us. We are so happy for you. We know how much being a mother has been a dream for you, and now you get to do that. But we also are nervous. I'm sorry I overreacted. But when I saw who I thought was Clay—again, so sorry—with another woman, I just got so mad he'd disrespect you like that."

He bows his head, and I know how much all this hurts for both of them. The distance is a lot for them to overcome, but we've done this before, and it just takes time to adjust. We'll get used to it again.

"Listen, I know this is a lot right now, but we have so much to be grateful for. And I'm not alone. You met Kennedy. She's my friend, and I have Malloy, who's a firefighter and a friend of mine too." My mom looks up, hopeful I have a love interest, and I quickly dispel those thoughts. "Just a friend, Mom!"

"Okay, sorry." She puts her hands up in surrender.

"Clay is coming over soon with lunch, and I want him treated with respect. No storming the door on his arrival, Dad. Got it?"

I give my dad a pointed look, and he also puts his hands up in surrender.

"I promise, Abby," he says.

"Good. And, Mom, remember the promise you made me in California that you would put effort into giving Clay a chance when you saw him." I look at her.

"Yes, that was my promise to you."

"I really don't know what the future holds for Clay and me, but I want peace between us because this baby deserves that." I put my hand on my belly.

My parents watch the gesture, and the smiles grow on their faces.

My mom looks up at me, and our eyes connect.

"Abby, honey, can you show us a picture of the ultrasound?" she asks, and my smile doubles.

"Of course, Mom. I would love to."

I make my way to my purse and rush back to show them all the images we got that day at Dr. Amri's office.

I sit between my parents, and the way they gush at the images makes my heart grow. It feels a little more real knowing I get to see them in this role as grandparents in the months ahead.

# CHAPTER 18

## Clay

IT'S AN EXCEPTIONALLY warm day in Boston, and spring isn't officially here yet. This jog is exactly what I needed as I shed yet another layer after the meal I had with Abby's family last weekend.

I came off a long week of shifts, so I was itching for a run, and today, the sun is shining. I didn't hesitate to put my running shoes on and hit the pavement when I looked outside this morning.

Rios was exhausted and bailed on our run, something he's been doing more of recently since things with him and Malloy are hot and cold lately. But I'm also in my own world now that I'm coming to terms with the fact I'm going to be a father. I can't get over how smoothly everything went with Mr. and Mrs. Morris, especially Collette.

When I was clearing everyone's plate, she came up to me and surprised me with a huge hug and took the time to clear the air. Abby and her father went on a walk around the water while Collette spent nearly an hour talking about her first marriage and all she struggled with raising Frankie on her own before marrying Rick.

Then she apologized for the years of hardship she put me

through. She had treated me unfairly, and although it doesn't make up for all that time, it sheds some light on the why behind her behavior.

It doesn't hurt that I got a good laugh from hearing that River nearly got a beating when Rick thought he was me. I sort of wish I was there to see that disaster unfold.

I think, overall, it was a successful visit with Collette and Rick. I'm glad they saw Abby, and we were able to tell them about the baby. I think having them here was good for Abby, and I think she shed a bit of her nerves as well. I can see she felt relieved after they went home too.

But it doesn't mean I'm not slightly irritated still. As much as we got to smooth things over with her parents, and I hopefully got a fresh start with Collette, I'm no closer to figuring things out with Abby. I still feel like we're in the exact same place when it comes to our stance on our living situation. She wants to keep us on our sides of the fence, so to speak.

Honestly, I want things back with Abby, but she's hellbent on keeping things the way they are—in this damn friendship corner she's built for us. We're having a fucking baby together, and we're not in relationships with anyone else. I mean, I still love her, and I can guarantee she still loves me.

If only I could find a way to prove that point because, at the moment, I'm only theorizing. But I see the way she holds her gaze on me a little too long when I walk by or the smoldering look she hits me with sometimes when I bend over, and I swear she wants me to kiss her when I'm about to leave.

I'm jogging up the steps to my apartment when my cell phone starts to ring through my headphones. I'm panting from exerting myself on the run, pushing the extra mile because my frustration has been getting to me lately. I pull my phone out to see Abby's name flashing across my screen.

"Hey," I answer, trying to minimize my heavy breathing.

"Hi, Clay. Sorry to bother you. Did I catch you at a bad

time?" she asks, sounding somewhat regretful that she is inconveniencing me with a call.

"I'm just getting back from a run." I get into my lobby and start to walk up the stairs, taking two steps at a time.

"Oh, shoot, I can let you go," she says, and I can bet she's gnawing on her bottom lip.

"Abby, what's wrong? Is there something wrong with the baby?" I'm about to turn around and make my way over to her.

"No, no, nothing like that. I just, ugh, I'm sorry. I just, I can't get my damn washer to work. And I have a whole load in there, and it's already wet, and I just need this to work." She sniffles.

"Are you crying?" I ask.

"Yes, Clay! I'm fucking hormonal, okay? I really wanted to do laundry today, and now I can't. And my day is ruined! You don't understand!" she whines, and I'm really doing everything in my power not to laugh.

"Okay. Give me a few minutes to get cleaned up, and I'm headed over," I say.

"No, it's fine. I shouldn't have called. I'll call someone else." She continues to sniffle.

"It's fine. I will be there in thirty minutes, okay?" I reassure her.

"Okay. Thank you."

"See you soon," I tell her before hanging up.

The moment I end the call, I smile to myself because she called me first. This might just be the in I need.

---

"Wow, this is really upsetting you, isn't it?" Abby is fully bawling when she opens the door.

"Well, my day just keeps getting worse. I sat down to have some of my favorite ice cream, and I forgot I ate it all last night." She continues to cry, and I can't help the horrified look I give her in return. "Don't look at me like that, Clay. I'm growing a human! I can't control what's happening," she says, and I put my hands up in surrender.

"I didn't say anything," I explain.

"You don't have to. You're saying it all with your eyes."

"Why don't you show me the machine that started this horrific day for you," I say, and she glares at me before turning on her heels and walking back toward her washer and dryer.

She points to the machine, and I inspect everything before assessing the damage.

"Do you happen to have a flashlight?" I ask.

"I think Malloy left one here last time he came over," she says as she looks around.

"Malloy's been here?" I can't help the irritation in my tone.

"Clay, stop with the jealousy. I told you, he's my friend. I'm allowed to have friends." She opens cabinets in the hallway, finally finding the flashlight I need.

"You're right. I just don't love that it's Malloy, that's all," I reply as she hands me what I need.

"I don't know why you don't like the guy. He's been nothing but kind to me," she says, watching me inspect the machine.

"I don't get the best vibe from him, that's all."

"Well, he's not the one I have an issue with."

"What's that supposed to mean?" I ask, looking over at her.

"It just means that I think you're not giving Malloy a chance. You're judging him too quickly. And I think you should give him a shot. He's a good person."

I stop what I'm doing. "He was making a move on my girl, so I don't really feel like being so kind."

"First of all, Clay, I'm not your girl. Second of all, he

wasn't making a move on me. He was just hanging out with me. It wasn't what it seemed. I told you this so many times already." She rolls her eyes.

She's fucking high if she thinks she's not my girl.

"Really, Abby? That's what you think?" She nods her head with a finality. I know her stubbornness to dig her heels in the ground. My ex-wife thinks she has won this battle. Little does she know I can play dirty.

I take one final look at the machine and confirm what the issue is. I put the flashlight down and grab the tools I need while Abby watches me attentively.

"You think you can fix it?" she asks, hopefulness oozing in her tone.

"Mmhm," I answer casually.

Before I say anything else, I reach my arms behind my head and grab the collar of my shirt and yank it over my head.

"Clay, what are you doing?"

"I made the mistake of wearing a white shirt, and I don't want to get it dirty." I move into her living room and drape the shirt over her couch so it doesn't get wrinkled.

"It's a plain white tee. I know you have a ton of those," she says, crossing her arms, feigning annoyance.

I take my strides mindfully toward Abby, moving slowly so that with each step forward, she's walking backward until she's leaning against her dryer.

I know my muscles are a huge turn-on for her. It doesn't hurt that since she's left, I've had a lot of extra time and pent-up aggression to tone up a bit. Soon, I'm pinning her against the machine, my arms caging her in, my breath inches from her skin.

"Abby, it's been too long for you to know what's in my closet. You can't say for certain what I do and don't have, sweetheart. Like I said, I don't want to get this one dirty. Also, regarding you being my girl." I lick my lips, and I swear I hear her swallow. "You will always be mine. Don't forget whose baby you're carrying, sweetheart."

I see goosebumps break out along her skin, and I know she's turned on. If there's one thing I remember Ashton telling me from Samara's pregnancy, it was how hot and bothered she was once she got to her second trimester. If my calculations are correct, Abby is hitting that point right about now, and she's probably feeling pretty turned on at the moment.

I quickly push off the machine and start going through my toolbox to find what I need to get her washer up and running again. It takes Abby a moment to compose herself. Before long, the machine starts working, and I swear, I think I catch happy tears pooling in Abby's eyes.

"Do you want me to make you a sandwich before you go?" she offers. "It's the least I can do."

"Uh, yeah, sure. Thank you," I say as I make my way through the kitchen and wash up.

"You can put your shirt back on, you know." And just for that comment, I'll be keeping it off a little longer.

"Yeah, sure, no problem." I wink at her and go to grab my shirt from the couch. "On second thought, I think I'll keep it off because I don't want to get any of my meal on my shirt either. I hate mustard stains." I make a face.

"You hate mustard," she tosses back.

"But what if today I want to try it and love it?"

"You're infuriating."

"I don't think you mean that," I say, following her into the kitchen.

I saddle up next to her and help where I can. I start to stack her sandwich the way she usually would eat hers, and she grabs my hand. "Please don't put pickles on it."

"But you love pickles," I protest.

"Not this week, I don't." She nearly gags.

"Oh shoot, the baby is revolting against your favorite snack?" I make a face, and she looks like she might cry again.

"I know, right? I was so bummed when I realized it. I almost called you, but you were on shift, so I didn't want to bother you." She chuckles.

I grab her hand and interlace my fingers with hers. "Abby, you can call me anytime. Day or night, even if I'm on shift. I want to do this with you." I bring her hand to my lips and kiss it softly. I see her melt into me slightly, then pull her hand away.

"We should sit down." She hands me my plate, and we walk over to the table. We start to eat in silence until I decide to put my foot in my mouth.

"Have you given any more thought to me moving in?" The moment I say it, I see her stiffen up.

"No, because I didn't realize it was still up for discussion, Clay," she says.

"Abby, this is ridiculous," I begin, putting my sandwich down. "We should be living together so I can be here to help. I mean, today is a perfect example. I could have been here already. I can be here and help prepare for the baby and get the nursery ready. All the things that need to get done, I'd be here."

"Where would you sleep?" she asks.

"There's the baby's room for the time being, and it's not like I can't sleep in the same room as you when the nursery is ready."

She cuts me a look, and I stare at her.

"You can't be serious? You think we can't be in the same room together?" I ask her.

She points down to the barely there belly she's sporting. "I think exhibit A proves my point. No, I do not. It would get messy. You know it would," she says, and I roll my eyes.

"Fine, then what if there was a bed in the baby's room, and I slept in there?" I suggest.

"I still think that's a no."

"Always being the final say, Abby."

"That's not fair, Clay! I don't want to fight. Please." She breathes and then continues eating.

"I'll drop it for now." I put my finger up. "I am only saying for now. This will be revisited. But let's at least swap keys. That would be useful, and I should have a key to this place. What if something happens and you need me or vice versa?"

She chews her bite, thinking over what I suggested, and finally relents. "Fine, I'll agree that's a smart thing to do."

"Okay, good. I already have a spare key to give you," I say. "I'll grab it before I leave."

"Okay, let me grab mine now, or I'll forget. This pregnancy brain thing is real. I always thought people were exaggerating, but I have forgotten so much stuff. I have to make lists for everything—I swear I had to make a note when I forgot to refill the toilet paper roll in my bathroom the other day. And all I had done prior to grabbing a new one was wash my hands." Abby does this cute little laugh to herself, and it's hard not to fall in love with her a little more, watching this little moment between us unfold.

"I'm sorry I didn't fight harder for you, Abby," I tell her, bringing a heaviness to our meal. "I just want you to know that I should have fought harder for you when you left. I crumbled, and I assumed you'd be back. I'm sorry I didn't do more."

She's about to get up to grab the key but stops halfway up from her chair. "No, Clay. I needed to figure things out. I'm still figuring myself out. It's just how our journey had to be. I appreciate you saying that, but this is on me," she says, and it doesn't make me feel any better about how things turned out.

"I'm going to go get that key. I'll be right back." She scurries off to her living room.

Maybe if I had put more effort into getting her back, we could have worked things out and avoided where we are today. But then again, here she is, carrying our child, and maybe there's still a shot at the two of us being together, even if she doesn't see that future together.

"I had the keys made with these funny designs. You'll know they're mine. Don't laugh." She hands me a SpongeBob key. She always loved that damn cartoon.

"The guys will have a field day with this on my keychain," I say as I grab it and inspect the design. I tuck it into the pocket of my jeans before gathering my dishes and hers.

"Well, you said you wanted to swap keys, so you get what you get." She smiles, and I won't lie; I would do anything to see that smile directed at me more often.

I help get everything in order in the kitchen before heading out for the afternoon.

"The machine should be all set. Let me know if you need anything else or if it starts acting up again," I tell her, feeling a little uneasy as I head for the front door.

"I appreciate you coming over. Thanks again," she says, leaning against the door as she holds it open for me.

I grab my shirt and finally throw it over my head. I thought it would have more power of persuasion. Baby steps, I guess.

We were never this uneasy with one another. From the moment we started dating, we came together so effortlessly. This feels strange, this limbo we are living in. Now that we have the baby coming, we need to find a way to coexist, but all I want to do is go back to being married, and I can't even touch her.

I run my fingers through my hair, needing to keep my hands busy, or I'll pull her in to kiss her. I see her look down at my lips, and her cheeks turn that light shade of pink that I used to love when she'd get shy around me at the beginning of our relationship.

"I guess I'll see you at the next appointment?" she asks, trying to figure out how to part ways.

"Yeah, sounds good," I say, turning and walking further away from her, wishing I didn't have to say goodbye.

I finally press the button to the elevator. The moment I walk inside the metal box, I hear the door to her apartment close, and I swear I can take a full breath again. I don't even know how I'm going to go months like this, having to keep my hands to myself. All I want to do is touch her and feel her in my arms.

The elevator ride is filled with thoughts of the months ahead. I'm about to walk out the elevator doors when I realize I forgot to give her a key to my place. Whoever said pregnancy brain was reserved for the person carrying the child alone was an idiot. I am apparently having sympathy symptoms, which is ridiculous to even think, so I walk myself backward and press the number to her floor.

I tap my foot impatiently as I ascend the elevator back to her level. The moment I get there, I knock on her door, but she doesn't answer. There is no way she left. What if she fell and hit her head? What if she's unconscious?

I reach into my pocket to text her when I feel the key. I pull out the ridiculous SpongeBob contraption and decide to make use of it while I can.

The moment I get inside the apartment, I yell out for Abby. She doesn't answer, but I do hear the water running. I remember Abby mentioning she was going to take a shower, so she must have gone straight there after I left.

I can't help but feel the parallels of this scenario to my brother's encounter with Kennedy when he walked into her hotel room the day they first started things together. That brings a smile to my face. That sort of catapulted everything to a whole new level for them, and he's never been the same.

I decide to grab my keys to pull my extra set off. I'm about to leave mine on the console table when I hear my name in the distance. I turn around to see if Abby may have heard me, but she's not in the hallway, so I'm about to leave when I hear it again, this time with a soft moan.

"Oh, *Clay*." She definitely said my name.

What the fuck is going on?

I decide to move closer to the main bedroom, the sound of my heart pounding in my ears. Abby is going to kill me for invading her privacy. But I swear I heard my name come off her lips, and now my curiosity is piqued.

I get to her bedroom door, but I find it empty. I'm about to turn back, feeling a little uncomfortable that I've taken this scavenger hunt too far, when I hear another moan. The water is still running, and this time, I note it's a stream more like the faucet of the bath. Again, I'm losing my mind because my feet take over, and I simply follow the sound.

I find myself standing at the bathroom door, and the vision in front of me has me gaping. My dick has a mind of its own, so I'm hard as a rock within seconds.

Abby, in all her pregnant glory, which only means a small little bump, naked, in a bubble bath, water running with a small amount of water in the tub, is holding a little teal vibrator, which is buzzing on such a low level I can barely hear it. Her eyes are closed, her chest is pushed out, the bubbles coating her olive skin, and her nipples pebbled, almost asking for me to suck them into my mouth. Fuck, she's perfect, and all I want to do is devour her.

And here I am, standing near the door like an absolute stalker. Fuck. I'm still taking in her beauty when she opens her eyes, and I swear she is processing what she's seeing, and it all happens in a matter of seconds. She starts screaming, and I panic.

"Fuck, Abby, I'm so sorry, baby." I put my hands up, trying to calm her down.

"What are you doing, Clay?" she yells, then proceeds to throw the vibrator at my forehead. It bounces and hits the wall opposite me and lands on the ground, but it doesn't turn off and continues to stay on and vibrate across the floor. We both stare at it because the thing is now on full blast. That thing can really be quite powerful.

"Wow, that thing can get pretty intense, huh?" I give her that cocky smile that drives her crazy.

"Fuck you, Clay! What are you doing back here?" She tries to cover her breasts, but she fails to realize the bubbles are not hiding her in any way down below. My eyes are glued to her pussy, and I am not ashamed that I'm staring. It takes her a minute to realize where my focus is.

"My eyes are up here, Clay!" she yells.

"Yes, I'm well aware, but my focus is down there." I jut my chin to her bottom half, apparently feeling bold and like a death wish is on the agenda for this afternoon.

"How did you get in here?" she asks, then throws a hand up, cupping both breasts with one hand, losing control and slipping a nip out, screaming and then suctioning her body against the tub in hopes of hiding herself from me. Too bad I have memorized every inch of her body from head to toe. She can try to cover herself, but I know every little freckle and scar she holds on that perfect skin of hers.

"I have a key, remember?" I smile.

"Shit," she whispers, forgetting she just gave me a damn key. Wow, she really is forgetful now that another human is taking over her brain cells.

The longer I stare at her in that tub, even just the little bit of skin that's showing, the more my dick thinks he's going to get some, so he's making himself known.

"Get some control of that, Clay!" She's motioning toward my dick.

"Abby, I can't. It's been a while! What do you want me to do?" I move my hand over my jeans, and I swear even a slight touch to the area feels like it might set me off.

"Don't act like you haven't gotten any since that night." She rolls her eyes.

I look away because I haven't touched anyone since I've been with her.

"You can't be fucking serious." She chuckles.

"You think this is funny?" I wave my hand over my junk because the more I look at her, the more my dick strains behind my zipper. The discomfort is only mounting.

"It seems you have just as much pent-up frustration as me," she says, this time a sly smile painting her lips.

"You're fucking naked in front of me, and you think I won't react?" I tell her, throwing my hands in the air.

"I didn't invite you in here, remember?" This time, she stands up, and I can't help the confusion in my expression.

She doesn't even try to cover herself as if all the timidness she had just a few minutes ago is replaced by a boldness I am not expecting. Then, she takes a step out of the tub. At first, I think she's going to come at me, but she turns to the vibrator, grabs it, and returns to the tub, sitting back down in the water.

"Well, are you going to leave me alone so I can finish what I started?" she says while I stand there, my jaw permanently on the ground because this is not the woman I married. She was never this forward when it came to sex.

"What if I said I'll stay right here," I throw back, sort of curious how she'll respond.

"Suit yourself." She grabs her left breast and squeezes, poking her tongue out to graze the bottom of her lip. Fuck, I just want to kiss the hell out of her right now or plunge my cock down her throat. Not sure which one, actually.

I can't form words because I think I'm short-circuiting as I watch her move the vibrator into the water. We never did toy play when we were married. My eyes follow it to where I assume is down the apex of her thighs, but then she surprises me with what she says next.

"You want to play too, Clay?"

I must be fucking dreaming right now. My mouth is as dry

as the Sahara. There is no way she's asking me to join her. Before I can ask her what she means, she elaborates.

"If I'm going to get myself off, you might as well do the same." She smiles, and right then, she must put the vibrator to her clit because she arches her back, closes her eyes, and makes the most beautiful sound come out of her mouth.

I don't even try to clarify if she's serious, so I rush to unbuckle my jeans and push my pants and boxers down. I've got my dick in my hand, and the moment I stroke myself, I already know it won't take much to get me to the brink.

Abby is a goddess in that tub. The water, along with the moans that take over the bathroom, it's fucking bliss. I watch her free hand glide along her body, pinching her nipples, her chest rising and falling faster the closer she chases her high.

I want this to last a little longer because I know the moment I fall off this cliff, she's going to build that fucking wall again, and I'll have to leave. But there's no escaping the feeling that's building up along my spine.

Abby's just as mesmerized, watching me stroke my cock, her eyes fixated on my length as she keeps one hand under the water, where I imagine the vibrator works her clit. I bet watching me is turning her on just as much as watching her is getting me hotter. I wish I could take over and bury myself deep inside her.

I'm moving my hand along my length faster, and Abby's moans are getting louder.

"Clay, I'm going to come," she says and arches her back, calling out my name as her eyes close. I'm following right behind her, ropes of cum flowing out of me as I say her name and wish I was burying myself deep inside her where I know I belong.

As we are both coming off our high, we start to slow our breaths, and I grab tissue to clean myself up. She pulls the vibrator out of the water and places it to the side, moving her hands up and trying to situate the bubbles around to cover her breasts. She turns the nozzle, in what I assume is an effort to warm the water a little more.

I pull my boxers and pants up, moving to wash my hands, looking at her through the reflection in the mirror. She doesn't seem uncomfortable by my presence, which is a relief after what we just did.

In all our time as a couple, we've never been this sexually adventurous together. We were always comfortable in the bedroom, but I can't say we ever pleasured ourselves in front of each other. And there's something incredibly hot about it. Seeing her come undone like that was freeing and beautiful.

I finish washing my hands and turn toward her while I'm drying them. "Abby, that was different for us."

"I think everything we've done is a little different these days," she says as she takes the bar of soap and lathers her arms.

"I can't argue with that. But that was hot," I tell her, throwing the towel on the bathroom counter. "Where did that come from?"

"It came from a need. I have hormones coursing through me, and let's be honest. Seeing you there, imagining you without your shirt on, did things to me. Then seeing you half naked just now helped me get my needs met. And I think you got something out of it too." She smiles.

I lean down, my arms straddling each side of the tub. "Yeah, but you can't deny the chemistry, Abby. We were made for each other, baby. And you know it's not just about needs being met. You and I both know you want more than just a good view. That vibrator isn't going to cut it the entire time during the pregnancy," I whisper into her ear.

Goosebumps erupt along her skin, and I see her breath hitch. It takes everything in me not to say fuck it and just submerge myself into the water. Instead, I let my gaze trail down to her breasts, which already look a little bigger from the pregnancy, and my lips graze her jaw. She moves her head over, letting me trail open-mouth kisses down her neck.

"Someone really is horny. Imagine if you let me fuck you right now. Imagine if you were on that bed right now, how wet you'd be for me," I say as I poke my tongue out and lick her neck.

"Mmmm," she moans, closing her eyes, her breath accelerating, and I know she'd be ready to go again if I asked her to. But I need her to want me to come back. I can't give in too easily.

"Maybe next time we can play a little longer," I say, and I pull away.

"Where are you going?" she yells as I retreat.

"Abby, your fingers are going to prune, sweetheart. Plus, you don't want that water to get too hot. Remember what the doctor said."

My laugh escapes, and I hear her frustrated grunt as I leave her bathroom, then the apartment. I can't lie and say I'm not hard again because everything about Abby turns me on, but I have to keep her wanting more, so I'll play the long game until she's writhing for more.

Because winning my girl back is still endgame.

# CHAPTER 19

*Abby*

I'M LOST IN THOUGHT, watching a mom push her baby in a stroller outside when Malloy walks up to the table.

"Hey, Abby, sorry to leave you waiting. My mom needed some help with stuff at the house," he says, pulling up a chair to join me.

We decided to meet for lunch at a small diner down the street from my apartment. Spring is trying hard to make its way through after a tough winter. Who am I kidding? Every winter in Boston is tough.

Luckily, today is a nice day, and I'm starting to feel the warmth of the sun breathing through the clouds. I thought it would be a good time to break the news of my pregnancy to Malloy. I'll be showing more as the weeks creep forward.

"It's good to see you. I haven't been here long, so don't worry about it," I reassure him, and he gives me a small smile, seeing right through my lie.

I've been here for thirty minutes. I hate being late, so I got here extra early to get a seat. I wanted to make sure I got a spot with a nice view of the street so I could watch people walk by.

"You're a shit liar. You know that, right? I'll make sure to play poker with you." He winks and grabs his water.

I'm about to say something when the waitress comes over, and I swear she drools at Malloy. "Hey, can I grab you something to drink other than water?"

"Oh, I'm good with this, thanks." He holds up the water while I roll my eyes, and he chuckles at my reaction.

"Okay, just wave me over when you're ready to order. Our specials are the turkey club and tomato soup. My name is Amanda, and I'll be helping you today." She winks. This would usually be her cue to go, but she's still standing there, and it's sort of uncomfortable.

"Alright, Amanda, we'll let ya know when we need you to come back," I tell her, really needing some privacy so I can let Malloy in on my secret.

She swings her head over toward me, and I swear it's like she just realized I'm sitting here. What am I, invisible?

Malloy laughs because I think he's thinking the same thing as me, and I glare at him. She sets her sights back on the handsome firefighter but luckily takes the hint when he doesn't return her gaze and leaves.

"My goodness, obsessed much?" I huff.

"Someone's got her panties in a wad," Malloy teases, and I stick my tongue out.

Ever since that night last week when Clay was over and we had our little "show-and-tell," I can't stop thinking about how much I want a repeat. These hormones of mine are making me hot and bothered constantly. I've got an itch that I cannot scratch alone anymore, and it's driving me nuts.

"I need to tell you something," I finally spit out.

"I guessed as much. I've got some stuff to update you on too. Why don't you go first. You look like you're going to combust." He gives me a look like he's scared of me.

My glare doesn't seem to scare him off, so I throw a napkin at him and decide to spit it out already.

"Fine, I'm pregnant," I say nonchalantly, looking down at my nails because I'm trying to play it cool, even though I'm anything but.

"I'm sorry, say that again." Malloy puts his cup down and I can feel his eyes on me.

"You heard me. I'm. Pregnant," I repeat.

"Oh really. And who is the father?" A small smirk forms on his lips. He knows exactly who the father is. Fucker is going to make me say it.

I look up to meet those forest green eyes and quickly look away, the smile that's threatening to break free on my face too difficult to hide.

"You are sly, Ms. Morris." He sits back in his seat.

"It was one night," I say in return.

"Yeah, I hear that's all it takes." He laughs.

"Well, I tried for more than one night, and it never took, so this was a surprise for both of us," I admit, taking a drink of my water.

We're quiet, Malloy processing what I admitted to him. I have never really gone into immense detail about how things went down with Clay and me after the bar.

"So what does this mean for you two? It must change things?" he asks.

"Not really. I mean, we're still living our lives the way they were before I found out," I admit.

"*Come on*, Abby." He looks at me, shocked.

"What?"

"The guy loves you, and it's completely obvious by the way you're telling me you're pregnant with his child that you still have feelings for him. You're being foolish," he says, and I can't help but feel attacked.

"Excuse me?" I put my water down and look at him with my mouth agape.

"Listen, you know that when it comes to me, I'm going to be honest, and that's just what our friendship means. I'm not going to sugarcoat it with you. You're being foolish thinking you can have this man's baby and ignore that you still love him. Because you do. And he loves you. You're going to what? Have his child and just be miserable, for what? To prove a point? To be stubborn?"

"You have some nerve," I say, grabbing my things, about to storm out.

"No, Abby, you don't get to walk away because I'm saying things you don't like to hear. No, sorry. Marissa can tell you she doesn't agree, but I can't? That's not fair. Also, as much as Clay may think I'm not his friend, I actually see his side. I see why things were hard for you too. I can be on both of your sides from what you've told me and be your friend," he says, grabbing my wrist, trying to keep me from leaving.

I hate that he's right. He's entitled to his opinion, but it pisses me off that he's not wrong about how I feel about Clay. And I think I hold a lot of guilt that I can't just let go of and run back to Clay—that a part of me is holding on to this need to stay firm in my decision to be in this solitary life I have chosen. I deserve to suffer because I did this to us. I'm using this as a punishment, which is just cruel for both of us.

Does it make sense? No. Am I doing anything to fix it? Still no. Am I hormonal and letting it continue to rule my decision-making? Yes.

I put my stuff down and sit back down. "Sorry, I overreacted."

"It's fine. You're pregnant, so I'll let it slide. I've watched three of Rios's sisters go through it. They were nightmares. You're just beginning, and this is just the tip of the iceberg." He gives me crazy eyes, and I swear I want to throw something at his head. I'm contemplating the napkin holder, but there are witnesses, so I decide against it.

"Rios is the one who figured out I was pregnant, actually."

"You ran into Rios, huh? Well, the fact he figured it out doesn't surprise me. He's got some weird sixth sense about it," Malloy says as he waves the server over. "I hope you're ready to order because I need food. If not, we need to get fries or something. Amanda keeps giving me the stalker vibes, and we can't be here longer than the regular diner allowed time—if you catch my drift."

"What can I get you?" Amanda says. She showed up so quickly I barely had time to process what was happening.

"Yes, we'll get a basket of fries to start. Abby, do you know what you want, sweetie?" He looks over at me to play along. The moment he brings his hand to touch mine, I see Amanda deflate.

"Yes, *pumpkin*." My tone is dripping sarcasm. "I'll have the chicken Caesar salad with the tortilla soup. Thanks," I say, handing over the menu.

"I'll have the ultimate burger with onion rings." He gives her a tight smile, then winks at me.

She scurries off, and once she's out of earshot, he pulls his hand away. "Thank you. She wouldn't stop looking at me, and I swear she was freaking me out a bit there. I had to make her think we were together." I swear he shivers a bit at the end of his statement. It's hard not to laugh at his dramatic behavior.

"Okay, what's your update?" I ask because I need to know what's going on with Baylee. I haven't gotten to see him much since we last hung out. Life has been a bit hectic for me, and he's been working crazy hours lately.

"Oh, quite a bit. Not good news like yours though." He pulls his hat off and moves his hand through his ginger hair, then puts his ball cap back on backward. "My mom has cancer."

The lump that forms in my throat is immediate and I can't control the tears that start to form in my eyes. I wish I could blame the damn pregnancy hormones, but I can't. I'm devastated for him. Malloy's father is not in the picture, and he was raised by a single mother. It was only his older brother and mother his entire life. His brother is a lawyer out in Ohio, so he's been closest to his mother. This is devastating to hear.

"Oh, Malloy, I'm so sorry." I grab his hands and squeeze. "What kind? What stage?"

"It's stage three, they just found out. Lung cancer." He swallows thickly, and I can see the devastation across his face. He looks absolutely grief-stricken with the news, and I'm gutted for my friend.

"What's the prognosis? Can they give you any information?" I know nothing about this type of cancer.

"That's the thing, it's not great." He bows his head. "There's no cure for this kind of cancer. She's never smoked a day in her life, but she got lung cancer. She'll have to do a few rounds of chemo. Then we'll reevaluate and see if she needs to do any other type of therapy, but they gave her about five years."

His eyes are shining with unshed tears, and my heart is aching for my friend.

"I don't even know what to say. What can I do?" I ask because I feel helpless.

"Nothing. Just listening is enough." He looks out the window, lost in thought. "I'm asking for a transfer closer to her. Right now, it's too much being twenty miles out. It doesn't seem like a lot, but I don't want to be that far away. Some guys don't mind the commute, but right now, living where I am, outside the city, the traffic can delay me quite a bit, depending on the time of day. I just put in the papers, and I'm waiting to see where I'll go. As long as I'm closer to home here in the city, it's better than being out in Dover. It's just too far right now from my mom.

"My brother can't be here right now. He's about to propose to his girlfriend, and I just don't want to put his life on hold. He's done so much to help raise me throughout the years. He deserves his time now. I just can't interrupt the life he's built." He moves his hands down his face, and I can see the turmoil.

"But if you need the help, you should ask for it," I tell him.

"Eric has done so much for me, Abby. I was a tough kid growing up. I was resentful because I never had a father figure around. I gave my mother and brother hell. Rios and I were always stirring up trouble. I don't know how we ended up making a career out of our poor behavior because we were little shits." He chuckles at the memory.

"Well, this version of you that I see in front of me is quite exceptional. And you're not giving yourself enough credit. You're relocating to be there for your mom. That's pretty amazing," I tell him.

He seems uncomfortable with the compliments about him, so I decide to deviate the conversation in another direction.

"How are things with you and Rios? Things get any better?"

"I think so? I mean, I'd say, once I told him about my mom, yes. Sadly, it took something so severe to get him to snap out of it, but yes, he's acting like things are better now. But I think it also has to do with the fact that Baylee has a new boyfriend. They met after she went back to school after the holidays. It seems serious." He shrugs, and I notice how hurt he seems with the revelation.

"How does it make you feel?" I ask him, hoping he will give me an honest answer.

"I want to say I wish things could be different, but now that my mom is sick, I can't really give her the attention she deserves. Plus, I value my friendship with Rios too much. He's my friend, and he's been super helpful with my mom's diagnosis. Right now, I'm still not back in the city full-time, so he's been visiting her and making sure she's cared for while I can't be there, which means a lot." I get how that could be hard on his emotions.

"That makes sense." I have no idea how you balance that, and he's in a tough spot.

"Don't get me wrong. I know I didn't imagine things with Baylee, but at the same time, the timing and circumstances weren't right, so here we are." It seems like he's trying to convince himself more than he's trying to convince me.

Right then, Amanda shows up with our food, and I can't help how hungry I am all of a sudden. I make grabby hands once everything is deposited on the table.

"Careful, Abs, I think you're drooling," Malloy comments, and he's back to his cheerful self and gone is the seriousness from earlier.

"You shush and get used to it. It's only going to get worse as I get bigger," I say as I grab some salad with my fork in one hand and some of the fries with the other. I think I'm mastering this multitasking thing.

"I promise you aren't alone in this," I say while chewing, trying not to show him my food and be inconsiderate while I scarf it down.

I'm chewing my food for a few minutes in silence until I look up and see Malloy watching me with a look of disgust on his face.

"What? Do I have something on my face?"

"How are you taking the fries, dipping them in tortilla soup, then adding a forkful of the salad?"

"It's perfection. Want to try it?" I get everything on a forkful and shove it toward him for a big bite.

"I'm good, thanks." He moves his mouth away, nose up in the air.

"Suit yourself," I say with a mouthful and smile in contentment. I have never been this happy with food before. I swear this is the best meal I've ever had.

That meal was the worst possible idea ever.

Why would anyone mix chicken Caesar salad, tortilla soup, and French fries? As the meal is coming back up, the acidity is just an added bonus, and it's not fun.

I think this is what death feels like. The baby is revolting and probably hates me for my meal choice. At first, I thought it was just possibly a food I needed to avoid, but it's been over twelve hours that I can't keep anything down.

I finally got the strength to call my doctor, and the obstetrician on call told me to go to the hospital to get some IV hydration. It's the middle of the night, and I don't want to inconvenience anyone. I checked my shared calendar that I have with Clay, and it shows he's working tonight, so I'll just shoot him a quick text and let him know I am going to get myself checked out because dehydration isn't good for the baby.

I don't feel any cramping, but I'm incredibly lethargic after so many hours of being unable to keep anything down. I've tried to suck on ice cubes, but even those are hard to keep in my system. The minute I start to suck on those or even try a few sips of water, I bring them right back up. I must have food poisoning.

I find a plastic bag I can stuff in my purse to take along in the Uber with me, then send a quick text off to Clay, explaining the vomiting hasn't subsided. When he started his shift, he knew I was under the weather, but I wasn't this bad. I have no clue if he has access to his phone. It all depends if he's out on a call. I try to make it sound less serious to keep him from freaking out.

> Hey. I need to get checked out. I can't keep any food down, and the doctor thinks I need fluids. I might have food poisoning. I don't want you to worry. Hope the shift is going well. I'll keep you updated.

Now that Clay is informed, I grab my things and order my Uber. I get downstairs, and at this late hour, my ride gets here pretty quickly. I get in, and the way this guy keeps slamming on the brakes, I feel like whatever bile I have accumulated so far is going to make an appearance, so I plead with him to take it easy.

"Hey, any chance you can simmer down on the brake," I say as kindly as I can manage.

"You don't look so good," he says, glancing back at me through the rearview mirror. Then he sees me pulling things out of my bag in search of the one I hid in case I felt ill on the way to the hospital. It's dark back here, so I'm not able to find it.

He turns to address me this time. "Do not throw up in my car! No way!"

He rolls the windows down in an attempt, I assume, to keep me from throwing up, and all it does is make me exceptionally cold in the process.

"Listen, just get me to the hospital, please," I beg, just needing him to get me to Boston General, which is not that much farther. I would have walked if I could, but I'm exhausted from hours hugging the porcelain throne.

Shit, that metallic taste is making a comeback, and the vomit is inevitable. Right when the panic sets in that I'm going to vomit all over this guy's back seat, my hand feels the plastic of the bag, and I pull it out just in time. I grab it, and I'm about to hurl into the bag when I hear a horn ahead of us. I look up and scream. My driver looks in the direction of the horn.

The car swerves, but the impact is inevitable.

# CHAPTER 20

## Clay

WE ARE a guy short now that Jamison decided to move back to Minneapolis. He and his wife recently moved back to his wife's hometown for the extra help, and I can't blame them. But fuck are we feeling his loss at the station.

Being a man down and having a night like this feels like being kicked in the face on little sleep. It doesn't help that Abby isn't feeling good either. I can't be there to console her, which isn't helping matters. We are riding in the back of the fire engine, the sound of the siren alerting those on the street of our presence.

We have been on back-to-back calls since I walked into our station tonight, and I haven't had a chance to check in on Abby. As much as we can have our phones on us if we are sitting around, when on a call, we can't have our phones for personal communication while out.

I look over at my brother, and he can see the agony on my face because he understands what it's like when one of us is in pain. We wear the other's pain in moments like this, and he knows how much I want to be with Abby right now. But my mind needs to be on the guys tonight. They depend on me, and I have to be focused on them.

We pull up to the scene and find two vehicles involved in what looks to be a motor vehicle accident. It doesn't look too bad, but I can see onlookers on their phones, and one of the drivers seems to have a gash across his forehead.

The truck stops, and we hop out, walking over to the wreck to assess the damage to the vehicles and to take note of how many victims there are. My guys are walking around the car to the right, which sustained the biggest impact, while I'm taking in the perimeter. I look down and note something by the rear tire, which looks familiar.

I bend down and notice it's a key that looks much like one I have on my own key ring. I bend down to grab it, and I feel all the air in my lungs escape.

It's a fucking SpongeBob key, eerily similar to the one I have. What are the chances someone has the same damn taste in keys? I'm hopeful someone just loves SpongeBob as much as Abby. But my panic doubles when I look up and take in my brother speaking to someone in the back seat of one of the vehicles in the accident.

As I move toward him, it feels like everything around me goes eerily quiet. The only thing I can hear is the blood pounding loudly through my ears. The alarm I'm feeling coursing through me is beyond anything I've ever felt. I can't lose her. I know he's talking to her. The way his expression holds tension in his muscles, I know he's holding it together for me.

I reach River, and his focus is on whoever is in the backseat, so he doesn't even look at me. He's blocking my view into the car, speaking to the person, but now there's so much damn noise around me, along with my heart pounding, I can't make out much from his communication with the victim in the car.

But now that I'm closer, I can focus enough to hear it's a female's voice.

I want to shove my brother out of the way and take over,

but he's rooted in place. It's like he can read my mind in this moment, and it confirms my fear that it's Abby in that seat. That key isn't a fucking coincidence. She's there, and I need to get to her. My life is in this car.

"River, move out of my way." I grab his bicep, urging him to move.

Without looking at me, he tries to free his arm away from my grasp. He stays trained on the person in the car, his focus solely on them. The way he keeps his face trained on her, he's treating her beyond a victim—he's treating her like she's family. I feel it down to my core. It's this damn twin thing others just don't have, and it's fucking powerful. Right now, it's fucking pissing me off.

"River, move out of my way. Now!" I yell.

"No," he roars, something I've never heard from him. He's commanding, and it's confirmation of why we don't treat family. He knows that if I get in his way, I'll throw everything out the window. And he needs to keep a clear head between the two of us.

He looks back into the car, this time addressing her by name, "Abby, look at me. I know you're scared. Does anything hurt?"

"No, I just can't get the door open. I think it's stuck," she says. "And I can't stop throwing up." I can tell she's been crying from the way she's catching her breath.

"Did you hit your head?" my brother asks her.

"No. I was throwing up before the accident. I just don't know what's wrong with the door," she says as she tries to open it.

The way the cars hit one another, the airbags deployed on the sides of the vehicle. She was, luckily, wearing her seatbelt, but it must have jostled the latch on the doors in some way, keeping her and our crew from easily opening the doors on either side.

After a few more minutes, our guys are able to get to her.

They're gentle with her, and once I'm able to see her in the light, it's evident she doesn't have a scratch on her.

Her eyes are puffy from the tears, and she looks exhausted, but you wouldn't guess she was involved in a car accident. She's placed on a stretcher by the paramedics. Luckily, no one stops me from running to her.

"Abby, baby, are you okay?" I move my hand through her hair.

"The baby, Clay," she says, tears falling, fear evident as she looks at me, and all I want to do is take the pain away. "The driver looked back when he noticed I was sick, and he took his eyes off the road. He ran the red when he wasn't paying attention." She struggles to catch her breath, likely from crying. "But luckily, the light had just switched, so the other car wasn't going too fast. The windows were open. Things went flying everywhere. Then the airbags. It all happened so fast. It could have been a lot worse, but I'm still worried."

"We're going to get you looked at, alright?" I reassure her. "I'm going with you."

I look around me until I spot my captain.

"Hey, Cap, I'm sorry to do this, but I have to—"

"Go, Nichols, I got you covered," he yells to me, and I don't hesitate. I hate leaving my guys in this position, but they seem to have it covered. I nod over to my brother and run back to Abby. My mind wouldn't be in the right place if I stayed back.

I hop in the rig, and we're off. I try to stay quiet beside her, but it's hard not to check on her, making sure she's not bleeding or injured in areas she may not be feeling due to the adrenaline coursing through her body.

Once we get to the hospital, I follow her into the emergency room, and we get transferred up to the maternity floor.

We arrive in triage, and thankfully, the floor isn't too hectic tonight. She's quickly hooked up to monitors, and the baby's heartbeat is strong. It's a relief to hear the baby's heartbeat on the monitor, and I see the tears flow down Abby's cheeks as she must be feeling the same relief I am.

Now I can check that off my mental list. I can see some relief on Abby's face as well, even though she still looks a little green from whatever she's fighting from the food she ate earlier.

A nurse comes in with an ultrasound machine, asking questions regarding the accident. Abby reaches for my hand, and it's hard to miss the way her body tenses as she rehashes what happened. Hearing the baby's heartbeat is reassuring, but I know so much can still be wrong. Most of all, the biggest concern after a car accident is a uterine rupture.

The nurse explains the ultrasound to us and begins imaging. Even under these tough circumstances, it's difficult not to get excited about seeing our baby on the monitor. The baby is moving a ton, even if Abby isn't feeling movement yet. The nurse explains everything to us as she measures the fluid and prints the images for the chart.

Once she's finished, she tells us that she's going to speak to the doctor on call and return shortly.

"It's hard not to be scared. I wish I had just stayed home, Clay," she says, regret marring her features.

"Abby, how would you have known? It could have been worse. Being dehydrated has its own list of complications too." I need her to understand there's no fault here.

"I'm so scared, I just want—" She's interrupted by the doctor coming in.

"Hi, Abby, I'm Dr. Elkerela, the OB-GYN hospitalist tonight. I hear you were in an accident. I'm sorry you had to go through that," she says as she walks over to the fetal strip to look over the monitors showing the baby's heart rate and the contraction monitor that shows no contractions at this time.

"Well, the good news is there are no signs of a uterine

rupture," she smiles at us both, "and the baby looks great on the ultrasound. Of course, this does not mean I want you getting up and celebrating just yet.

I want you to take it easy. You need to monitor for any bleeding or cramping, and make sure you get some rest. You still suffered a trauma tonight. Now I hear you were on your way here due to some severe vomiting, is that right? Can you tell me more about that?"

I sit back and listen to Abby speak to the doctor about her symptoms relating to her food poisoning, and I'm incredibly comforted to hear she's going to be okay. There is an immense amount of relief washing over me, knowing Abby and our baby are going to be okay. My heart feels like the bulldozer that was resting over it can be lifted slightly.

We stay at the hospital until the doctor feels comfortable enough to discharge her. After getting some IV fluids and some medication for the nausea and vomiting, Abby is feeling relief from her food poisoning as well. Before the doctor signs off for us to officially head home, I can't hold back any longer, and I speak up.

"Dr. Elkerela, I'm sorry to bother you with yet another question, but Abby and I don't live together, and I'm just wondering—is it safe for Abby to be alone after the accident?"

I can tell Dr. Elkerela is taken aback by my question, and her eyes volley between the two of us, while Abby looks like she might smother me with a pillow. I have no shame in my question, so I stand a little taller and throw a smug smile her way while the doctor directs the answer at both of us.

"I am not too sure I'm going to make you very happy with this response, Abby, by the look you're giving Mr. Nichols, but I'd feel more comfortable if you weren't alone for the next few days until you follow up with your regular OB in the office." With that, she gives us one more curt smile and heads out.

Satisfied, I turn to grab my turnout coat, while I notice Abby stays still and is likely planning a way to murder me in my sleep.

"Looks like you just got yourself a new roomie." I wink at her. "I'll make sure to get my stuff into the spare room tomorrow. You won't have to lift a finger." I blow her a kiss.

"You know, I could ask Malloy to sleep over instead of you," she says, and I laugh.

"Over my dead body, princess. Get dressed. I'm taking you home."

There's a finality to my tone. I leave no room for discussion. Abby once loved it when I took command, mostly in the bedroom, and as things started to shift during the end of our marriage, I got soft with her because I thought she was more fragile.

I guess I saw her as more breakable. Maybe that was wrong of me; I see that now. But I'm done handling her with kid gloves. I want my wife back. All she's talked about is wanting herself back, the person she was before all the treatments started. So I'm giving her the Clay she once had as well.

# CHAPTER 21

## *Clay*

IT'S BEEN a week since the accident, and the sexual tension is at a record high. Each time I walk into a room, I feel Abby's eyes on me before I look for her.

Her family came out the minute they heard about the accident and stayed in a nearby hotel until we got the all-clear from the doctor that she and the baby were going to be okay. They left this morning, and I've been out on a run since the sun came up. I don't know what to do about these feelings that are coursing through me.

Each time I'm near Abby, all I want to do is claim her. I want to run my hands through her hair, demand she take me back, and call her mine again. But I know that the minute I show that side of me, she'll retreat, and we'll be further back than where we are now.

I have to play this right. She keeps saying she doesn't want to go back to the person she saw herself becoming when she left me at the end of our marriage. I get it. She wasn't whole anymore. She felt lost and buried from the individual she once was. I don't think she understands that as much as she felt like she was no longer herself, she was still the person I loved, just further from the surface.

When I look at Abby, I see every bit of her more clearly and fall in love with her even more than I thought possible. Now that she's pregnant, it's hard not to love her, knowing we'll have this little part of us to add to the world. And now that we are together in the same house again? I get to fall in love with her all over again, with the person she is slowly rediscovering within herself and who she is becoming in that process. She will never be the same Abby I met in that cafe all those years ago; she has been through too much life since then and is becoming so much more than that. A person who has been through trauma and is learning to rise from the ashes.

The sweat is cascading down my chest and my back, my shirt long forgotten. I reach the building and click the button to the elevator, catching the eye of Veronica, Apartment 8A. She doesn't hide her attraction each time she watches me pass, and today, she rushes to catch the elevator with me. I cringe as I try to stand in the farthest corner possible, away from her advances.

"You've worked up quite a sweat there, officer," she drawls with her southern accent.

"Um, I'm a firefighter, not a cop," I say dryly, my gaze watching the numbers moving up the floors. I honestly feel completely uncomfortable by her advances. She knows I'm not interested.

"You could pat me down any day," she says, a little breathy when she says it.

I keep my gaze forward, my jaw ticking in irritation. This chick does not take the hint. She's seen me with Abby, and even if I'm not affectionate, she doesn't know the extent of our relationship.

I'm about to say something when the door opens onto our floor, and Abby's in the hallway when I arrive. She looks over her shoulder and sees me coming out of the elevator. Her eyes catch sight of Veronica, and I see her smile falter, but she plasters a fake one on all the same. I want to laugh because I know she tries to hide her distaste for Veronica, but she won't admit she's jealous.

"Oh, hi, Abby. Good to see you. You're a lucky girl having this one all to yourself." Veronica giggles. Does this girl not have a filter?

I walk out into the hall and can feel the tension radiating off Abby's shoulders. She balls her hands into fists, and I can't help the smile that creeps over my face. If I was looking for confirmation that she's not over me, I got it in this one little interaction. The elevator doors close, and I see her watching it even after Veronica is gone.

"She wants me to claw her eyes out," Abby seethes.

"Careful, wildcat. You're acting a bit jealous over your ex-husband. We don't want that now, do we?" I say, looking at her expanding bump in her tank and the short shorts. I grab my bottom lip with my teeth and think about how much I want to touch her.

"I'm not jealous. Don't be ridiculous, Clay! I just can't stand when women throw themselves at men who aren't showing them any interest." She juts her chin in the direction of the now-closed elevator where Veronica was just flirting with me.

I move toward Abby, causing her to step back until her back hits the wall behind her. "Sweetheart, you don't have to keep fighting this tension. I can make you feel better, you know."

Her breathing picks up, and I see her pupils dilate. I know she's turned on, and her eyes trail down my torso to my basketball shorts. It's hard to miss my growing erection.

"I think the only person looking to find a release is you, Clay," she says with a coy smile.

"I think with the way you're nearly salivating for me, you wouldn't mind me feasting on that pussy of yours and calling my name." I move my face closer to the crook of her neck.

She makes room for me to nuzzle that space of her neck, and the minute I bring my lips onto her skin, she moans, making me want to lick her all over. It's like a fuse goes off, and her nipples pebble at the contact.

We're in the hallway, and I don't want to risk one of her neighbors coming out, so I pick her up, my sweat not bothering her in the slightest, and take her inside.

I kick the door closed, walk us to the kitchen, and set her down on the kitchen table. She brings her knees wide, panting as she stares at me, her eyes big as saucers. I stand in between her knees, pushing her head back and staring into her eyes, looking for the permission I need to kiss her.

"What are we doing?" she whispers, apprehension in her tone.

"I don't know, but I will admit, it feels right, whatever it is."

She brings her hands along my sides, sliding them up my ribs, and if the sweat bothers her, she doesn't show it. The press of her fingers along my skin feels like she's igniting a match. The pads of her fingers move a few more inches, then she changes angles, and it's her nails that move along my back and shoulders. Without another word, I pull her hair back and claim her lips.

She opens for me, and we both moan. It's like coming home. We're feral for one another. She uses her feet to push my shorts and boxers off of me. I'm not gentle with her top, tearing the flimsy tank and ripping it off her, grateful she went without a bra this morning. I toss the cotton fabric aside. It's like we're desperate for one another, much like we were that night when we reunited all those months ago.

I trail my hands down her neck, moving along her collarbone, then grabbing her breasts. I pinch her nipples, and her reaction spurs me on.

"Yes, don't stop." She pushes her chest out, resting her

arms at her sides, and rolls her hips, looking for some friction to rub her clit against.

My shorts are still pooled at my ankles, so I chuck them off, along with my running shoes and socks. I still have Abby in her tiny shorts and panties, but I may as well have a little fun with her because watching her beg is half the fun.

"Why are you naked, and I'm still half dressed?" She pants, frustration lacing her tone.

"Because I want to hear you beg a little more. You made me wait this long, adamant you didn't want me." I trail kisses and nibble down her chest as I descend until I reach right above the elastic waist of her shorts.

"Clay, please," she starts.

"Please what, baby?" I say, looking up at her. Her gaze is drunk with desire.

"Please make me feel good, Clay," she pleads, and I don't wait for her to say it again.

I peel off her shorts, then her underwear, until she's exposed to me. My dick is hard and waiting for some attention, but right now, this is about making her feel good, so I focus my attention on what's in front of me. Fuck, my girl is wet and ready.

I lick my lips and get down on my knees. I bring her legs over my shoulders and bite the inside of her thighs. She's watching me, and the moment I connect my teeth to her flesh, she whimpers.

I pebble kisses up the inner portion of her legs until I reach the area where they meet, and in one fell swoop, I lick her folds. Her head falls back, mouth opening, and her moan reverberates off the walls.

"Yes, fuck," as she sighs.

She's good for my ego. I lap her up, each moan spurring me on to chase her high. She reaches one of her hands forward to grab my hair and pulls, the pain only making me harder.

Soon enough, she's yelling that she's coming, and I swear I see stars of my own. She's riding my face, her feet resting on my shoulders as she rubs her clit on me as I lap up her juices.

She giggles as her hips start to slow.

"Mmm, that felt good," she says, a soft smile spreading across her face.

I move to stand in front of her again, my lips quickly finding hers. I can't get enough of her, and the way she pulls my body closer, I know she wants me even after just falling apart a few seconds ago.

I pull away, trying to show some restraint. "If we don't stop, I'm going to fuck you on this table." I nibble her bottom lip.

"So?" Her eyes are full of desire as she looks at me like she can't go another second without me inside her.

"Is that what you want, Abby?" I move my hips forward, my tip gliding closer to her center. How I haven't plunged right into her, I have no idea. I guess I have more restraint than I thought.

"I want to feel good."

"I already made you feel good," I say, not moving away but also not giving in completely to relieve that ache between her legs. My dick is inching closer, the tip grazing the folds without plunging in.

She bites down on her bottom lip, looking at my cock, then moves her hand to grip my dick and squeezes, pulling a moan out of me. She looks up at me and smiles, knowing damn well what she's doing—toying with me, pushing me closer to the edge.

We used to do this to one another years ago when things weren't so heavy in our relationship. When life didn't remind us how hard it could be. There's a lightness between us right now, and I like this side of her that's come out.

She's guiding my cock to her center, and we both watch in fascination as I disappear inside her, and the moment I'm fully seated, we both moan. I rest my forehead on her shoulder and breathe her in. I don't move for what feels like hours, but I know it's only a few long seconds.

She's holding me in place, her hands on my ass, and I know the moment I start moving, I won't be able to stop.

"You fill me up so good, Clay. You're the only one who fills me up like this." The thought of anyone else ever filling her up makes me see red.

I pull her head back until her eyes are on me. She knows she struck a nerve because her smile is saccharine.

"This pussy is mine, and you fucking know it," I say as I pull out almost all the way, then slam back in.

I do this at a punishing pace, pulling moans from her that are nearly pornographic. I'm holding her by the hips, watching her tits bounce, and it's bringing me closer to the edge. But I won't fall off until she climaxes again.

She grabs onto her breasts and pinches. I know she's sensitive because the minute she grips her nipples, she moans. It's the hottest thing, watching her take charge of her body this way. Then she lets go, one arm bracing onto the table and the other moving down to flick her clit.

The minute she presses that sensitive nub, I feel her walls constrict, and her chest pushes out, her head falling back while she calls out my name. She comes so loud, I swear it lasts minutes instead of seconds.

It's euphoric watching her climax. That's when I let my movements take over. I start to pump erratically, and soon, I feel that warmth move down my spine, and I come inside her.

"Fuck, Abby, baby," I scream, with sweat all over my body once again as I let the pleasure wash over me.

The high is heavenly; my senses are at an all-time high. Once I get my sight back, I take in the beauty in front of me. Abby has laid her upper body down on the table, her hair splayed out, those chestnut waves a mess, with her eyes closed and a soft smile spread across her face.

I bend down and plant soft kisses up her body, starting at her navel, then up her sternum, paying close attention to her breasts, then moving up her neck to her jaw, and finally resting on her lips.

"By the way, good morning," I say.

She laughs but can't seem to form words. She moves her arms up and runs her hands through her hair. Finally, she opens her eyes and takes my face in her hands.

"Good morning," she finally says.

We stare at one another, and it's hard to ignore the way she's processing the emotions going through her mind.

I know she's not sure what comes next.

"Clay—" She's about to ruin this moment, and I refuse to get in a fight.

"Don't, Abby—" My tone has a finality to it, and I hope she doesn't push.

"We should talk about this," she tries to push, and I move off her and straighten, grabbing my shorts and pulling them on.

"Why? So, you can ignore what we just did?" I throw back at her.

"That's not fair!"

"Wow! That's rich coming from you. What's not fair is you ignoring we have something more than a living situation going on here before our baby is born." I move around the table, picking up her thrown clothing.

"You act like I haven't explained myself," she says, pulling the clothes out of my hands as if I'm the one she's irritated at.

"No, what you've done is not give this a chance. You've given me excuses, Abby. Don't you get it? You're not the shell of yourself anymore." I throw my hands out, annoyed she doesn't see what's in front of me. "You're the person you always were."

She covers herself with the ripped tank, along with her underwear, her shorts forgotten. She stands in silence, not cowering to my words, but still not able to respond, so I continue.

"I don't understand what you're so afraid of with me. Is it me? Am I what you're afraid of? I mean, you think being with me again, as a partner, will dull something in you?" I finally ask, somewhat afraid of what she'll say.

She bites her bottom lip and looks away. I see her chin wobble like she's holding back a sob, and I feel a mix of anger and hurt, but I don't say anything. If she has something to say, she needs to use her words. I'm not going to outshine her if that's how she was feeling prior to our marriage crumbling.

She finally finds her voice and speaks. "Maybe?" It comes out more like a question than a statement.

"Elaborate," I say, waiting for more.

"When we got married and decided to throw away the birth control pills, it was freeing for me. I remember feeling like a true adult." She has this soft smile on her face as she looks off in the distance to the water like she's thinking back to that day. I don't remember it with that much clarity. Maybe for her it was a special day, but for me, I was just excited to start a life with her. I decide to stay quiet, folding my arms across my chest, and let her speak further.

"I was sheltered most of my life. I was confident I would be a successful artist but wasn't sure in what capacity. I was always good at art—be it on a canvas, on paper, or whatever medium. When computer design, then web design, was something I mastered, it took off for me, and I fell in love with it. My confidence only grew. I was good at that.

"But I remember always dreaming of being a mother. I babysat all the kids in my neighborhood growing up. I think it was the one thing I knew I was better at than my mom because I connected with kids better than she did. When we started dating, and I knew we would get married and want children together, it felt like the universe brought you to me.

Clay, I dreamed of our kids, and the moment we started trying, I had never felt more alive."

She walks closer to the window and leans against the glass, crossing her arms across her chest, mimicking my gesture.

"At first, I assumed it could take us a few months. I heard stories of some couples taking a while to get pregnant. I spent the nights you worked at the firehouse looking up cute ways to tell you. I remember dreaming of the announcement we would do. Even little boots we could get and maybe using the firehouse as the background to take a photo. I mean, I had the whole thing planned out."

She looks up at me as a lump forms in my throat. She's never told me any of this—in all the years we tried, she never shared an ounce of her plans with me. She always kept it close to the chest. I'm frozen in place, feeling exposed as I feel the weight of her pain from all those years ago. I begin to understand how much she carried; I never really absorbed what she was feeling, even though I thought I did.

"Yes, I love you, Clay. And back then, I loved you so much that each time we went into those appointments, I smiled and acted like I would do anything to try another type of treatment. I'd take an injection; I'd take whatever hormone I needed to in order to try because I was fucking desperate. But what I didn't tell you is that each time you poked me, I lost a piece of myself. Each time I peed on that damn stick and it was negative, it felt like a piece of myself died, even though there was no baby."

She sighs, putting her hand on the bump, on the life she now carries.

"This baby, our baby, it holds so much meaning to me. It's a piece of all those little lives we didn't get to meet. It's not just a part of us, but it's a piece of all the layers of me I lost. And yes, I want to run right back to you and forget about all the parts of me that felt so shattered. But I also don't want to ignore all the progress I made. I feel conflicted, Clay. I feel like I want so bad to run toward you and fuck all the feelings of the past, but I also want to remind myself that I've made it so far."

I blink and finally let a tear fall, wiping it quickly. Hearing Abby explain how she feels, the way she teeters from how she feels like her past and her present keep battling with her is a struggle for me. It's hard to know that despite this chemistry that obviously exists between us, she can't simply accept it. She fights it. But now I can't argue with her. I see her side. I don't like it, but I see it.

Now it's my job to woo her back and remind her that she won't lose herself in us. I did it once. I just have to find a way to do it again.

# CHAPTER 22

## Clay

RIVER HAS to drag me to my next shift, and I'm not even exaggerating when I say I don't want to head into the station. Luckily, Kennedy is staying the night with Abby while I'm on my shift. It gives me peace of mind knowing she won't be alone. This is my first shift since her family has gone back home.

On the drive over, River tells me his plan for proposing to Kennedy, which is happening in the weeks to come, and it's absolutely ridiculous, yet on par for the two of them. It involves a penis purse and a disagreement over not having the right menu options, two things that I would never do, yet something that I think Kennedy will somehow appreciate. I roll my eyes and try to hide my smile while he gives me his whole plan.

"You love it, so don't try to pretend you don't think I'm a genius." He points at me, then turns his head to focus on driving.

"The jury's still out, but you're bordering lunatic and comic," I say with a chuckle.

"Well, I am the funnier twin, so it sort of fits," he says, and I roll my eyes.

"Mom really didn't need to push you out. She had perfection after she delivered me," I say, buffing my nails and rubbing it on my shirt.

"Your life wouldn't be half as fun without me, Clay, and you fucking know it." He socks me in the shoulder.

"I think the word you're looking for is less stressful. It would be less stressful." I laugh, and he gives me the bird, his eyes trained on the road in front of him.

Once we arrive at the station, we see the guys huddled outside, Rios at the center, with the rest of the guys holding him back. River parks the truck in a hurry, and we make our way over to see what the scuffle is about. It isn't until we get closer that we notice Malloy is opposite him, his hands up, trying to calm his friend down.

"Dude, I put in the transfer, but I didn't know it would be here," Malloy says, his voice calm as he talks to his friend.

"I don't want you here, man!" Rios shouts.

"I thought we were past this," Malloy says back.

"Yeah, well, now we aren't."

"Dude, get over it. Nothing happened. You're being a fucking dick over nothing. I'm your best friend, and you're acting like I did something to deceive you and our friendship. Be a fucking man, and listen to me. You're like a brother to me," Malloy shouts. "Put this behind us."

Rios's nostrils flare as his eyes are like pinpricks glaring at Malloy. "Don't tell me you're like a brother to me when you definitely had something going on with my sister," he retorts, and my eyes go wide. Shit, this goes deeper than I thought. Malloy and Rios's sister?

Watching them yell back and forth, it's like watching a tennis match. All of us are just surveying this yelling match, making sure they don't take swings.

I had no idea they had this animosity toward one another. Abby had reassured me nothing was going on between her and Malloy, yet I never believed it was possible. I guess this is why. I still assumed something could happen between the two of them. Jealousy plays tricks on us when we feed it. Maybe this was why she was adamant nothing would happen with her and the firefighter from Dover. She knew about Rios's sister.

"Listen, I just wasn't expecting this, man. I just, I need some space, alright?" Rios throws his hands up, moving passed Malloy and into the station.

The guys disperse, following Rios inside. Some of the guys give Malloy a reassuring nod, and some even pat him on the shoulder, I guess feeling a bit sorry for the guy.

River looks over at me, his eyebrows shooting up in shock and disbelief. I share his sentiment. I stay behind, hoping to speak to Malloy. Malloy watches Rios's retreating form, defeat evident in his features.

"I really thought this would be good for us when I saw where I was stationed." He sighs. I'm not even sure he realizes I'm the one stuck out here with him.

"Give him time, man," I say. "Is it true though? You and his sister?"

He swings his gaze to me. "What? No!" He does a double take, then asks, "Clay, right?" I give a slight nod, and he continues. "Sorry, I just had to confirm. I honestly don't know how to tell you two apart yet. Abby said it takes time." I can't help the laugh that escapes.

Then his shoulders sag, and he closes his eyes, maybe reality dawning that he may as well come clean. "It's not what Rios thinks. Nothing happened. I swear. We didn't do anything. Plus, she's with someone now. I thought we were good. I mean, we were starting to hang out again. I even told Abby last time we hung out that we were finally doing better, but then this reaction makes me think it was all a farce." He looks back over at the door Rios walked through, his brows furrowing in concentration.

"I assume we're talking about Baylee, right?" Rios is the

only brother, surrounded by sisters. Baylee is the youngest and the only one of his sisters who isn't married.

"Yeah. I've known her since she was born. I mean, I don't think I have a memory without her in it. But I swear, nothing happened." He scratches his beard, worry taking over his features.

"But you wanted it to?" I ask.

"I mean, yeah, for a minute there, sure," he says without hesitation. "It came out of nowhere and surprised me. I mean, I didn't plan to catch feelings. But I have my friendship to think about. I mean, he's like a brother to me. I love him like family. And now, none of that matters. She's with someone else.

"My mom is sick, and I have her to think about. That's why I transferred back into the city because I needed to be closer to her." The more he talks, the more I'm starting to like the guy. I guess he's not as big an asshole as I thought. Damn it.

"Like I said, give it time. And you've got the rest of us," I say, smacking him on the back and pushing him to walk inside. If he needs a friend, I can welcome him in. Plus, he's been there for Abby when she's needed someone. I know she's going to have him by her side, so he's someone I'm going to have to get used to having around. May as well start now.

I am in no way insecure about my size, but Malloy is much taller than me and built. I still reach my arm around his shoulders the best I can to make sure he knows I want him to hear what I have to say.

"Let's get one thing straight though." I stop us before we get inside the firehouse. "You lay one hand on my wife in a romantic way," I look him straight in the eyes, "I'll fucking kill you." I smile, letting both my dimples pop out.

"That's fucking disgusting. I don't see Abby like that,

man. Plus, she's having your baby." He shivers like the thought makes him cringe.

"Perfect. Welcome to Station 10!" I slap his shoulder, about to start walking again.

Malloy stops and speaks so only I can hear him, "But just a friendly reminder, she's not your wife anymore."

"Motherfucker! Just when I thought we were going to be friends." Malloy laughs as I flip him off.

———

The rest of the shift is uneventful, and thank fuck. I got a few texts from Abby with selfies, mostly at my request. She was rolling her eyes in most of them while Kennedy was giving me the finger. I hope I can do the same pose in her wedding photos as payback.

River and I go back to Abby's apartment in the morning. He's just as anxious to see his girlfriend as I am to see Abby. He hurries ahead of me, and you'd think Kennedy is the one carrying his child.

"River, stop acting like a sad puppy," I say as he walks through the front door using my spare key. The moment he gets inside, he's calling for his girls.

"Kennedy, Lola, Daddy's home," he yells.

"Gross," Kennedy and I say at the same time.

"Oh, come on, you both love me," River says.

"Debatable," I respond, while Kennedy walks out with her stupid contraption to curl her hair.

I will be the first to admit Kennedy is gorgeous. Even with the heatless curler attached to her head, and even without makeup, she turns heads. Kennedy already has a fresh cup of coffee, makeup done and her work clothes on, but has saved the hair for last. I bet she left it on just to give something for River to comment on.

"Skipper, did you save this lovely thing just for me?" he asks as he buries his face in her neck.

"Yes, it's always about you, Riv," she answers and laughs as he mumbles something into her neck.

"I assume Abby's up?" I ask, jutting my chin as I walk down the hall.

"Yeah, she's working on her computer in bed," she responds, a Cheshire cat smile donning her features as I pass her. What the fuck is that about?

I give Kennedy a look but let it go as I pass her.

It all makes sense when I knock on the bedroom door and walk in once I hear a faint "Come in" from Abby's response.

Sitting on the bed is Abby, with her laptop sitting in front of her. That's not what's concerning. It's the contraption on *her* head. In addition, she's got these gold things under her eyes. Lola perks up for a second, then lies back down because the early morning just isn't for her, apparently.

"What the actual fuck did you do, Kennedy?" I yell down the hall.

River and Kennedy come running in, and my twin starts laughing.

"Skipper, I told you to keep her company, not convert her." River laughs.

"What? Kennedy said it's better for my hair, plus I could do it while I'm in labor, and it will keep my hair out of the way. Then, right before the baby comes, I just pull the rod out, and I'll have perfect curls. It's a win-win," she says, sipping her tea while I'm holding back a laugh.

"So you plan to go into labor and put this in your hair before heading into the hospital?" I round the bed to kiss to top of her head, around the rod. It's hard to keep a straight face.

"Yes, Clay, I do," she says, determination in her voice.

"I see; I look forward to that moment then," I say, winking at her. "Can I get anything else for you before I go shower?"

"No, I'm good, thank you." She smiles at me.

"Well, we're going to get going," Kennedy says.

"Lola, come," River says. Lola stays rooted in place. Abby gives Lola a few extra scratches and then gives her permission to go off with River and Kennedy. She finally relents and takes off.

River looks at us like he's taken offense that his dog doesn't want to leave.

"That's low, Abby, stealing another man's dog." River brings his hand to his heart like he's wounded.

"So dramatic, River." Abby rolls her eyes.

Kennedy rounds the bed, gives Abby a hug, and whispers, "Lean on me whenever you want." Kennedy kisses her cheek, and I can see the two of them have grown close in a short amount of time.

River grabs the bags Kennedy had brought, and once I hear the front door close, I turn to Abby. "Are you sure you don't need anything before I grab a shower?"

"No, thank you. I'm not on bed rest, Clay. I can get up, remember?" she says with a wink, sipping her tea and taking a bite of her toast.

"Right. Still feeling alright?" I ask, probably for the hundredth time.

She rolls her eyes, likely annoyed by my pestering, but I don't even care. "Yes, drill sergeant. Go!" She shoos me off, and I start to walk away.

"What time should we head out? Ten forty-five?" We have an appointment with her regular obstetrician. It's a fun one because we get another ultrasound. Any opportunity to see the baby is one we look forward to.

"Yeah, that should be enough time to get to the office," she says, already focused on the screen in front of her.

I'm about to walk out of the room when she screams.

"Oh my gosh, what is it?" My heart may literally leap out of my chest.

"I think the baby just kicked. I have been feeling little movements. They're more like flutters for me. Samara told me, last I spoke to her, it would feel like a fish swimming against your skin at first. But this one felt like a limb. Oh my gosh." She's got her palm against her belly, her smile so wide, tears instantly pooling.

"Do you think I could feel?" Even though we've been intimate, I still don't know where we stand. Everything feels fragile between us, so I'm tentative as I approach her.

"Of course," she says, one hand still splayed on her belly while the other motions for me to come over.

I walk around the bed and sit down opposite her.

The minute I take a seat, she grabs my hand and presses it against her warm belly, directly against her skin. At first, I don't feel anything. She makes a face, disappointment etching her features.

She uses her hand and guides mine around her belly, hoping to capture the movement again.

"Come on, little one, let Daddy feel you move," she coos at the baby.

This is the first time she's spoken to the baby in front of me, and it's the first time the acknowledgment of *daddy* is made from her to me. A lump forms in my throat. I try to tamp it down but find it futile. It's hard to hide the emotion.

She presses my hand against her belly, and I try to resist, not wanting to hurt her.

"It doesn't hurt, Clay," she says, as if reading my mind.

Before I can protest, I feel it, this little kick from the inside. I take a breath in, my eyes go wide, and I am not even the least bit embarrassed to admit I cry. The tears fall down my cheeks as our baby kicks against my hand, and that life that I believe brought us back together makes it known to us both.

"Our little miracle," Abby whispers. She's looking down at her belly, which is still so small in comparison to something so powerful, yet it holds so much love.

"Yes, truly a miracle," I say, bringing my other hand to hold her belly on the opposite side, and on instinct, I kiss the center. Abby moves her opposite hand through my hair, and I relish the feeling.

I whisper a soft, *I love you* to my little son or daughter and hope they hear me. Nothing sweeter has ever existed.

———

"Do you mind if we stop at a coffee shop on the way home?" I ask, headed back from our appointment.

We couldn't have asked for a better appointment. In reality, after the scare Abby had the other week, things have gone smoothly. I'm so relieved. She could have gotten hurt, but I don't allow my mind to wander to the worst-case scenario.

The baby was bouncing on the screen today, and each time Abby giggled, the baby reacted on the ultrasound. We were surprised to find out the technician could see the baby's gender, even with all the movement.

We had gone back and forth on finding out, not sure if we were going to wait until the delivery day to know for sure. We decided to put the results in an envelope and find out later. Abby said getting pregnant spontaneously was a pretty big surprise. She thought getting the nursery ready together might be a fun project.

We're torn whether to find out with the family or just make it about us looking in the envelope at a later date. I'm leaning toward it just being me and her because this has been about the two of us coming back together, even though that seems to be a slow-moving process.

It feels like we have taken two steps forward, then ten steps back when it comes to where we stand, but I'm hoping what I'm about to do helps us somewhat. I think I've figured out how to start anew, and my plan is starting now.

"Sure. Is there a spot you have in mind?" she asks, looking

down at the images that were printed, not the ones where the gender is revealed. She's not even paying attention to where I'm driving us. "Isn't it crazy how big the baby is getting, and yet, I am not showing that much?"

"They say everyone carries differently," I repeat what her doctor said. She's forgotten about the coffee shop, so I simply keep driving.

The moment I pull up to the spot, I cut the engine and open my door. I walk around and open her door. She's still too enthralled by the ultrasound pictures to look up, but I go to grab her, and it pulls her out of her thoughts enough to get her gaze to shift toward the spot I've brought us.

Amazonia's Bean Co. is displayed up above, and her mouth hangs open.

"What are we doing here?" She uses my hand to stand and shifts her gaze from the sign in front of us to me.

This is where we met years ago, and it's where I first saw the woman I would fall in love with.

"Abby, I have loved you, probably since the moment I laid eyes on you. I was a stupid twenty-year-old kid who needed something warm on a cold day, and I left this place with more than a cup of coffee. I left with my heart full. You keep saying you were a shell of yourself at the end of our marriage. I'm here to remind you that's not how it has to be.

"Life is about navigating the changes it brings. It's about weaving through the hard parts and figuring out how we want to adapt. You've adapted. You're not hollow; you're adapting. But I get it. For you, it felt like you were on empty. I'm here to recharge you. This baby will be a symbol of all the pieces of you that have overcome the hardships you have in the past. But it will also be a symbol of the parts of our future we still get to live. Piece by piece, I'll give you these little glimpses into the past so that together, you can still be you. Because I think we can still be us, just as much as you can be yourself when we're apart."

I see her eyes fill with tears, but she holds back from letting them fall. She keeps looking from me to the sign in front of us.

"Please, Abby, just give me this shot. Give us a chance again. Let me try. Let me try for us. I get you're scared. But for all the moments you're scared of being lost *with* me, I'm petrified that I can't live without you." I put my hand on the bump that's growing this life of ours.

"But what if I lose this version of me I already lost before?" she says in a whisper.

"Then I'll be right here beside you, ready to help you find your way back. But what if you soar higher than you ever thought possible?" I say in return, moving that chestnut hair that blows in her face, those bright-blue eyes looking back at me, and I feel like she's warming my heart with her gaze.

She beams at that response and then grabs my hand. Before she drags me into the cafe, I pull her toward me and grasp her cheeks.

My hazel eyes lock onto hers, and I feel like I'm having an entire conversation with her as I lose myself in her gaze. And then I bring my lips down on hers, and that zap of energy I've longed for takes over, and I kiss the woman who was made for me.

Her hands grip the sides of my shirt and pull me closer. The little moan that I pull from Abby spurs me on, and all I want to do is deepen the kiss, but then I remember we are on a public sidewalk, so I pull back. A soft smile grazes her features when I pull away.

I think she might actually be falling for my charms.

Again.

# CHAPTER 23

*Abby*

"WHAT DO you mean I have to leave?" River protests.

"Riv, I told you, it's a buddy read with Abby," Kennedy explains as her fiancé whines in the kitchen while Clay laughs in the corner.

"But Malloy gets to stay!" River points, and Malloy is enthralled in the book I read with Kennedy, so he's not even paying attention to the conversation.

"He's not here for the book; he's here to update me on his mom," I chime in, enjoying my craving for cookies and sriracha, my newest obsession.

Kennedy is eyeing me, disgust evident in the way she's watching me savor each bite. "You're worse than Samara. You know that, right?"

I flip her the bird and continue to enjoy my latest delightful treat.

"Let's go and leave them be. You don't want to be here for this book talk anyhow." Clay pats his brother on the shoulder. "I looked the title up online. The book is boring as hell."

Clay walks over to the couch and, without thinking, kisses me goodbye.

The room goes silent, and it's only then we realize our mistake.

We keep messing around like these lovesick fools, and I've enjoyed everything about it. It's been sort of fun, sneaking around and getting hot and heavy behind closed doors without anyone knowing about it. Everything about our little secret has felt very dirty. I don't know why. It's not like what we are doing is forbidden and I'm not pregnant with his child.

My hormones are driving me batty, so any chance we get, we are on top of each other. We are still keeping a low profile until we figure this out between us. At least, that was the plan until Clay just outed us.

"You fucker!" Malloy lets out.

He reaches into his back pocket and pulls a fifty and throws it at Kennedy. "I've known you two point five seconds, and I'm already giving you my money. Goddamnit!"

"Yeah, she's sneaky like that. I told you not to let that pretty face fool you," River says, glaring at his wife-to-be.

She blows a kiss to her fiancé.

"You're still betting on us, and you got Malloy in on it?" I punch Malloy in the bicep.

"Damn, Abby. I bruise like a peach!" He rubs his arm. "I've got a date tomorrow, so lay off spots where she might see my valuable assets." He flexes his biceps and waggles his brows, then opens the book and keeps reading.

"To clarify, we are taking it slow," Clay says.

River is about to interject when Clay continues, "And do not add another bet on how long it takes for us to put a label on this, you assholes."

River slams his mouth shut and then winks at Kennedy, meaning those two will have a bet going by the end of the night. Then I see a slight nod from Malloy, and I know the three of them already have a fucking plan.

"Get the hell out, Nichols twins!" I point at both of them.

"See what you did!" Clay says to River. "You made her mad, and now I won't get any."

"You probably weren't getting any after you outed your little secret!" he taunts, and Clay gives him the double bird in response.

I roll my eyes, and they finally leave the apartment. Lola gets comfortable at my feet, and Malloy looks up from the book.

"What is Clay talking about 'boring'? This book is hot as fuck." He flips the pages to the front and then compares the cover to the table of contents. "What the hell?"

Kennedy and I laugh. The dust jacket is removed to reveal the actual book we are reading. The book Clay thought we were reading looked to be a self-help book, but in reality, we are reading a smutty book. It's all over social media, and we thought we'd throw the guys off and replace the dust jacket. It worked, and we've been carrying it everywhere.

"The scenes are out of control. This is not possible. I mean, how is any man supposed to live up to this in actuality?" he says, opening it again and reading even more.

"I mean, I tried a few things out," Kennedy admits, her face turning a bright shade of pink.

"Shut up!" I poke her with my foot.

"Well, I was curious. Malloy, this doesn't leave the room!" She glares at him, and I think, as strong as Malloy might be, he could be scared of Kennedy. She's got her boardroom face on, so she's quite intimidating at the moment.

"I swear, I won't say a word. Also, how do I get admittance into this book club?" he asks.

"Oh, this isn't a book club," I say.

"Then make it one," he says, grabbing one of my cookies, unfortunately, faster than me because I try to slap it out of his hands.

"Don't steal food from a pregnant woman," I seethe.

"You have a whole sleeve, Maleficent," he teases.

"You know, it might be fun to have a book club," Kennedy says. "Dom here has a point." She thumbs over to Malloy.

"Dom? What the fuck?" Malloy protests.

"You sort of remind me of one of the alpha males in those Dom/sub books I read. You're built like one."

"Thank you?" He looks at me, not sure if Kennedy is being kind or a jerk. I think that's her way of welcoming him into the group. I smile in return. I think she likes him.

This might be exactly what Malloy needs to distract him, not only from his mom's illness, but from everything going on with the Rios and Baylee debacle. I think so much is crumbling from the life he's used to, and he needs a new normal to acclimate to. Hopefully we can be his new support system to lean on.

———

I'm brushing my teeth later that night when I hear Clay walk in. I'm all worked up after talking about the book and I will admit, I started an audiobook that is just as dirty. I have been waiting for Clay to get home because I sort of need a release.

"Abby, where are you?" I hear him yell from the front.

"I'm brushing my teeth," I say, rinsing my mouth out. I was going for a sexy look, so I rush to spit out my toothpaste. Luckily, I have already changed, so my plan is halfway there.

I was on the smaller side when it came to my pregnant belly, but in the last week, it popped. I am no longer able to hide the fact that I am expecting. I am embracing every aspect of this look, and Clay eyes me each chance he gets.

As ravenous as we've been with one another, he's been letting me set the pace with how fast we move. He's been sweet, taking me to the farmers' market, something we did often when we first moved in together. We've also been going on walks after dinner, which we did after getting married, and making some of my favorite meals together.

Tonight, I decided to do something I used to do when we first started dating: I put on some sexy lingerie. I used to wear the cutest sets before I began to feel like having sex was a chore. I opted for one that still fit: a red and black ensemble. My boobs are going to pop right out the minute I bend over, but I doubt Clay will mind. If Clay is going to put effort into little pieces of our past pushing into our future, I think I should do the same.

The confidence boost this gives me is uplifting. I feel sexy and seen in this outfit, not just knowing Clay will love it on me, but the fact that I feel good wearing it. The way my body looks, each curve in it, even the roundness of it, is making me feel bold and powerful. The extra weight I might be carrying now that I have a baby inside me is something I'm embracing.

Clay rounds the corner from the hallway, and I know the moment he spots me because he's mid-sentence and stops. He must have his phone in his hand because I hear a thud hit the ground.

"Hey, baby, I was wondering if you could help me out with a few of these pieces of fabric," I say, acting all innocent as I look over my shoulder at the strap of lingerie like I'm completely clueless.

I threw some heels on, loving the way my legs look. I am on the shorter side, but having the added inches gives me the confidence to stride across the room toward Clay while he just stands there, his eyes trailing down my body. I love the way his eyes trail down my skin, feeling like it might catch on fire from just his gaze.

"What's wrong, Clay? You feeling alright?" I pout for added role-play.

I can already see him stiffening behind his jeans, so I reach him and immediately cup his dick and rub him from the outside of his pants. He moans at the contact and takes a deep breath in.

"Fuck, Abby, you look edible."

"I'd hope so," I say, biting down on my lower lip. "You see, I'm feeling a little needy tonight. You think you can help me out with that?"

He moans, and I think he whimpers a low "Yes, please" under his breath.

I put my hand against his chest and push him up against the door. A loud thump ricochets against the wall where the door connects. His mouth hangs open like he's still in shock at what he sees. I'm amazed nothing has fallen out of place from my bra yet.

I keep my eyes on him while I move my hands down his shirt, slowly letting my nails scrape down his abs. His hard body is such a turn-on, and the way his muscles tense under my fingers is spurring me on.

I reach his belt buckle and start to undo it, then unbutton his pants. Then I push his pants down, his boxers going with them.

His erection springs free, and I lick my lips. I see Clay look down, and his breaths increase, the anticipation evident as he realizes what's about to happen.

"Abby, baby, are you sure?" He moves his hand through my hair.

I answer by getting on my knees and licking the slit at the head of his cock.

"Fuck me." His head falls back, hitting the wall.

His response only gives me the reassurance I need to keep going, confidence running through my veins. I open my mouth wider and take him all the way in, his head hitting the back of my throat.

"Fuck, fuck, fuck, Abby, fuck." He breathes in, I assume to keep himself from coming, and I start to fuck him with my mouth.

I peek up at him and see him looking down at me, moving his hands through my hair, making sure to have a full view of me moving along his shaft. Although I'm on my knees, I know I'm in full control right now. This kind of power is so intoxicating.

I moan, and that causes him to moan. I know the vibration only makes him moan louder, so he is lost in bliss at the moment.

I'm holding onto his hips, his hands in my hair, tears falling down my face. I'm so wet right now, so I take one of my hands off his body and start to move it toward my clit. I'm about to pleasure myself, to get myself off so we can fall off that cliff together, when he pops me off him.

"No fucking way. I come inside my pussy." He grabs me like I weigh nothing, pulling me into his arms.

I wrap myself around him, my legs locking behind his back, as he turns me around so that my back is against the wall. He moves so fast that I don't even realize what's happening until he slides my lace panties to the side, and I feel his erection at my center. In one fell swoop, he's inside me.

My nails dig into his back, and he begins to move, causing my breasts to start to bouncing until they pop out of the damn cups. He kisses me hard, his hand moving between us, pulling at my bra until he unclasps it in the back and tosses it to the ground. The animalistic way in which we go at it only spurs me on, and my orgasm rushes into me.

He pulls away slightly, leaving room for my growing belly but also giving space to see him moving in and out, and it's fucking hot. This is how we used to be, like we couldn't get enough of each other.

"Fuck, Abby, you're everything, baby," he says, looking up at me, then back down to where we are joined.

He's greedy tonight and wants another orgasm from me, so he moves his hand between us. He angles us, his cock hitting that spot deep inside me where I know I'll see stars. I grab onto his shoulders, needing the extra support. He moves his hand down to my clit and begins to stroke my nub while I move a hand up to tease my nipple. The combination is sensation overload.

"That's right, keep touching yourself like that. Take control; you're so fucking sexy," he chants, and it's a turn-on to hear him talk to me like that.

"Yes, Clay, right there, you fuck me so good," I say as I arch my back, hitting my head on the wall behind me, and we both keep moaning. The pleasure is at every corner, almost all-encompassing. I swear I can feel my orgasm creeping up, and when I fall off the edge, I see the colors of the rainbow paint my vision.

I scream so loud and arch off the wall. Clay grabs me and licks me up my sternum, then bites my nipple. It only intensifies the entire experience, and then I feel his climax coat my insides. Ropes of his cum feel like they go on forever, and I swear we stand there, panting for what feels like hours.

Once we come down from our highs, my legs feel like jelly when my feet hit the ground.

"I swear, it has never been that good, Abby," he says, his head against my shoulder, his breaths tickling my skin.

I pull his head up so his hazel eyes, those green flecks slightly visible with the hallway light coming through the doorway, are looking right at me.

"I think we are just finding our way back to each other." I kiss him, sliding my tongue into his mouth, and I swear if I wasn't spent, I could probably get him hard again.

He squeezes my ass, moving my underwear back into place.

"Sorry if I ruined your bra." He winks.

"No, you aren't." I laugh.

"You're right, I'm not." He bites the side of my boob. "Also, these are getting bigger, and I'm not mad about it." He runs his tongue along my breasts, turning me on again. I swear these hormones are insatiable.

"I think they get bigger after I deliver too," I tell him.

"Mmm." He uses his palms to squeeze them together and runs his tongue between them.

"I know you're thinking of doing dirty things to them, aren't you?" I ask because he's got a dirty mind in the bedroom.

"Maybe." He smirks.

"I know you." I laugh.

"Want me to give you a sneak peek in the shower? I have a few ideas already," he says as he starts walking naked toward the bathroom. It's hard to resist that toned body. Years of firefighting, that heavy equipment and training, definitely makes for a nice body. It's something I haven't complained about when it comes to the view I've had at home. Now I get it all to myself again.

I start removing my underwear.

"Yeah, what do you have in mind?" I say, then Clay surprises me when he sprints back to grab me. He gently picks me up and takes me into the shower, where I start laughing when he turns on the water, puts me under the shower head, and gets me dirty all over again.

# CHAPTER 24

## Clay

MY KNEE BOUNCES as we sit in Abby's therapist's office. Dr. Beskow looks at me. Her purple glasses come off as artsy, and for some reason, she seems like someone Abby would have as an art professor and not a therapist.

"It's nice to finally meet you, Clay. I hope you don't mind coming down here today. I asked that you come to this session," she says, and her voice is soothing. She could definitely teach an art class. But now that she has started speaking, I can see the therapist side too.

"It's no problem," I say, pressing my palm against my leg in hopes of stopping the bouncing.

"You don't have to be uncomfortable. I'm not here to judge your relationship with Abby. I'm here for the two of you," she says, a soft smile on her face.

I look over and find Abby smiling. I feel like Abby and I have finally come to a good place, and I won't lie and say I'm not a little scared. What if Dr. Beskow tells us we're moving too fast? Fuck, I'm really scared, I guess.

"Okay," I say, blowing out a breath.

"Why don't we start with why you think you're here," she

says, and my eyes go wide in panic. I look at Abby, and she squeezes my leg in reassurance.

"Uh, well, I guess, to see if Abby and I are moving in the right direction?" I say it more as a question instead of a statement. It feels like this is a test, and I sort of hate it. I don't mind the idea of therapy, but I still don't know what's happening, and I don't know if there's a wrong answer. I feel like my relationship with Abby hangs in the balance.

"No, I'm not a marriage therapist. I'm here for Abby, primarily. But my goal here is to ensure Abby is able to express to you how she is feeling at this point in her journey. I started working with Abby a while ago. And I felt it was time for her to bring you in so you could hear what she had to say." Dr. Beskow nods, and I nod as well, not really sure why I'm doing so. Fuck, I'm like a puppet.

She continues, "Abby, why don't you start." She motions toward Abby, and I look at my ex-wife. Abby turns her body toward me, and I return the gesture, hoping I'm looking a little more even, though I probably look stiff as fuck.

"Clay, I know I've been a little hard to understand as I've tried to figure out all the things I've been going through emotionally. I was really trying to give myself space to find who I am again. I need grace to get out of the darkness I was in when I left you." She looks down at her hands, and I can tell by the way she's intertwining her fingers she's just as anxious.

I move my hands to interlace with hers, and she smiles up at me.

"Clay, I love you." Hearing her admit that brings me comfort. I never doubted that she loved me, but hearing her say it to me in this setting is reassuring.

"And when I first realized I was pregnant, I felt relieved it was you who I love. I never stopped loving you. But I think that when I left our marriage, I may have stopped loving myself. And that's what I had a hard time saying to you. But today, when I tell you I love you, I am also telling you that I love myself. I want to move forward, and I want us to welcome this baby together. I want to have a family with you."

She takes a deep breath and looks over at Dr. Beskow, and the relief in Abby's shoulders is evident in her posture.

"Clay, how does that make you feel, what Abby is saying to you?" Dr. Beskow asks.

"Of course, that makes me feel good to hear. I never, not for one second, doubted my love for her," I say.

"There seems to be a *but* in there," she notices.

"Um, yeah, there is," I say, unable to look at Abby with my next confession.

"This is a safe space. Please tell Abby how you're feeling. This won't work if you two aren't honest with each other," she pushes, and I may as well let this off my chest now. It's been eating at me since we reconnected.

"Well, starting back up with Abby is something I've wanted for, well, since she walked out on our marriage. If I'm quite honest with you, I never wanted the divorce. But with the space, I was able to reflect. And now that she gave me the other side of how she was feeling, I can't help but have questions." I turn to face Abby. "I want a fresh start. I think we can have that. I want this baby to have that. I think this baby deserves that. I think we both deserve that, too, you and me. But I am worried.

"What if one day, we're at the park, and you see a family of four and get it in your head you want two more kids? If we can't have that naturally, what happens then? We did the IVF route, and that didn't work. You didn't really give surrogacy a shot because before we could, you walked away. Adoption wasn't even talked about because, again, you turned your back on our marriage. So, it's hard for me to be all in when I feel like I have to be ready for that other shoe to drop."

I turn to look at Dr. Beskow, rubbing the back of my neck,

nerves taking over my bloodstream because I am uncomfort-able bringing this up. Did I just fuck this up with the only woman I have ever loved?

"Abby, why don't you talk to Clay about this?" Dr. Beskow addresses Abby directly.

"Clay." She grabs my hand to pull my gaze to her. I turn my head to face her again. "I know I scared you, and you have every right to feel that apprehension. I think it will take time to earn that trust back. I think the love part came easy for us. It always did before, and it might always be the easier part of our relationship. The baby-making part? That might be the part that brings some hardship. And that's something that I am sorry I struggled to handle.

"I am going to be honest. It hurts to know I can't carry a baby easily." She rubs her belly. "But I am lucky in this moment. I know that. And I think surrogacy should be some-thing we discuss next time. I think that's something we should go to right off the bat. Now we know. If by some miracle this," she points at her belly, "happens again, then I think we are going to truly get a lottery ticket." She laughs. "But I think it's time to consider surrogacy as the next step for us to expand our family. I'm open to it. I should have talked to you about it. I was just angry, and instead of being vocal, I shut down. It was my coping mechanism. I admit it wasn't a healthy one, but it's what I did at that time."

"And if surrogacy doesn't work?" I have to have a backup plan for that as well because this is something I now have anxiety over, I realize.

"Then adoption is our final step," she says, bringing her hand to my cheek.

Dr. Beskow chimes in, "I think this is a great start to open communication between the two of you. Remember that when things get tough, it's okay to be vocal about what the other needs. The two of you have been through a lot together. Abby, just because you went through the physical pain of IVF does not discount the emotional pain Clay may have experienced, okay? Remember what we discussed. It's important to acknowledge that."

Abby nods.

"If I can also say that I don't think I was aware of how much pain Abby was suppressing regarding the IVF struggles. Emotionally, she held on to a lot, and I wasn't understanding how hard it was for her. That was on me," I admit.

"It's hard for you to know how I'm feeling if I'm not telling you," Abby says.

"Clay, Abby and I have talked a lot about how hard it is for you to know how she's feeling without her using her words. I think she knew how much you two were connected, so she expected you to read her thoughts. You're not telepathic, and many couples expect that kind of behavior after years together. It's just not possible, as much as Hollywood depicts it in movies." She smiles.

I squeeze Abby's hand, and luckily, the discomfort I felt upon coming into the office today has subsided. I feel myself relax and sit back a little further into the couch.

"Now, I have a little something I need you two to do for me in the next week. My patients hate when I say this, but it's a little homework," Dr. Beskow says, a smile painting her features.

Damn it, there's the tension taking over my shoulders again. I've always hated homework.

# CHAPTER 25

*Abby*

LAST NIGHT, Clay and I sat in our living room together with two wine glasses and sunk them into a white cake to find out the gender of our baby. It was just the two of us, and it was a moment I will treasure.

We both laughed and cried together. We smeared cake on one another and simply soaked up the moment where we got to plan out our future. We didn't have to hear any stories or other people telling us their thoughts and feelings on the matter. We just had it as our own special memory.

For someone who had planned all the details of telling her husband she was expecting, to announcing her pregnancy on social media, to then doing a gender reveal, nothing was really going as planned. Even the way I would be soaking up this pregnancy, everything has been different.

I have spent a lot of hours in therapy talking it through with my therapist. During the early weeks when I found out, I panicked. I wondered about the what-ifs. The big one was, what if this didn't work out, and I lost the baby? And her response wasn't sugar-coated. She just said, "What if you do?"

I think that was the first time someone gave it to me straight. And we sat there and walked through all the scenarios, and somehow that was comforting. It was reassuring for my brain to know how I might react. It's awful, I know, but it's how a person who has dealt with the truth of trying to conceive might feel when everything has been hard to get to up to this point.

But now, I'm finally embracing this pregnancy. That's what she told me to do a few sessions back. I sat with the results of the gender for a little while, still a bit apprehensive. I think I was a little scared because knowing made it a little more real. Knowing I was holding back only led to her decision when Clay joined us at that last session.

The homework Dr. Beskow told us to do? A gender reveal if we cared to find out. She said it was a great way to bond and connect with the baby after struggling to get pregnant for as long as we had. And I'm so glad we did. The moment we saw the color of the cake in the glasses, we both dropped them onto the remainder of the cake, pulled each other into a hug, and whispered, "I love you" to each other.

All the other darkness of our past just faded away. It was almost like we knew right then that no matter what, we could deal with the hardship. It doesn't mean we wouldn't have difficult moments, but we knew we would be okay. I just knew I would have to be honest with not only Clay but with myself.

Now we are driving to see Clay's mother, Mary, River, Kennedy, Samara, and Ashton. The twins are getting bigger, and I haven't met them yet, so I'm finally getting a chance to meet them and visit with Sam and Ash.

The moment we pull up to their house, Sam runs out, and that sunshine personality graces me. Apparently, while she was pregnant, she was incredibly difficult, snapping at everyone who crossed her path. I don't know what everyone is talking about; she isn't feisty at all.

I give Clay a look, and as if he can read my mind, he responds, "Don't give me that look. She was unbearable at times. Now it seems Ash has taken on the attitude himself."

I have no time to say anything before she pulls me into a hug that might take all the air out of my lungs.

"Shit, Sam, you're going to squeeze her too tight," Clay yells.

"Damn, sorry." She pulls away from me and taps the bump. "You're adorable. I was the size of a double-decker, but this way," she says and brings her hand forward because of the twin belly size.

I giggle and bring her in for another hug. "I missed you, Sam. It's been too long. Thanks for not hating me." I truly missed her, and I'm so glad we can still be friends. She has every reason to disown me as one.

"Of course I don't hate you," she says, giving me a kiss on the cheek.

"What am I, chopped liver?" Clay whines, and Sam rolls her eyes.

"Between you and your brother, I don't know who is more needy," she responds, and Clay immediately says, "River!"

Once we're inside, it's pandemonium. Everyone is hugging, and Mary is laughing one second, then crying another, and money is exchanged back and forth because there is always a bet going about something. It's chaos, and I stand back, wondering how I thought I'd live without this.

———

"Balrog is not a word!" River yells.

"The fuck it's not!" Ashton yells across from him.

I rest my forehead down on the table. Every fucking time we play this game, it's the same thing. I swear to god. Years of playing and I swear this happens every. Single. Time.

I look over to Kennedy and Samara, and we give each

other the same look like we want to stab ourselves in the eye with a pencil.

"We do this all the time. I'm not going through the Scrabble rules again. It's not in the dictionary," Clay says, rubbing his temples.

"It's a fucking word!" Ash says again.

"But it's not a word, goddamnit! Kennedy back me up!" He looks at her, and she throws her arms up.

"Oh, so now you're quiet, Skip?" he protests. "You weren't last night when—"

"Don't you dare finish that sentence, Riv!" she yells.

Clay covers his mother's ears while River says, "Sorry, Ma!"

Kennedy buries her face in her hands, and I can see her ears turning red. I don't know why I thought this would go any differently. It's hard not to laugh.

"Okay, can I go yet?" I ask.

Clay removes his hands from his mother's ears, and she pats them in appreciation while glaring in River's direction.

I get a nod from Clay for me to go ahead, and I begin laying my square pieces on the board, spelling my word out. I get a few pieces out, and, as expected, River starts to pipe up.

"How many pieces do you have, Abby?" He throws his hands up. He is so damn competitive.

"What are you even spelling?" Ash chimes in.

I don't even acknowledge either of them and keep going. Once done, everyone stands from their spot, and it takes them a second to figure it out. Sam is the first to scream, which only sets off the twins to start wailing.

"Oh my god, no shit, what? Really?" Mary says, looking over at Clay, then at me, then at River.

River is looking at the game board, then at me. "Can you play a phrase like that?" He looks at Clay. "I think she can only play a word, not a phrase." He looks back at the board.

"Kennedy, baby, check the rules because 'It's a girl' is a phrase and not a word."

Kennedy is ignoring him, and she's running over to hug me, and Mary is crying as she makes her way to her son. It takes River another second to realize what the fuck is going on, and then he belts out, "I'm going to have a niece!?"

Everyone breaks out in cheers, and we are laughing and crying all around. Clay and I couldn't think of a fun way to tell our family and friends, so we thought this was a cute yet competitive way to break the news. This gathering was already arranged so we worked it in. We had this game at home, so we snuck the pieces in my jacket and viola! The suggestion of the game was an easy sell because everyone loves to play.

"When did you find out?" Kennedy asks.

"Last night. We found out together with a cake. We wanted it to be just us." Clay comes up behind me and kisses my cheek.

"What about your parents? Do they know?" Mary asks.

"We FaceTimed them right before we drove here. We didn't have a fun way to tell them, so we just saved a piece of the cake and showed them the color on the call. Did the same for my brother and sister-in-law." I smile.

"A little girl." Mary nearly has hearts in her eyes. "I always wanted a girl, and then I got these hooligans."

"Hey!" River and Clay protest. "We were angels!" That comes from River.

Ashton laughs hard, and Mary joins him.

"Sure you were. I nearly had a heart attack on a weekly basis. You two gave me a run for my money," she says, and I believe her.

These two are a handful now. I don't know how their sergeant handles them at the firehouse on shift. They're exhausting just for a few hours at a time together.

The game is forgotten, and the guys go off to the kitchen to have a celebratory drink while we take the twins to the living room and talk about plans for my daughter, which still feels surreal to think about. I still can't believe I'm going to be holding a little girl in my arms in the months to come.

# CHAPTER 26

## *Clay*

"HOLD ON, you proposed with a penis purse?" Malloy asks as he places the final touches on the peel-and-stick wallpaper in my daughter's nursery.

"Yeah, isn't that awesome?" River says. The smile he's sporting is proud, while I'm mostly embarrassed I share DNA with him.

"It's something. Not sure awesome is the description I'd use," Malloy says while giving me a look. "Also, how did Kennedy not cut your balls off after that? She sort of terrifies me."

"Skipper? She's harmless!" River laughs.

I look over at Malloy and admit, "I swear there was a time I thought they were going to kill each other."

"Speaking of killing each other, how are you two friends now?" My brother points at Malloy and me, questioning the friendship that's blossomed.

I won't lie… I'm kind of surprised as well. But Malloy is sort of a cool dude. I can't even pretend not to like him more than Rios. He is just easy to hang out with, and when he's here, he fits right in with us.

We both shrug.

"Don't get me wrong. I mean, I'll be the first to say that I completely misjudged you. But my brother here was going to rip your head off when he saw you with his girl. So, what was that about?" River continues.

"You mean Rios didn't talk to you?" Malloy asks. "I thought that's why you were cool with me. I thought he came clean."

"Came clean about what?" That makes me pause. What is he talking about?

Malloy rubs his beard, and I can see he's uncomfortable. "Dude, I do not want to get in the middle of this. Abby knows what's going on, but I asked her to stay out of it. I thought Rios would have done the right thing and spoken to you."

"What are you talking about?" I put my tools down and stand tall. "Why don't you clear the air now?"

River stands between us. The tension in the room is palpable, and I can see the discomfort in Malloy's posture.

"Fuck man, I swear I thought Rios would have talked to you by now." I swear Malloy better explain himself.

"About what? What does Rios need to tell me?" I ask again.

"Dude, it's best you talk to him," he says.

"Why don't you tell me what you know." I gesture for him to move it along.

"Abby's friend Marissa called Rios. I guess she has his number. She was trying to play matchmaker to get you two back together. She was trying to get you jealous, and when she called him, he said he had someone in mind to set Abby up with for a date. From Marissa's standpoint, that's all she knew. Marissa was in the dark from there. She had no idea it was another firefighter.

"He then came to me and asked me to take Abby out. He knew I was sort of into his sister, and it was a dig to prove a point. So I went for it, not because I had something for Abby, but because I wanted Rios not to be pissed at me. I came clean to Abby early in the date. Rios is the one who set it all up, having me show up at the bar that night. I thought you already knew. Abby didn't tell you because she knew about Baylee, and she was just respecting that whole thing with Rios, so she wanted you and Rios to sort of talk it out. I bet she hoped he would have spoken to you about it or didn't want to stir the pot further."

What the fuck was Rios doing? And why didn't Abby say anything? Most of all, why the fuck did she purposely go there knowing I would already be there?

My head is spinning. I'm trying hard not to be pissed at Abby, but she knew I'd be at that bar. Then again, she came running to me to clear the air that night. Although, talking was minimal because we were ripping each other's clothes off. Tensions were high.

That doesn't explain Rios's actions. I get he's pissed that Malloy might have a thing for his sister, but is he blinded by so much rage that he'd fuck up a relationship with someone at his own firehouse? This violates so many unspoken codes between brothers. How can I trust him if he'd do this to me so easily?

My brother comes in my line of sight, knowing all too well I'm pissed. "Clay, don't rush to judgment. Don't fuck things up without thinking things through." He lays his hand on my chest, trying to calm me down.

My jaw ticks, feeling anything but calm, and I swear it's taking everything in me to keep from storming out of this nursery and finding Rios. I deserve answers. What the fuck was he thinking, messing with my relationship with Abby? He barely knows what went down between us.

I get if Rios wanted to see Abby and me back together. But getting another firefighter mixed in all this is below the belt. Why do this? Why get me fired up like this?

Marissa is a whole different story. I know her. She is a hopeless romantic. After Abby left me, she kept reaching out, trying to convince me to run after her, to try and work things out. I was the one who said Abby needed to work her shit out. I honestly thought Abby would come running back days later. I bet she thought this was her last hope to get us back together before one of us moved on with someone else for good.

I run my hand through my hair, my mind going a mile a minute. It's then I hear the front door open and laughter pour through. Fuck, Abby's home with Kennedy and Samara. Ashton couldn't join us because he stayed back with the twins to keep them on a schedule. Something about nap time being valuable for them at this age.

"Clay, you won't believe this onesie set I found for the baby," Abby yells from the other room, delight evident in her tone.

I swallow the bile that's creeping up. I'm trying not to be pissed right now. Why didn't she at least say something more about Rios? Why didn't she give me a hint that he was a prick because I've spent months acting like the guy was my fucking brother at the station? Top that with the fact I was going on runs with him, acting like we had this deeper connection, and I felt bad he was upset his friendship with Malloy wasn't on solid ground. I had no clue he had something to do with that night at the bar.

She walks down the hall, and the minute she's visible in the doorway, she freezes. The tension is palpable the moment she sees me. Malloy's discomfort is radiating off him, and I've never seen someone flee from a scene quicker.

"Fuck, you know what? I forgot laundry in the machine. I have to go!"

He throws down the tools he was using and the instructions for the nursery furniture he was working on and waves a goodbye in our direction, then mumbles a faint apology at Abby. She crinkles her nose, not quite understanding what transpired while she was gone.

River has shifted to my side, looking at me, hoping I take his advice by not overreacting.

"Kennedy, Sam, let's get out of here. I'll drop you off at home, Samara," he says in their direction. Before leaving, he squeezes my shoulder and gets in my line of sight. I give him a slight nod, and it's enough to let him know I'll be okay.

The girls rub at Abby's shoulder but don't say much else. I'm rooted in place, still trying to think of what to say. There are so many emotions rushing through me right now, but hurt is at the center of it all.

Once the front door closes, the silence is eerie. I finally find my voice.

"Why did you go to that bar that night, Abby?" The moment I say it, realization for my mood causes her shoulders to tense.

She takes in a breath. "It's not what you think, Clay," she whispers.

"I know the date meant nothing to Malloy. You said the same thing when you came to my place that night. I now realize Rios is a dick. But one thing doesn't make sense to me." I rub at the back of my neck as I walk a little closer to her. "Why did you go knowing I would be there? Did you want to hurt me that night?"

No matter how you look at this, I still don't understand why she went, knowing I would be there.

"What? No!" she says, surprised I would suggest such a thing.

"So, you didn't think it would be hurtful to show up on the arm of someone else? Because even if it was a friendly night out for you, it's looking like anything but that for me," I say, sort of dumbfounded she didn't think this through. "Think about it, Abby. How do you think it would feel for me? Especially a firefighter, nonetheless!" I can't help the emotion in my tone.

"I don't know, Clay. Once I knew what Rios's plan was, I'll

admit, a part of me was a bit curious," she acknowledges, and even saying it aloud, she's taken aback.

"Curious?" I repeat. "What the fuck does that mean?"

"I don't know, okay? I guess I came back to Boston, and I was confused. I then heard this whole fucking plan Rios and Marissa had concocted, and when Malloy told me about the bar, I just thought to myself, 'What if you started dating someone, and I saw you move on?' So I let my insecurities take hold of the reins. I get it, okay? It was selfish. I was being an absolute brat. The minute I walked in there, I regretted it. That's why I went to your apartment afterward. I felt awful. But I guess I just wanted to see if you would still care if you saw me."

I laugh at that last statement. Is she fucking serious?

"I know, okay? I know I was dumb. But I'm human, Clay. I left you, and the reality that I returned to Boston and was now going to have to live in the city I loved without the man I still loved was setting in. So, I panicked."

She chews on her bottom lip, and I admit it's hard to stay mad at her. It was a bad decision on her part that night, but it's not catastrophic. That night changed everything, and if it wasn't for her curiosity of sorts, we might not be here right now.

I reach down and grab her hand, pull her to me, and bend down, bringing my lips to hers. Her soft lips meet mine, and as much as I was seeing red a moment ago, my world rights itself the instant I touch her.

I pull away and guide us along to the living room, sitting on the couch, then moving her to straddle me. I intertwine our hands.

"You're not mad?" she asks, surprise in her voice.

"Oh no, I'm pretty pissed," I say, a smile on my face. "But I'm choosing to see your side and understand you were also confused. Do me a favor though." I look over at her. "Let's not play these little games anymore. We're about to have a baby. I think the sleep deprivation might play some tricks on us, and we don't need to add to that, alright? I know we talked about this with the therapist, but I'm just reiterating it now. I don't want you to think I don't love you. I have always loved you."

I lean over, first lifting her shirt to plant a kiss on her belly, then bringing my lips over her collarbone, this time dragging my tongue over her skin, pulling a moan from her. I trail my lips up until I'm at her mouth, locking my eyes with hers, those bright blues pulling me in much like they did years ago.

"You've captured me since day one, Abby. It's only you," I tell her, and she leans into me, kissing me, and I open to her. Our kiss starts soft and quickly turns into something more.

Abby hasn't been shy about how much she wants sex as she has gotten closer to her due date. We are now a month away from meeting our daughter, and as much as most complain about the discomforts of those final weeks, Abby says she still feels all the hormones coursing through her veins.

"I need you, Clay." She breathes into me as she moves to straddle me.

"Take what you need, baby," I tell her, moving the strap down from her flimsy tank top. I have no problem showing my love through physical touch.

Her breast pops out on one side, and I knead it with my palm. She moans and throws her head back, gyrating her hips at a steady rhythm, trying to soothe that ache down below.

My cock is hard for her, and it's doing a shit job of hiding behind the shorts I'm wearing. She's in a long flowing skirt for the warm day, and it's perfect for what she has planned. She doesn't even attempt to remove it. She simply moves it up, desperate to get me inside her.

She shifts my shorts down enough to spring my cock free, and the moment she lines me up, she slides down. She moves achingly slow, watching my face and moaning the entire time until she's fully seated.

"Fuck, Abby, you are so tight for me," I say, this time, holding both her breasts with my palms, pinching both nipples to get a reaction from her.

She grabs her bottom lip with her top teeth and begins to rock. Her movement must hit perfectly against her clit because she's quickly telling me how perfect it feels.

I slide my hands down to grab onto her hips. I take over and start to pump up, hitting that spot inside her that drives her mad. Her tits bounce in front of my face, and with the size they are now, the fullness is calling for me to suck on them.

I do exactly that. I pull one of her nipples into my mouth and suck hard. The moan I get from her only urges me to take her a step further, and I bite down, and she yells, "Fuck, Clay, I'm going to come!"

Right then, her walls constrict around my cock, and without warning, I'm coming right along with her. I pump into her erratically, my cum going off into her pussy, and I swear my vision goes black for what feels like hours.

Once my vision returns, Abby is breathing heavily, her breasts in my face, and I lick and nip at them. She's sensitive all over, so she laughs, pulling herself upright.

She sits back, still straddling me, her belly on full display, her tank pulled up, her breasts still spilling out. I can't help but bring my hands to cup them and knead them. She moans and moves her hips again. Her hair looks like she's been well fucked, yet her smile is easy across her face.

"Let's go take a shower, baby," I tell her.

She's too tired to answer, so she just nods.

I hold her hand while she slowly gets up, and I pull her skirt down.

I know I've gotten through this conversation with Abby, but it doesn't really settle that restlessness inside that I still have to deal with Rios because he betrayed a trust in our brotherhood.

———

"Hey, man, what was so urgent you had to see me?" Rios says as he opens the door to his apartment.

I remove my ball cap and run my hand through my hair. I left Abby chatting with Marissa and headed over shortly after we had dinner. I had unsettled business, and I couldn't leave this up in the air with Rios. May as well speak to him and see what he has to say.

Marissa said exactly what Abby and Malloy had already told me. She was playing matchmaker. She had no idea Rios was planning on setting Abby up with a firefighter. That was never the intention. Although Malloy knew about it, he had explained it was a bad idea to Rios. The way he told it, Rios seemed unaffected, or per Malloy, Rios gave absolutely zero fucks he was hurting his fellow crew member.

Malloy thought it was better he went out with Abby, who he knew he'd likely not catch feelings for, than risk Rios setting her up with someone else where sparks might fly, and things go completely wrong. I'm even more in debt to the guy because he's shown more compassion as a friend in a short amount of time than Rios, whom I've considered a friend for years.

"We need to talk," I say, and I can see the tension overcome Rios immediately.

"Abby okay?" he asks as I walk into his apartment.

"Yeah, she's great. She's at home. Baby's fine." I brush it off. Luckily, I took my brother's advice and didn't screw things up. I will admit, I wanted to be an absolute dick and run away earlier. I could have, but she's pregnant, and upsetting her would have definitely been a shit way of handling things. Talking to her was the right way to go about it. If we are going to move forward, that's the only way we can work together if we are ever going to make our relationship survive.

"I know about you setting her up with Malloy." I get straight to the point. I'm sick of beating around the bush.

"I don't know what you're talking about." His eyes start to dart around the room.

"So that's how you're going to play this? Don't be a tool, Rios," I say. After all these years, he's going to treat me like a fucking idiot?

"All this time, you made Malloy out to be the ass, and you've sat on your throne like we should feel sorry for you. But you're the asshole." I point at him. "I trusted you, day in and day out, with my life. All of us did. That's what this job is about. That's at the core of what we do. Come clean, Rios. Now's your shot."

He runs his hand over his head, that buzz cut grown out a bit. He finally blows out a breath, and I'm hoping he'll just be the man I thought he was. "He was fucking around with my sister behind my back, man! He needed to prove to me I could trust him! So yeah, I made him go out with Abby!"

"So, you threw my ex-wife in my face with another man! And you fucking let me think she was out on a date with him? Even better, you didn't even let me in on it? That's fucked up, Rios. This isn't high school! Man up, dude! Who fucking cares if he likes your sister? Malloy is a good person. You'd rather she date a random guy than a person with some integrity like him?" I yell back.

"You don't get it! You don't have a sister!" he throws back.

"Yeah, you're right. You handled it with class. I have no idea what it's like to feel betrayed by people I thought cared for me!" I throw my hands in the air. "Rios, you're so fucking selfish, you can't see straight. I came here giving you the benefit of the doubt. But fuck you!" I get close to him, my finger in his face. "You don't deserve my respect. I'll keep you safe when we're out on a call. In that firehouse, I will do my job. But outside of it? Fuck. You."

I'm breathing hard. I don't need this shit. I've been through enough shit in my life to have to deal with people like this. Life is too short for this petty drama. My father lost his life surrounded by his brothers. If his life showed me one thing, it's that each moment is precious. I will not waste my time on people who don't care about the value of friendship and family.

I storm out of his place, slamming the door. He calls out for me, but if I ever decide to bring Rios back as a friend, I think there will always be a piece of our relationship that will be fractured.

Each mile home, I leave a piece of that anger behind. My focus is on this new chapter. I have a woman I love and a daughter who needs every piece of her father whole. That is my focus and my love. The two of them are my everything.

# CHAPTER 27

*Abby*

A WEEK after the Rios fiasco, I'm at my baby shower. My family flew in, and even after months of feeling the baby kick, seeing my belly all round in front of me, and reconnecting my love with Clay, I still feel like all this is a dream.

"You can thank me anytime," Marissa says as I pop another pretzel in my mouth.

"Oh really?" I laugh at her humbleness.

"Yes, this is all because of me." I swear she's standing a little taller. Is her nose sticking up in the air?

"Get over yourself." I snort. "You know Clay and Rios got in a huge fight, right?"

"Rios did that to himself. I had an innocent plan in place. Rios did himself dirty, not me," she says. "Also, your little plan to get Clay all hot and bothered got you knocked up. I mean, your egg and his angry swimmers were on a mission that night." She laughs and begins to saunter off, a little too proud of herself. I can't help the eye roll.

"Also, my painting looks amazing in this apartment. It brings the whole place together," she tells me before joining everyone else.

I wish I could be mad at her, but she's been my ride or die, and I absolutely love her through thick and thin. So much has happened since that lunch with her in Los Angeles on that rainy day and that paint night. It's hard to believe how quickly life can change.

I'm going to be a mother. I'm going to be welcoming a child in what could be a matter of days. Most would have had a baby shower at this point, but I kept resisting it. I didn't really want a baby shower. My mother, along with Clay's, thought I wasn't going to give in, but I finally did at the last moment.

It might sound strange to some, but after years of trying to get pregnant, my focus shifted once I found out I was pregnant. I realized I just wanted to treasure my inner circle. I wanted to savor these moments. Much like it wasn't about the baby announcement, the social media post, or the little outfits, it isn't about the games, the little foods we serve, or the party favors.

I want to sit and talk with my friends. I want to take pictures with my friends and family. I want to soak up this time with them while they're here visiting with me. I don't want to just have my girlfriends here and ignore their partners. I want my brother here, mostly so he can stare at my baby's father like he hung the moon. He is one hundred percent hanging off every word Clay is saying right now, and I want to savor that when I look back on today.

From what I hear Mary say about Clay's father, life is absolutely too precious and fleeting to get caught up on the little things that won't matter later. I want to enjoy her laughter as she watches her sons argue over who the baby will love more because she won't know who the father is versus the uncle. I love hearing Kennedy tell everyone about her winter wedding while Samara jumps up and down about how pretty her best friend will be in a white gown.

This is what life is about, not the little details that so many, including myself, get caught up in. I am choosing to live this life in the present because I have already walked away from it once before.

My dad walks up to my side and brings his arm around me. I lay my head on his shoulder and breathe him in. He still smells like the cologne he wore when I was a little girl coming home from preschool. I can still close my eyes and remember bouncing on his knee, giggling as I begged him not to let me fall off.

"I can't believe you're gonna be a mama, Abigail." He kisses my chestnut hair.

"Believe me, Daddy, I'm shocked each time I wake up and see this mountain of a belly." I pat my stomach as the baby does summersaults from the pastry-induced sugar rush she got a few minutes ago.

"Still keeping those lips sealed on the name?" My dad looks down at me, and I smile.

"Oh, I almost let that slip. Clay would have been none too pleased with that pregnancy brain slip-up on my part." I laugh.

"So close." He snaps his fingers, then looks over at River and does a quick shake of the head.

"You have a bet going, don't you?" I ask him, squinting at my former brother-in-law.

"What, me? Never." He places his hand on his chest as if that's completely out of character for him.

"Sure, Dad," I say, sipping my water.

He laughs as he hugs me tighter. I soak in the people around me, knowing any minute, everything about my life is going to change in the best way, and my little girl is going to bring a little more life to each piece of it.

———

*Clay*

I'm grabbing more waters to put out on the counter when Frankie finds me to say goodbye.

"Dude, I'm so glad you're back with my sister. There are no words to describe the relief I'm feeling." He's smiling from ear to ear.

It's only then it dawns on me that I haven't really had a true conversation with Abby about being completely back together with her. Maybe that should be something we do before we have the baby.

"I heard you took the divorce pretty badly," I say as I put the waters down on the counter.

"I may have had a bit of a temper tantrum." He brings his index and thumb together and laughs. "But seriously, man, I'm happy for you two. You're going to be the best parents. I mean that." He hugs me and says his goodbyes. They'll be in town for a few more days. He's got some work to do in Boston before they head back, so I can grab a beer with him and River and Ashton before he heads back to New York.

The party starts to dwindle, and my mom is helping Abby get the last few gifts put away in the nursery. We didn't register for much because we already bought a majority of the bigger items. Her parents wanted to gift some of the bedroom sets, and my mother had purchased some other items for the baby, so we simply asked for clothes and other essentials. This was about togetherness and making memories, especially being this close to the due date. I loved the idea of just gathering for the sake of being with our loved ones.

My brother comes around the corner with a bag that says, "World's Best Uncle" across the front.

"Super subtle, Riv," I tell him.

"I know, right?" he says, his smile taking over his face.

My brother seems to be ecstatic in the role of uncle, and it's really special to share this with him. We missed out with our dad, being so young when he died. We will never get that back with him, but we can give my daughter the best relationship possible with the people we consider family, and I know she will have the most amazing uncle in River. He loves hard and with his whole heart.

"Did you get the baby a special gift?" I ask him, pointing at the bag.

"No. This one is for you, man." He smiles, his dimples popping out. My brother is the most considerate guy I know, and I wish everyone in life had someone like this they could call—

"You absolute shit!" I tell River as I look inside the gift bag. "No fucking way. I don't want this."

"Yes, you do," he says, nodding his head vigorously. "I think it should be a tradition we pass down."

Horrified, I look up at him. "You want me to give this to my fucking daughter?"

"Ew, no, you lunatic! Like a tradition we give our friends, you sick fuck!" He smacks me upside the head.

I hand the bag back over to him, trying to return it.

"Nope, I've deemed it bad luck to give it back, and now you have to keep it and do exactly what I did with it." He throws his hands up, not accepting the bag as I chase him into the kitchen with it.

Kennedy walks in with Abby and my mom. "What's going on in here?" Kennedy asks.

I throw the bag behind my back. "What? No, nothing!" I yell an octave too high.

"What's behind your back, son?" my mom asks.

"Ma, nothing."

"Clay, what do you have behind your back?" Abby asks, rubbing her belly.

River looks over at me, his eyes pleading for me to keep my trap shut.

"River gave me his dirty underwear." Why in the fuck did I just say that?

All three women wrinkle their noses, and River looks at

me like I've got shit for brains. I internally roll my eyes at the stupidity of the lie I just told, and River looks like he's going to fall over with the laughter he's trying to contain. Fucker.

They decide to leave us be, and the minute they're out of earshot, he whisper-yells, "My fucking underwear? What the fuck, Clay? Haven't I taught you anything?"

"I panicked, okay?" I bring the bag up in his face, and he glares at me.

I shove the bag in the back of the pantry, hoping Abby doesn't go looking for it and consider it forgotten for now. I can't deal with this nonsense right now.

---

Sitting outside on the balcony, the warmth of the season is just right.

"Today was perfect, wasn't it?" Abby says as she closes her eyes and rests her head on my shoulder.

"Yeah, I think so. The baby shower was exactly what you wanted, baby?" I ask, kissing the top of her head.

"Mmhm." She sighs. "You know what would make this even more epic though? A foot rub." She then proceeds to readjust herself and pushes her swollen feet over to me so I can massage them. She's getting closer to her due date, which has brought on the sausage-toe phase of pregnancy. Her words, not mine.

"I like the color you chose. This bright color can be seen from space, I think." I chuckle as she wiggles her toes with the neon pink toenail polish.

"Don't make fun of my toes." She laughs, keeping her eyes closed, but her smile widens.

"You know, I wanted to talk to you about something," I say, pressing my thumb deeper into her muscles, and she moans.

"Okay, I'm all ears. But speak fast because I might fall asleep."

"My lease is up soon. I sort of need to make a decision." My eyes are fixed on her for a reaction.

I've been avoiding this conversation, a little hesitant due to the way Abby has been trying to find her footing since moving back from Boston. I just want to make sure she is comfortable along the way.

"Oh yeah? And what do you want?" she asks.

"I think it's pretty obvious what I want. But I don't want to leave any room for interpretation. I want you. I want us, as a family, under one roof. I want to wake up with you in my arms. I want to hold our daughter in the middle of the night when she cries, not as a part-time father." In no way do I want to be visiting. I want to be with her, at some point as her husband, if she will have me.

"I would like that too." She sits up and moves her hand up my neck and onto my cheek. "I think it's time you go grab your stuff and bring it here... permanently. Come home, Clay."

I cup her face in my hands and kiss her. "I love you, Abby."

"I love you too," she says. "I can't wait to—ugh." She looks down, panicked. "Oh my god!"

"What?" I have no idea what's going on.

"Either I peed myself, or my water broke," she admits and then stands. "I'm going to go check in the bathroom."

She gives me no time to say anything and rushes off to the restroom. I sit there for a second, sort of stunned in silence. What just happened? Should I be doing something?

Soon, Abby is yelling from inside, "Clay, it's my water." Which isn't surprising because Abby doesn't just pee on herself.

I snap out of it and hop up from the patio furniture.

I run inside and grab our hospital bag. Once I pull that out of the front closet, I grab my phone.

"I'll text your parents, brother, and my family. Anyone else?"

"Yes, text Marissa!" she shouts. "She's still in town."

I frantically pull out my phone and get to texting everyone. One full text thread will have to do. My phone is going to be going off tonight, but I don't even care anymore.

As I'm about to text, I see movement in the hallway. I walk toward the bedroom doorway and see Abby in our en-suite bathroom. She's staring at herself, a contraption on her head.

"What the hell are you doing, Abby?" I can't help but ask.

"What do you think? I'm getting the heatless curlers in. I told you, I want to have my hair ready, like Kennedy showed me." She looks over at me like I've gone mad.

"You've got to be fucking kidding me right now, woman!" I yell.

My future sister-in-law is not going to hear the end of this. I cannot believe Abby is in labor and she's worried about curling her hair right now thanks to Kennedy and her weird hair obsession.

I walk away and return to the task of texting our friends and family.

Here goes nothing:

CLAY

It's go time!

# CHAPTER 28

## *Clay*

"YOU THINK forty-five is a good age then?" I ask as Abby is getting a concoction of apple juice, cranberry juice, and Sprite. The way she sips and moans, you'd think it's an alcoholic beverage.

"Clay, she's going to date before she's forty-five." She rolls her eyes.

The nurse taking Abby's vitals chuckles. I can't stop looking at our daughter as she lies on my chest, sleeping skin-to-skin against me. I can feel her little heart beating, and I swear, I have never felt more at peace in my life.

She's got a little cap on her head, and I keep lifting it to see her soft chestnut hair. She's got so much of it, and each time I see it, I can't help but smile. She is absolutely perfect in every way. Each time she smiles in her sleep, I see a little dimple pop out, resembling my brother and me.

She gave Abby a run for her money though. I thought we were going to rush to an emergency C-section near the end. Her heart rate kept dropping, but luckily, right at the last minute, she must have gotten in the right position, and Abby was able to push her out.

The moment she let out that scream on her arrival, I

looked over at Abby, and we were both in tears. She was placed on Abby's chest and looked up at her mama. Those eyes locked on her, and I've never seen a more beautiful sight. All that hard work, hours of labor, righted itself.

Our families have been out there, incessantly texting me and asking for updates. I promised I would let them come back here once our two hours of bonding time were up. I begged if they could all come back for the name reveal. Our nurse is pretty awesome, and she said she'd make an exception, but only for ten minutes.

She said she'd go get them in a few minutes. I hate to get up and disturb her, but I know I need to move her over to Abby. I want to stand up and make sure I have the camera set up to get everyone's reaction to her name. It's something we put a lot of time and effort into. Hopefully everyone loves it as much as we do.

I get our little girl situated on Abby, her swaddle more like a burrito than anything, then get the video set up in the corner. Abby is beaming at me, glowing in a way I never could have imagined when we started this journey years ago.

My mother and Collette are the first to sneak in, and the instant they see my daughter's sweet face, they both start crying. I let them have their moment and soak it up. Each one of the family members comes in, and I'm glad this happened before they flew home. It's special to see them take in our little girl in this way.

Once everyone is gathered and we finally have their attention, I begin.

"Well, it seems our little girl must have known she wanted an audience. She must be more like her Uncle River than we were prepared for." Everyone laughs, and of course my brother fucking bows. I control the eye roll and smile at him.

I continue, "We've kept her name a secret. I know that has been hard for most of you. As you all know, for Abby and me, having our baby has been a miracle, our blessing. And now that she's here, it's hard to imagine a life without her. But there are some people who can't be here today, yet a life without them feels hard to imagine each and every day as well."

I look over to Abby, and tears fall down her cheeks. I clear my throat and move past the lump that feels like it's lodged in there.

"As all of you know, my father Gabriel died when River and I were very young, being a hero. He is a man we have always looked up to. He is a man who our little girl will never personally know but whom we hope she will never grow up feeling untouched by. But in some stroke of kismet, Kennedy met our father hours before his passing, on a day she too lost her own parents. So today, we honor not only our father but her mother. We would like to introduce Gabriella Christine Nichols."

Since we learned the baby was a girl, Abby and I wanted to honor my father. We had come up with her name within the first hour, easily deciding she would be named Gabriella. Her middle name was something we kept coming back to. It wasn't until she was on the phone with Kennedy, talking about names, that Kennedy mentioned her mother's middle name and how we should use it. I don't think Kennedy thought we'd take her up on it, but she was seriously offering it. We found ways of bringing it up in conversation, and once we felt comfortable Kennedy would be okay with us using it, we decided it would be fitting.

My mom brings me into a tight hug. When she pulls away, she grabs my face and whispers, "Your father is looking down on you and smiling. I can guarantee it."

My brother comes up next, gripping my shoulders and then pulling me into a tight hug. There is nothing more special than the bond I feel with him. He has been my best friend, and I can't wait to go through this part of life with him. I know he will be an absolutely wonderful uncle, showing her everything fun this world has to offer.

"I'm proud of you, Clay," he says into my ear.

"Thank you, Riv," I whisper. I hug him a little tighter, feeling our bond growing even deeper.

We pull apart, and soon, Gabriella is being passed around, first to the grandparents, then to my brother. Kennedy gets a turn, and I swear, I sense her heart growing. Her smile doubles, and I see the love this girl brings to all of us. I walk over to Abby and kiss the top of her head.

It's hard to imagine this love not surrounding us because it feels so pure and so much a part of our fabric now that she's here with us. Even just a few hours old, it's like she's been a part of us for much longer.

## CLAY

THE DAYS BLEED INTO WEEKS, and we are moving into fall sooner than we ever expected. Gabriella is growing faster before our eyes as each day passes.

Abby took her out today to get some stuff with Kennedy for her bridal shower, which isn't for some time. The wedding is scheduled for next winter, so there's more than enough time until the festivities, but the girls are getting a head start on the planning.

It's fun to see my brother in this phase of life though. He looks at Kennedy, and I see him anticipating the next step. I can't wait to see him standing at the altar, looking at his bride and hopefully losing his cool.

"Clay, what about this?" He holds up the one item I've kept hidden, but that fucking twin thing means he finds shit.

"Goddamnit, River, no! I don't want to use that," I yell.

Lola thinks it's a toy, so she's jumping, trying to get a hold of it. I say go for it and toss it so she tears it to shreds.

"Listen, I get it's hideous, but it's comical, and it will bring you luck. This thing will make her say yes, I swear!" He hands the object to me, and I stare at it.

"Okay, fine, I give up. Where should I put it?" I relent.

"Put it right at the center there." He points at the center of the bed. "It will make her laugh."

"I swear, River, if she knees me in the balls, I'm going to fucking bury you with this. Then I'll tell Mom, this was all your fault!" I point a finger at him, and he smiles. I want to wipe his smug smile right off with this stupid thing.

I walk into the bedroom and place the item in the middle of the bed, rolling my eyes and wondering why I listen to my brother. I'm about to change my mind when I hear my brother yell, "They're on their way back. I'm going to head downstairs and sneak out!"

I hear him speaking to Lola, then gathering her leash and heading out with a quick "Good luck" before he closes the front door.

My heart is racing. I'm taking a huge gamble doing this right now. I mean, I haven't let much time pass since Gabriella was born to let things settle, but I want to do this. I want to unify us again in this way.

River sends me another text; the pieces of my plan coming to fruition.

RIVER

Just got Kennedy downstairs. My Gabby girl thought I was you. 😊

Also, thanks for helping me out today.

RIVER

Always brother.

I stand in place until I hear the elevator ding outside, staying on the inside of our apartment until Abby opens the front door.

The moment she swings the door open, she's surprised to find me waiting for her. Gabriella's eyes sparkle when she sees me. She's in the baby wrap, one of her preferred ways of being carried right now. This week's freak-out of choice is the stroller, in which she has chosen to scream at a frequency I did not know she could reach.

Abby takes in the scenery of our foyer.

"Clay, what's going on?" She swings her gaze around, taking in all the little knick-knacks I've placed on the walls and surrounding areas.

I go to grab the diaper bag, but she wraps her arms around our daughter, moving her hands up and down, giving her body a little bounce as she smiles and bends to look at everything.

There are pictures from our first dates, some stubs from movies, notes I've written, and items I had saved along the way from our years of dating. I had things saved I found when I was cleaning up boxes from the apartment a few months back. It jogged my memory to some items I had left at my mom's place, and I went there to get a few more things as well.

We move further along, and then, going deeper into the apartment, we find pictures from our engagement, where I printed the photos and lined them up.

"I have loved you through so many stages of life. I couldn't pick just one," I say, and she looks over at me, her smile growing.

I grab her hand and plant a kiss on her lips, then place a soft kiss on top of our daughter's head as well. Gabriella's legs kick in excitement, even if she has no idea what's going on.

We continue to move through the hallway as I hold her hand. She knows where this is leading, but we simply smile at one another. I have butterflies multiplying in my stomach as I know what's coming. I'm nervous about what I've put together in our room for her. I continue with my speech in hopes that she understands why I've decided to highlight our journey in such a way.

"I know we had some difficult times in our past that we do not love to reflect on," I say, feeling the nerves skyrocket as I move her closer to the bedroom, "but I still think we can't go forward ignoring the past hardships. So, we must move through those times together too."

I can tell she's unsure where I'm going with this because I'm blocking her view into our doorway, but then I move out of the way and guide her inside.

I wavered on this part of our story when I came up with the plan for our proposal this time around. I bought a ton of syringes representing our IVF struggles. I've seen so many people have children after a long journey through IVF, and they surround the baby with their empty syringes.

But has anyone told the story of their marriage after IVF? Because that's what my story is with Abby. We lost a lot, and we returned together. Our story may have a baby that came out of it all, but IVF took our marriage down a different path the first time. This represents a traveled path that has led to a different outcome. I thought it was poignant to put them in the shape of a heart on the bed to ask her an important question.

I continue to move her into our room. I did something similar when I asked her to marry me the first time. It was outside, near the harbor, on a warm day in June. This is different because we've come a long way since that warm summer day. I get down on one knee, pulling the box from the middle of the bed.

She keeps her eyes trained on the center of the bed, and I quickly grab her attention. "Eyes on me, baby."

"But is that—"

"No, no, Abby, sweetheart, look here, baby."

She keeps her eyes trained where they were but finally moves her gaze toward me, and I begin to speak.

"We lost track of where we started. Life got hard, which is normal. We just needed a few little reminders. When life gets tough again, we will have to do a better job of taking a step back and redirecting each other. We need to remind one another where we came from. We started this journey together, and there is no place I'd rather be than in your arms, battling it out with you." I open the box, and she breathes in.

I updated the ring I first got her. What was once a solitaire is now three stones, with the original solitaire in the center and a stone on either side.

"We started as one, which is represented in the center. Gabriella is now added as the new stone on the side, and we now have another stone on the opposite side, which will symbolize whatever comes in our future. I love you, Abby. Please, will you be my wife again?"

She's nodding and then finally whisper-yells, "Yes, of course!"

I place the ring on her finger, then stand and pull her in a hug, careful with our little girl between us. I pull back and kiss her, feeling her soft lips against mine.

We move apart, and she looks into my eyes—her blue eyes shining so bright, my heart soars. Finally, she looks at me and opens her mouth, ready to speak, and I wait in anticipation.

"Clay, why is there a penis purse in the middle of our bed?"

*The End*

*Malloy*

"I DON'T KNOW how you eat that crap, Rios." After nearly twenty years of friendship, you'd think I'd be used to seeing the guy eat fucking anchovies on his pizza, but I still want to fucking gag.

"Get the fuck over it, big guy!" he says as he's moving his player around the game in front of him. The latest *FIFA* game, which is now *EA Sports*, is out, and we never miss an opportunity to play.

The ritual is ordering pizza and playing until our hearts' content. We've taken the entire day to eat and play games, making it feel like old times again. It's been strained for us. In all honesty, things have been strained for Rios between him and all of the guys at the station. He fucked up, and he knows it since he intervened with Abby and Clay.

I think deep down, he understands he fucked up, but he's too stubborn to own up to his mistake. The problem is that Rios is like a brother to me. And life has been a dick to me, so I need some normalcy in my world. I need my friend back, so I'll take what I can get where I can get it. If he will give me this, I'll take it.

We play a few more hours, and soon, we look up to see it's

after midnight. I grab a water and rub my hand down my face. We both still have tomorrow off, and I'm relieved because our last shift kicked our asses. This summer has been absolute hell. Luckily, Clay is back on rotation. It's hard to have your guys off. It throws the entire house off our equilibrium.

"Didn't you have a date last weekend?" Rios asks, taking a swig of his beer. That's his third one. Thank goodness he is taking an Uber home.

"Yeah. It was alright. She was interesting." I leave out the part that she was pretty much trying to hump me from the moment the date started. I'm certainly leaving out the part where, each time I closed my eyes, all I saw was a dark-haired girl who I kept fantasizing about. I'll definitely leave out the fact the fantasy girl was his sister. Fuck, fuck, fuck.

Since Rios suspected he saw something between his sister and me, I have kept my distance. I have not spoken to Baylee, not even breathed in her direction, since the day I agreed to go on that fake date with Abby. She made assumptions, and I didn't try to clarify either.

Baylee's usually in town for the summer, but she stayed at school in Connecticut this year, stating she wanted to be near her boyfriend and get a summer internship. She came back during the holidays, but I took on extra shifts and only saw my mother, then hurried back to Dover at my previous station for work.

It's best this way. After she left, she tried to reach out a few times, but I stopped responding to her texts. Then she took the hint. I heard from her brother she found herself a new boyfriend, and they've been getting more serious ever since. And I've made sure to keep my mind occupied with other things. It doesn't mean I keep myself from thinking of her because she's always on my mind.

Does it mean I've been celibate? Absolutely not. I compartmentalize. I date. I see other women in hopes I can find someone to distract me. Yes, it's an asshole move. I just don't do a great job of it when I'm on a date. All I do is compare how my date isn't Baylee: pouty fucking lips, tiny waist, dark brown hair, dark eyes that feel like they look directly into my soul.

"You going to see her again?" Rios keeps pressing, pulling me out of my thoughts, and I honestly don't want to keep talking about this date of mine.

"Not sure." I shrug. If I play this as indifferent, maybe he won't be so pushy. "We'll see."

"You should. It might be good for you. Look how happy my sister is. She found someone who's perfect for her." He reaches behind him and pulls out his phone. He presses a few buttons, then turns the screen to face me, and I'm assaulted with photos of Baylee and her douche boyfriend. Something about him just rubs me wrong, but I say nothing.

Whenever she posts on social media, I can't help but check up on her. I'm a fucking masochist, I'll admit. When I look at her, though, there's something off in her demeanor. And she's dressing differently now too—dresses covering her up when she'd always wear things that showed her toned arms and legs. And what's up with these fucking tight hairdos? She'd always have her dark locks down past her shoulders. And I hate that her smile never reaches her eyes anymore. Her bright smile was so beautiful, and I barely see her teeth showing in photos these days.

I can't say anything to Rios because he'll know I'm checking up on her, so I keep my damn mouth shut. Her smile doesn't seem genuine, and it kills me I can't say anything. I want to shake Rios and tell him his sister looks miserable, but if I even hint there's something off about them together, he'll read it as jealousy, so I leave it be.

I smile and give my generic, "I'm happy for her," comment and turn to toss my bottled water.

Rios orders his ride, and soon he's headed out. I shove his

pizza in his hands because I do not need that pie sitting in my fridge, stinking up the joint. I've made the mistake of forgetting it here, and I couldn't get rid of the stench for days. Just the reminder makes me shudder.

I walk through my apartment, still finding boxes in corners because I have to unpack. I've been here a few months, but life has been busy between shifts at the firehouse and taking my mom to appointments, so unpacking boxes is the last thing on my mind. Plus, if I have extra time, I'd much rather soak up the nice weather while Boston hasn't frozen over yet. The winters are brutal here.

I'm brushing my teeth when I hear the faint sound of my phone. I rush to grab it, concerned it might be my mother with an emergency. I finally find it in the living room and see it's from the last person I'd expect. I press accept and put the phone to my ear.

"Hey, you okay?" I ask into the phone.

At first, I think she dialed it by accident because she never calls me until I hear a hoarse, nearly faint version of her voice.

"Tucker? I need you." Her voice cracks at the end as if she's holding back a sob.

"Where are you?" I answer.

"My place," she croaks.

"Stay right where you are. I'm leaving right now." In a rush, I grab my things, not even turning off any lights.

Luckily, it's summer, and it's the middle of the night because there's no traffic. I make it to Connecticut in record time. I pull up to her apartment complex, and her light is faint but on. She's lived here for the past two years. Thank goodness she hasn't moved. I helped her get settled here when she and a few of her friends found this place after moving her from the dorms.

I park my truck and lock up, running to her apartment. I'm getting ready to call her to come unlock the door when I see it's already open. It's then I realize the lock is broken.

I walk frantically into the apartment, my heart pounding, the whoosh of the blood flowing through my ears all I can hear.

"Baylee, it's Tucker. Where are you?" I call, taking in the scene in front of me.

The apartment is in shambles. The living room light is knocked down, and some of the chairs are tossed. She hasn't called out to me in response, but I hear a slight sniffle coming from the back room.

I try to tamper down my breathing because my blood is still rushing through my ears. What the fuck happened here tonight?

I finally go back toward the room that was last hers. When I push the door open, I find her in a corner, her knees pressed up into her chest, her hair a mess, and her arms hugging her legs into herself. Her mascara is running down her face as if she's been crying for hours.

What. The. Actual. Fuck?

"Baylee?" *Who did this to my girl?*

"I didn't know who else to call."

———

Want to know how Malloy and Baylee's love story unfolds in *Embers in the Dark*? Preorder now. Coming June 11, 2025.

Pre-order here or with the QR code below:

*Acknowledgments*

When I started this book, I knew it would be an emotional ride. Abby's infertility journey is one that holds a rawness I wanted readers to feel coming off the pages as they turned them. I wanted to honor her feelings as if she were someone you met drinking a cup of coffee. I am not a person that suffered the way Abby suffered, but I have hurt in other ways, and I wrote my struggles in the pages you just read.

Throughout this story, I left little morsels of my story within Embers in Our Past to show that everyone has pieces of themselves in books like these. I try to write my characters to feel as real as possible and I hope you have felt as if you can pull up a chair and immerse yourself within their life, much like I have felt as I write them.

I feel lucky I still get to dive in and continue in this world of the Boston Embers series as I continue writing this crew, moving on with Malloy and Baylee. But I think my heart will have a special place with Abby. I think when I left her behind in book one, many were unfair to judge her, but I'm excited to share her side of the story. And I hope now that you have gotten her side, you can understand how her struggles impacted her decisions, even if you reacted differently after leaving her in book one.

This book would not have been possible without a team to stand by my side. I had some incredible cheerleaders powering me through to help me get this work done. Joanna, Meghan, and Ashley really were three people that kept me writing. There were times I felt defeated, and I bet there will be times I still will. But they hype me up when I feel down. They push me forward and I am forever grateful.

Joanna, for being the one who really started me writing. She is that one that keeps with the the chant of, "ONE MORE CHAPTER!" You know that without you, there is no me. Thank you for being who you are. I love you beyond myself. Thank you sissy, for not only being an amazing person, but for always answering a call, text, or bat signal. No matter what stage of life, you are my person.

Meghan, not only being my amazing PA, but also for being my Christmas Wife 🎄 and forever loving on my characters and defending them to no end. Thank you for loving on my work and keeping me going with fun texts and buddy reading with me. It keeps me going when I need an extra push. And for introducing me to Ash.

Ashley, you are a gift. Thank you for being honest, true, and a cheerleader for authors. You are incredibly supportive and a beautiful person to work with. I can't put into words how much you have helped me grow in the short amount of time we've known one another. I am so excited to work even more with you with my future books.

Designing a cover is no easy feat and this new cover was a labor of love. Christiana at Concepts by Canea, you are a true artist and I appreciate you so much. Thank you for bringing life to Abby and Clay with your beautiful and unique illustration on my cover. I can't wait to see what you have in store with the rest of Boston Embers crew.

Thank you to The Author Agency for all you do with everything behind the scenes making sure my release is ready to go from pumping me up with the cover reveal, to my eARC sign-ups, to release day celebrations. I appreciate all you do. Working with you has been seamless and it doesn't got unnoticed.

Thanks to everyone at Kat Literary Services for all you do regarding your editing services. I have personally worked with Steph White for all my fiction books and the relationship we've built throughout this time has been really special. Thanks for the cheerful notes you've sent because they've kept me smiling from afar as I've gotten to read your edits as I've been moving along in my writing journey.

Thank you to my Beta readers, Hype team, ARC team, and readers! Without you, I could not do this. You make doing what I do worth it. Thank you for this journey. I love hearing from you, communicating on social media, and seeing reviews that my books make you smile. It pushes me to keep moving forward and it's a great way to connect as I make these characters come to life. I hope you know I do not take that lightly and I am truly appreciative and blessed to know that. Thank you from the bottom of my heart.

I cannot finish my acknowledgements without thanking my family. This past year in which *Embers in Our Past* was written was a tremendously challenging one for my family and I. They gave me space to write and I am so proud of all we accomplished despite all the hardships we faced. Thank you to my children and husband for the grace they gave me as I had to confine myself to write this. But they always provide me that endless support. And I'm forever grateful for the space. I love you so much.

Thank you again for picking up my book. As an indie author that does this because I have a passion for books, each person that picks up a story I wrote brings me joy. I love pouring my heart into telling a story. The fact that I have the ability to put my words out into the world for you to read is such a gift I will not take for granted. So when you take the time to pick up my book and read the words I have written, it does not go unnoticed.

From the bottom of my heart, thank you.

-Stefanie xoxo

# About the Author

Stefanie Castro is a Registered Nurse, certified doula and yoga instructor. She specialized in the field of obstetrics and loves everything about her career. She is a first-generation Brazilian American and is fluent in English, Portuguese and Spanish. Stefanie is a wife of 18 years and mother to her son and daughter, along with her very rambunctious Cavalier King Charles dog.

She has grown in her love of reading throughout the years and now it's hard to find her without her kindle by her side. Her favorite foods are popcorn and sushi. She is also very excited about Christmas and begins plotting her next year's decor on December 26th. Stefanie has started two bookclubs and is avidly reading whenever she has a free moment in her day. She loves to cuddle on the couch with her dog, along with a great book and a cup of tea.

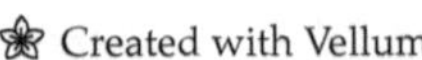 Created with Vellum